Verve Stones

The Legend of Spoon

Book One

James W. Aries

This book is a work of fiction. Any references to
historical events, real people, or real places are used
fictitiously. Other names, characters, places, and
events are products of the author's imagination, and
any resemblance to actual events or places or persons,
living or dead, is entirely coincidental.

ISBN-13: 978-1505815726
ISBN-10: 150581572X

This book is dedicated to my mom,
whom I miss very much.

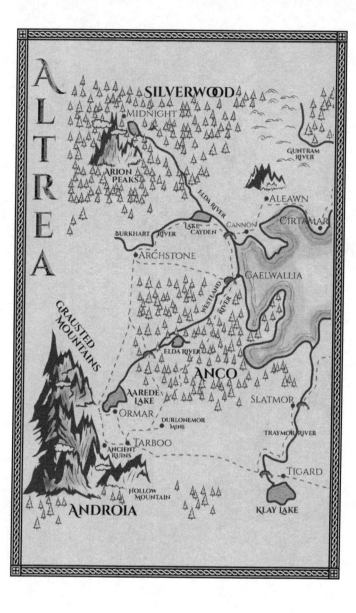

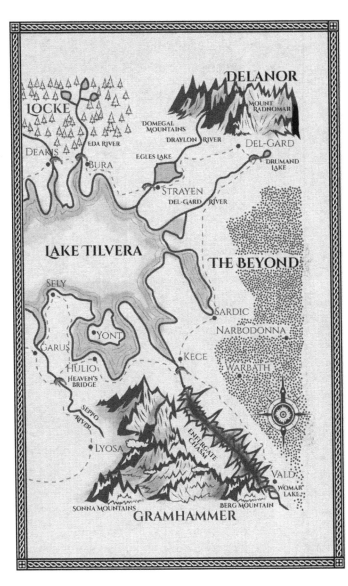

Prologue

"THIS WILL BE THE LAST ONE, General," droned a faceless man.

A guard with mud-colored eyes and a dazed expression on his face brought the last prisoner into the dungeon. The prisoner was barefoot, wore tattered rags for clothes, and had a foul bag slung over her head hiding her tangled black hair. The guard guided the woman to a thick, iron chair in the middle of the room and shoved her down. He tied the prisoner's wrists and ankles in place with strips of leather.

The faceless man removed the soiled bag from the prisoner's head. He then slammed a metal stand onto the stone floor at the prisoner's feet. The collision of metal and rock created a shower of sparks causing the prisoner to recoil and cover her eyes, as if the dark room had been flooded with a bright light.

"At last," said the general, securing his sword to the stand.

As the prisoner's gray eyes adjusted to the dimly lit room, she couldn't help but notice the uniquely shaped sword before him. The blade had three edges and was shaped like a star. Beneath the blade rested a black crossbar with a leather handle bound with silver thread. The blade's capstone, set in the pommel, was a green gem of unprecedented beauty and pureness.

The prisoner was scared and, yet, curious. She surveyed the numerous bookshelves that filled the walls of the gloomy chamber. Each was full of moth-eaten scrolls and dust-covered books piled high in no particular order. The prisoner then noticed five rectangular tables in front of her. Each was covered with a variety of gems, tools, and scientific devices. She quickly whispered a silent prayer, pleading not to be part of any strange experiments.

Over the years in the dungeon, the prisoner had seen her family and friends dragged from their cells and into this secret chamber. None ever returned. She had imagined the room to be more splendid than this dungeon laboratory. How thankful she felt that her husband had been spared this fate.

The faceless man grabbed a large, iron goblet from the nearest table and, with the help of the guard, filled the prisoner's mouth with purple ooze. The prisoner fought to no avail as the fiery potion coated her throat. She convulsed against her restraints, coughing and gagging. She came to rest hunched forward, almost lifeless. Unable to move her body, but fully aware of her surroundings, the prisoner stared vacantly through her new, mud-colored eyes.

The general cracked his knuckles and got into position for the final time. The faceless man and the guard exited the dungeon. After closing the door, an intense green light radiated from beneath. Once the light faded, and a soft thump resonated from inside, the general's associates reentered the room. They lifted their superior's limp-but-breathing body from the floor, unhooked his sword from the metal stand, and carried him up the many stairs to his private quarters; leaving an empty room in their wake.

Chapter
1

THE MAN HAD NO FACE. He wore a long trench coat with a hood that hung to where his eyes should have been. Instead of skin, I saw emptiness, as if someone had erased his features. And he was standing behind a blue minivan across the street from my house.

I'd stepped out my front door and there he was, staring at me. He made the hair on the back of my neck stand up. I fumbled for the silver key in my pocket. I found it, but immediately dropped it because my fingers were shaking. I picked it up off the porch and quickly locked the door behind me. When I turned around again, the faceless man was gone.

The feeling of being watched made my skin crawl. I found my bike on its side in the middle of the lawn. As I pedaled towards the blue minivan, I couldn't shake the thought of the faceless man jumping out and grabbing me. But he never did. The only thing behind the minivan was a couple of dandelions growing through a crack in the sidewalk.

I headed to my best friend's house. Alex and I met when we were seven, and over the next seven years we've become inseparable. He only lived a few blocks away. I cut across the neighbor's yard and down a trail through the woods. I rode over some dirt humps and around a high-banked turn. I rejoined the street at the faded salmon-colored mailbox. It used to be yellow, but I broke the old one during Alex's ninth birthday party.

A boy in a blue football jersey and jeans said, "Hey, Spoon, you made it."

Spoon isn't my real name, of course. It's Ethan Spooner. With a last name like Spooner, it didn't take long to get shortened.

I skidded to a stop and said, "Sorry I'm late." I kept quiet about the faceless guy. I didn't want Alex to make fun of me. "My mom said I couldn't leave the house unless I'd finished two chapters of the assigned reading."

"But it's only Monday," said Alex, looking at me sideways.

"That's exactly what I told her," I said, getting off my bike. "But you know how she gets about me putting things off."

Alex nodded. He was seated in the middle of his driveway, with the guts of what appeared to be an old weed whacker scattered around him. He touched the copper end of a red wire to the post of an old car battery. "What do you want to do today?" he asked, making a spark.

"You're going to electrocute yourself *again*," I said, watching a twinkle of pleasure in his eyes.

"This thing is mostly dead."

"Right," I said. I thought about his previous question. "We could kill some aliens."

"I'd love to, but we can't," said Alex, grabbing another wire, this one black. He touched it to the battery's other post. Nothing happened. His lips pressed together into a frown. "We broke the console."

"What happened?"

"We were playing the new racing game this morning," he explained. "I won three games in a row. I let my brothers know how great I was. They tackled me, and the console got kicked in the process."

This kind of thing occurred a lot with Alex and his two brothers.

"Now what are we going to do?" I said, happy to see him disconnect the wires from the battery's posts.

"I have just the thing," he said, smiling wolfishly.

Within an hour I was crouched in a lookout, which was nothing more than a few hunks of plywood nailed between two thick branches, way up in a Douglas fir tree. Being thirty feet in the air gave me a perfect view of the combat zone. Set in front of me was a bucket of ammo – pinecones soaked in water. They're heavier and easier to throw when they're wet. They also leave a nice welt on bare skin. If you think that's bad, we freeze them in the winter.

"Here they come," I called out to Alex. He was stationed inside a tree house fifteen feet below me with three buckets of ammo.

"I see 'em," he said.

Two boys came hurdling towards us. One was an eleventh grader, and the other was a sixth grader. Both were Alex's brothers. They wore camouflage shirts that they'd bought at a garage sale.

The older brother slipped behind a tree and chucked pinecones so fast that they whistled through the air. The wooden walls of the tree house thudded like drums with every hit. Alex's brothers had soaked their ammo, too.

The youngest brother hid behind a cluster of alders. He was the weakest thrower. What he lacked in velocity he more than made up for in foot speed. In a matter of seconds he was under the tree house and out of our sight.

We kept the two brothers pinned down with our barrage of pinecones. I hit Alex's older brother multiple times on the arms, legs, and shoulders, and his younger brother twice on the top of the head. Alex drilled his older brother's shin. My early success soon ran out with my ammo.

"Here comes Spoon," shouted the younger brother.

Alex's older brother rushed for the base of the tree house, zigzagging around ferns and trees. He reached his younger brother. Together they tagged me as I climbed down from the lookout. I finally reached the trap door in the roof of the tree house, welts and all.

The tree house was put together with two-by-fours and mismatched pieces of plywood. Alex and his brothers got the materials from a scrap pile next to a house that was being remodeled across the street. The tree house could hold six boys with ease. It was built with a Douglas fir tree growing through the middle. It had four walls, three lawn chairs for furniture, and a homemade zip line for an escape route.

Alex and I rotated between two of the windows, and two remaining buckets of pinecones, like a pair of snipers. I was able to land direct hits almost every time a head, elbow, or knee poked out below. A pinecone hit Alex on the forearm, causing him to yelp in pain.

"I'm almost out," I said, dodging a pinecone that ricocheted around the inside of the tree house.

"Me too," said Alex, showing me the last five pinecones in his bucket.

I hurled my last two pinecones, both hitting the youngest brother in the back. "Zip line?" I asked.

"Zip line," agreed Alex.

We climbed through the trapdoor and onto the roof. I reached for the first zip line handle, grabbed on, and jumped off the roof.

"They're taking the zip lines!" shouted someone from below.

Now I know what you're picturing in your head. One of those professional zip lines that people ride on vacations. But like I said, this is a *homemade* zip line. It was no more than a thick rope tightened between two trees with a rusty winch. Don't get me wrong, sailing twenty feet over the forest floor is fun. It's just that our zip line isn't made with wire cable. It sags terribly in the center, sucking the speed right out of the ride.

As soon as my body sailed through the air, a whizzing pinecone hit me in the elbow. Another smacked against the bone of my ankle. One more thumped me in the side of the head. It hurt so bad that I struggled to keep hold of the handle. Alex's brothers cheered every time I winced.

When I was close enough to the ground I released my grip. Letting my knees bend to absorb the fall, I gathered my balance and sprinted down a trail. Alex was right behind me. Last week, we'd stashed some pinecones in various spots throughout the forest. The closest was coming up on our right, hidden at the base of a green fern. All we had to do was get there.

Alex's brothers charged after us, their feet thudding against the packed dirt. I threw my last pinecone over my shoulder. Sliding over the forest floor, I thrust my hand beneath the fern. No pinecones.

"What's the matter," heckled the older brother, "out of ammo?"

Alex rushed up behind me while shouting back at his brother, "You took our pinecones!"

"Why do you think we agreed to have a pinecone fight in the first place?" mocked the younger brother.

We had no choice but to run. Making ninety-degree turns, we charged back towards the tree house. "Head for my backyard!" Alex yelled.

I nodded.

Alex's brothers used this time to tag us in the backs with pinecones they pulled from their fanny-packs. I hate fanny-packs. We sprinted over a rotting log, around a stump, and between two leafy bushes.

We reached the spot where Alex's cherry wooden fence connected to his neighbor's gray wooden fence. I planted one foot on the outside of the cherry fence, grabbed the top, and propelled myself into my best friend's backyard. Pinecones banged against the wooden panels of the fence behind me.

With two hands, Alex pulled himself up. He sat on the top of the fence that divided his neighbor's yard and his own. With his back to his neighbor's house, and his legs dangling above his own yard, Alex scanned the ground for a safe place to land. But he never got the chance. A pinecone cracked him in the base of the skull. His arms went to the back of his head, and his body fell backward.

"Alex!" I hollered.

I ran up the side of the fence that separated the two yards, grabbed a hold of the top, and catapulted myself into the neighbor's yard. Alex rolled around on his side holding his wrist. "Ouch, ouch, ouch!" he moaned, louder each time.

"Let me see," I said.

Alex removed his shaking hand from his injured wrist. It was red and swollen. Thankfully, no bones were sticking through his skin.

"Can you move your fingers?" I asked.

He wiggled them with a painful groan. "Barely."

Alex's brothers climbed into the neighbor's yard, too. "Sorry, Alex," apologized his oldest brother. "I didn't know this would happen."

Alex gritted his teeth. "Don't worry about it."

"Does it hurt?" Alex's younger brother asked.

"Yeah," said Alex, his voice sounding shaky. "I heard it crack."

His brothers shuddered.

An elderly Asian woman ran out of her house. She had ash-gray hair, a wrinkled face, and pink bunny slippers. She held a rolling pin behind her head like a samurai warrior. "Get off my flowers!" she shouted.

I looked down at my shoes. I was standing on a bush with thorny branches and red blossoms. Alex had landed on a cluster of flowers with yellow and orange pedals. Both plants were smashed to pieces.

"Let's get out of here before we get whacked," said Alex's oldest brother.

That sounded good to me. "We're sorry about your flowers," I said, apologizing to the old lady. "But I think my friend broke his wrist."

The older woman stopped and stared at me, frozen. "Your Japanese is flawless," she said, sounding amazed.

"What?" I asked.

"Where did you learn to speak it so well?" she asked. "You don't even have an accent."

I had no idea what the old lady was talking about. I turned toward Alex, who had a funny look on his face.

"What?" I asked, checking to see if my fly was open.

"You're speaking to our neighbor's grandmother," he said.

"So," I said. "She's mad because we destroyed her flowers."

Alex pressed his lips into a thin line, not appearing to be in pain at the moment. "She's speaking Japanese," he said slowly, as if to make a point.

"She is?" I asked.

My cheeks burned red hot as all three brothers nodded their heads.

I ignored their confused looks. "Whatever," I shrugged. "Let's get Alex out of here."

They helped Alex up, but kept glancing at me like I was an alien. The four of us made our way out of the old woman's backyard.

"Sorry," I said to her as we were leaving.

"It's alright," she said in perfect English.

Chapter 2

ALEX'S MOM DROVE HIM to the emergency room with his brothers. It would be their second trip in two months. Alone, I got on my bike and pedaled home. I rode the long way, sticking to the streets. I tried not to think about what happened with Alex's neighbor, but that was easier said than done. I was so thrown off by it that I almost forgot about the faceless guy. Almost.

Passing the blue minivan, I breathed a sigh of relief. The faceless guy was nowhere to be seen. I dropped my bike on the lawn, unlocked the front door of my house, and walked inside. It was Monday, the first day of summer break. I had the house to myself. Mom ran a checkstand at the neighborhood grocery store. She'd be home in three hours, according to the clock in the kitchen.

Pacing around our dining room table, I wondered how I might test whatever happened with the old lady. I didn't know anyone else who spoke another language. But I did have movies with language settings.

Our modest movie collection was displayed in the corner of the living room. I reached for a romantic comedy that my mom had seen a hundred times. I put the movie into our computer. I waited for the main menu to appear and went to language settings. I selected French, with English subtitles.

I hit play and watched as two people spoke to each other in English. They were talking about getting married. The subtitles scrolled across the bottom, word for word of what I was hearing.

I stopped the movie and went back to the language settings on the menu. To my surprise there was no problem to fix. The language was set to French. The subtitles were set to English. Nothing had changed. I set the language to Spanish this time, set the subtitles to Chinese, and resumed play.

The movie continued from where it had left off. I listened to the man and woman speaking all lovey-dovey in English, and English subtitles were scrolling across the bottom of the screen once again.

Goosebumps spread across my forearms. I ejected the DVD, grabbed a different movie, and waited for the menu. This time I selected Arabic with German subtitles. I skipped ahead to a part where people were talking. I pushed play and closed my eyes. I heard people talking in English. I opened my eyes and found English subtitles. The same thing happened when I tried Spanish and Italian.

I told my mom about Alex breaking his arm as soon as she got home, but I left out the part where I talked with the old Asian lady. I also kept quiet about my little language experiment. I figured telling her would mean I believed in all this nonsense. I wasn't prepared to go down that road yet.

Mom changed out of her work clothes. She put on an oversized sweatshirt and jeans, and pulled her dusty-blonde hair back in a ponytail. As she boiled noodles and stirred spaghetti sauce for dinner, she made me read two more chapters from my assigned reading. I tried to put up a fight, but there was no changing her mind.

We ate around a circular table in the kitchen. Mom treated our family dinner like it was sacred, and she would have no distractions. No phones, no texting, and no television. Only conversations.

She told me about these kids who decided to play hide-and-seek on the paper aisle. She talked about all the places they hid, and how they knocked over a towering display of toilet paper. I wasn't listening very well. I kept thinking about how long it might take someone to learn a new language, or two. Years? Decades?

Mom shifted gears and told me about a woman who came through her line before her lunch break. She said that the police were at my school this afternoon. My ears perked up at the mention of *police* and *school*.

"What happened?" I asked.

"The woman said that she was at the school's playground with her kids when a police officer drove up. He asked her, and the other two ladies at the playground, if they'd seen anyone suspicious wandering around," explained my mom.

"What did they say?" I asked, scooting to the edge of my seat.

"She told the officer that she hadn't seen anyone. The officer explained that a few hours earlier they got a call from someone in the neighborhood who'd seen a hooded man cutting across the playground."

I almost choked on my mouthful of garlic bread. "Did they ever get the guy?"

"Not yet," mom said. "But I'm sure it's only a matter of time before they catch up to him."

My stomach twisted at my own memory of the faceless man. I didn't want to make a big deal about it. But I knew that it would be much worse to keep what I saw a secret. "That hooded man was here today."

Mom's eyes widened, and she dropped her fork. "What!"

"I saw him hiding behind the Carlson's minivan. I stepped out the front door and he was watching me. It was creepy."

Mom put her napkin on her plate and pushed her chair back. "I'm calling the police. They must know what you saw," she said, standing up. Mom walked over to the telephone and dialed. She was put on hold twice. Finally, she was able to tell an officer what I had told her. "Thank you," mom said, hanging up.

"What did they say?" I asked.

"The officer said that there were two other reports today. They're sending out extra patrols tonight in case the person shows up again."

We finished the rest of our meal while I fought the urge to look out the window for the faceless man.

I woke up the next morning well after mom had gone to work. I showered, got dressed, and put on an orange hooded sweatshirt with jeans. As I brushed my teeth, I stared at my reddish-brown hair, pointy nose, and hazel eyes in the mirror. I flexed my muscles, laughing at my toothpick-like frame.

I'd prayed for a morning free of reading. A note on the counter shattered that hope. Mom's orders were to read two chapters before leaving the house. I considered going out now, and reading the chapters before lunch. Though, I couldn't bring myself to disobey her. I sat on the couch and read.

When my reading was complete, I wrote a note to my mom about going to Alex's house. I walked out of my house and locked the door. Out the corner of my eye I could see the blue minivan. I couldn't see anyone hiding behind it. Satisfied, I got on my bike and rode down the street.

Alex lived in a tan house with a two-car garage. I left my bike on his uneven driveway, hopped over a baseball bat and glove, and stepped onto a cement step. I knocked on the brown door.

Alex's mom greeted me with a forced smile. "Hello, Spoon." Looking over her shoulder, she shouted, "Alex, you have a visitor!"

The aroma of spices drifted out of the house. Stomping feet climbed the stairs behind Alex's mom. "What?" Alex's youngest brother asked.

"*Alex* has a visitor," she repeated.

"Okay," he said, making eye contact with me, but rushing off as if he might catch a cold. He disappeared downstairs.

I swayed back and forth on my heels. Alex emerged with a cast over his wrist. "What's up, Spoon?"

His eyes darted from me, to his mom, and back to me. Something was wrong. Alex's mom finally walked into her house with nothing more than a nod of her head. I tried to tell myself that she must have been having a bad day. The twisting in my stomach made me think otherwise.

"It's broken," said Alex, showing me his wrist.

His cast was blue, and someone had already signed it across the forearm. "Your brothers?" I asked, pointing.

He nodded, sticking out his arm so I could see it better. *To our brother, Humpty Dumpty,* was written in black marker. It took me a moment to figure that one out. *Humpty Dumpty sat on a wall. Humpty Dumpty took a great fall,* I sang in my head. I smiled at their joke, humming the rhyme under my breath.

"Don't you start singing that song, too," Alex said, glaring at me.

I put my palms up. "Can I sign your cast?" I asked, changing the subject.

"Absolutely," he said. "I still have the pen in my pocket."

Alex handed me the permanent marker. I signed, *Get Well Soon, Loser!*

"What do you want to do today?" I asked, passing back the marker.

He furrowed his eyebrows, sucked in a deep breath, and kept his eyes glued to his feet. "I told my mom what happened yesterday with our neighbor's grandmother, and she thinks that we should take a little break."

"What does 'take a little break' mean?"

"She wants me to take a break from hanging out with you," Alex said, rubbing the back of his head with his good hand.

"What about summer vacation?" I asked, my voice rising.

"I don't know," he said. "When my mom calms down you'll be the first person I call."

"Whatever," I said, rolling my eyes.

Alex made eye contact with me, a frown on his face. Then he stepped into his house and shut the door. I was left to sulk on his front porch.

Back home, I slammed the front door behind me and walked into my bedroom. I crashed onto the bed, shoes and all. I couldn't stop thinking about how Alex's mom didn't want me around, like I was some kind of mutant. We had an entire summer break ahead of us. Was I supposed to spend it alone?

I punched my pillow, rolled over, and put my hands behind my head. I don't know how long I laid there, but the sound of the front door opening brought me back to reality. The clock on my nightstand flashed 11:23 am. Sometimes mom would come home from work and have lunch with me. I didn't feel like getting out of bed though.

Staying in bed, I listened to her footsteps creaking on the floor. My bedroom door opened. Closing my eyes, I pretended to be asleep. This usually was enough to get her to leave. For some reason I never heard the door close. My curiosity got the better of me. I cracked open one eye, just enough to see... It wasn't my mom standing in the doorway. It was a man wearing a hood that hung low over his face, to where his eyes should have been.

Chapter 3

THE FACELESS MAN STOOD THERE, hunched forward, and unmoving. He wore a faded, leather trench coat that stretched all the way to his boots. It appeared to be held together with what looked like metal rivets.

"You're not my mom," I said, crawling backwards on my bed until my back pressed up against the wall.

The faceless man didn't say anything. He just shook his head from side to side, reminding me of the grim reaper. I scanned the room for something to defend myself with. A book on my nightstand was the best I could do. I quickly grabbed it.

"How did you get in here?" I asked, my words sounding shaky.

"The door was unlocked," said the man, his voice vibrating inside my skull.

I fought the urge to smack my own forehead. I'd slammed the door when I got home, but forgot to lock it. "You'd better leave before my mom gets here and calls the police!" I shouted.

"You need not fear me," said the faceless man.

"Says the creep who snuck into my house!"

"I needed to be sure who your father is, and considering you're speaking Lyosian, I believe I have my answer."

I arched an eyebrow. "What's that supposed mean?"

"It signifies that my search is complete," said the faceless man. "Your father's name is Kalven Spooner, or at least it was back where he was born."

A chill ran up my spine. My dad grew up in Amesbury, London, near the famous stone circles of Stonehenge. He didn't speak of his past much, but I definitely would've remembered him talking about a faceless guy from his hometown.

"So what, you know his name," I stammered.

"I know more than just his name," said the faceless man. "Your father is one of the more brilliant minds of his age, along with my brother. Kalven has an insatiable appetite for knowledge. He also has a pair of violet eyes that would be unique in your world."

My jaw clenched so tight that it gave me a headache. I don't know about my dad being some genius. He worked at the library. But he did have violet eyes. Mom said that was the first thing she noticed about him the day they met.

"Lyosian?" I asked, remembering how the old lady told me that I spoke perfect Japanese. "Is that some kind of language?"

The faceless man nodded.

"I thought they spoke English in London?" I asked.

"I'm sure they do," said the faceless man. "Your father, though, is not from this 'London' you speak of."

"Where is he from then?" I asked, trying to understand what in the world was going on.

"You will soon see," he said, with a different tone.

I shivered at his statement even though there was no unkindness in his voice.

"You came all this way for nothing. My dad died when I was two," I said.

The faceless man shook his head from side to side. "You're wrong."

The statement hit me like a blow to the stomach. Grandpa Collins told me that three middle school boys had seen the whole thing. They told the police that a young girl with glowing eyes stood in front of my dad, one palm out. She never touched him, according to the witnesses, but my dad struggled to break free of unseen hands at his throat. He eventually slumped forward and fell to the concrete.

The three eyewitnesses ran across the street yelling for help. The young girl escaped down a sidewalk, only glancing over her shoulder long enough for one of the boys to see that her eyes no longer glowed. They reported her with one green eye and one blue eye. My grandfather went on to say that the news ran an artist's rendering of the young girl's face every night for weeks. But she was never seen or heard from again.

"I'm not wrong," I said, louder than I anticipated. "He was murdered!"

"Please, do not misunderstand me," said the faceless man. "I am sorry to hear about your father's death. I would have loved to take him with us. But he isn't the one I've searched for these past three years."

"Who have you been looking for?" I asked, afraid I might already know the answer.

"You," echoed the faceless man as he removed his leather hood with his boney fingers.

Chapter
4

BENEATH THE MAN'S HOOD was a pair of tiny ears, a dimpled chin, and a bald head. That was it. No eyes. No nose. No mouth. Yet a vapor-like mass swirled, neither liquid nor gas, where his face should've been.

"Who, or what, are you?" I sputtered between gasps of breath.

The churning colors morphed from hues of gray and black to green and blue. "My name is Quaren," he answered. "I am to be trusted."

How could this... this creature, find me with no eyes, or talk to me without a mouth? The stress of it gave me a bloody nose. This wasn't something new for me. My nose bleeds whenever I get scared, like the day I tried a front flip on a trampoline; or nervous, like the afternoon I tried to talk with a new girl at lunch.

Reaching over to my nightstand, yet keeping an eye on the faceless man, I grabbed a box of tissues. I tilted my head back and used the tissue to help stop the bleeding. "What do you want with me?" I asked with one nostril plugged.

"I'm here to escort you to your father's home," explained Quaren, his face shifting from different shades of red and black, with a splash of pink.

I could make a run for the door, but the faceless guy would probably block my escape. I could jump out the window, but the image of me bleeding in the backyard didn't sound appealing. With no other options, I clutched the book in my hand a little tighter.

"Why would you want to do that?" I asked. "There's nothing special about me."

Quaren's face shifted to a mixture of pinks, oranges, and grays, reminding me of a mood ring. "Someone seems to think so," he said.

I wrinkled my forehead. He was a freak. A nutcase. And I was about to tell him just that when he reached into his coat pocket. I gasped, expecting him to pull out a knife, or worse.

To my surprise, Quaren produced a glass vial. It was topped with a clump of brown wax. A tiny stone clinked against the glass. I squinted at the vial. Then I felt a tingling sensation course through my body, as if I'd just been jolted with a tiny amount of electricity.

Quaren's face shifted to solid gray. "I've waited a long time to return home."

Reaching back into his coat pocket, he took out a leather bag with a drawstring tied at the top. He untied the bag and poured grainy, white sand into his other palm.

"You're going to drug me?" I asked, trembling.

"No," Quaren said, his face washing over with blue. "Nothing so straightforward."

With his boot, Quaren cleared away the dirty clothes lying at his feet. He uncovered a patch of brown carpet half the size of my bed. Then he began to make a circle on the floor with the white sand.

It might've been the burning feeling in my gut, or my hands shaking at my sides, but something in me snapped. I rocketed off the bed, straight for the faceless man. I smacked Quaren in the side of the head with my book. And the tissue popped out of my nose as we hit the floor.

I crawled for the door. I would have reached the doorknob if I were an inch taller. Quaren had me by an ankle. He yanked me backwards with one hand. He was stronger than he looked. And faster, too.

"I can't let you leave," said Quaren, his voice thundering inside of my head.

"HELP!" I screamed repeatedly. Hollering for my mom, or a neighbor, or anyone that could get me away from this freak.

"Please, try and calm down," he said somewhat patiently as his face shifted to deep reds and oranges.

"Yeah right!" I protested, continuing to kick and scream for help.

Quaren countered my flaying by grabbing my ankle with both hands and twisting. An explosion of pain shot through my leg. He had me in some kind of ankle lock. And no matter how hard I fought, I just couldn't break free.

"Your struggles are useless," he said calmly.

"I don't care," I moaned.

I continued to fight against his hold. When that didn't work I reached for a leg of my dresser. Stretching my body, and blocking out the pain, I tipped the dresser onto the faceless man. My piggybank crashed onto the back of his head. The thud sounded like it hurt, but he still didn't let go of my ankle.

Through tear filled eyes, I rolled to face my bed. My fingers found a tennis racket underneath. I swung it as best I could at him, but I couldn't get much force behind my blows because of the funny angle of my assault. I attempted to improve that by rotating onto my back, but the faceless man had another idea.

"Enough is enough," he declared, twisting my ankle another degree to make his point.

It hurt so bad that little beads of sweat formed on my forehead.

"I don't want to break your ankle, but I will if I must," he added, turning my ankle enough to cause my vision to blur.

Some part of me believed him, and with nothing else to attack him with, unless you count some smelly gym socks on the floor, I'd have to postpone my escape plan.

"You win," I admitted through gritted teeth, playing along for the moment.

Quaren released my ankle and stood up. I did the same, unable to put my full weight on my very sore ankle. We turned and faced each other. He was a full head taller than me. He picked up his leather bag from the ground and finished making the circle with the sand.

"Please, step inside," he said, his churning face now yellow and red.

"Why?" I asked, out of breath.

Quaren explained, "It's the only way for us to reach your father's homeland."

"I thought you had to *fly* to London," I said, scratching my head.

He pointed a pale finger at the white circle on my bedroom floor. "Trust me."

"Not a chance," I said, not moving.

The swirls on Quaren's face shifted to a dull orange. "If you do as I say, I promise to leave your home immediately."

My lungs heaved from my failed escape. I'd make another break for it the moment he let his guard down. "All I have to do is stand in your stupid circle, and you'll leave?" I said, playing along.

"That, and hold this stone," he said, showing me the vial.

I looked from the white circle, to Quaren, and at his glowing, red stone under the glass. I was one hundred percent positive that a pebble and some sand weren't going send me to London. Would he keep his word? I doubted it. I decided to take the gamble. I stepped into the circle.

Quaren picked off the vial's wax stopper with his fingernails. He brought the vial towards me. It contained a red, polished stone with no sharp edges. It grew brighter and brighter the closer it got to me. I checked the vial for a battery pack or solar panel. Nothing. I could always throw it at him.

"You're clearly Kalven's son," said Quaren as he turned the glass vial over and poured the glowing stone into my outstretched palm.

My breath froze in my chest the instant the stone touched my skin. A red light shined, and the tingling sensation exploded throughout my body.

"What's happening to me?" I demanded, no longer able to feel my fingers or toes.

"Don't be afraid," said Quaren, taking a step backwards, but staying inside the circle. "This is to be expected."

"Expected?" I shrieked.

The tips of my fingers shone from within, as if my bones were glowing. I shook them trying to make the light go away. That only made my skin light up, too. Suddenly, my fingertips began disintegrating.

"This isn't normal!" I screamed, as the stone fell from my hand. "What's happening to me?"

My vision turned red, my throat filled with what felt like burning coals, and my insides seared. I half expected my clothes to catch on fire. I wanted to punch the faceless guy, but that was impossible; I no longer had hands.

My body was breaking down into glowing, red sand. Now my forearms, biceps, and shoulders were disappearing, too.

The red sand began swirling around me. I felt like I was a sandcastle being attacked by a leaf blower.

I crumbled to my knees as my feet and lower legs blew away next. I stared at where my arms and legs should have been.

My nostrils filled with the smell of burnt hair, and I struggled to breathe.

Quaren's stone lay in the circle, and a tornado of red, glowing sand was getting sucked into it.

Just then my mom stepped into the bedroom. Her eyes widened, and her jaw hung open. She screamed. But I couldn't hear her over the roar of the swirling sand around me. I felt like I was being sucked through the eye of a needle.

As soon as my mom lunged for me, everything went black.

Chapter 5

I WAS NO LONGER IN MY BEDROOM. Opening my eyes, I saw that I was in a dark room with my face to the ground. Rays of moonlight shone through cracks in the ceiling, allowing me to see my breaths in the cold air. The glowing red stone lie in front of my face. I reached over and picked it up.

Rolling onto my back, I tried to stand. Every muscle in my body felt like rubber, and my lungs burned with each breathe. I got to my knees with some effort. My head was swimming, and I wanted to puke. I made myself sit up. I was alive, but where was I?

Looking down, I was in the middle of a circle of white sand. It had to be the same stuff Quaren used in my bedroom. Opening my right palm, I stared at the now dim stone. Had I been drugged? Had Quaren kidnapped me? Was I in London? I worked myself into a panic and got another bloody nose.

Leaning back, pinching the bridge of my nose, I watched patches of twinkling stars between the gaps in the ceiling. I had no clue how long I'd been unconscious. When my nose stopped bleeding, I stuffed Quaren's stone into a pocket in my jeans.

Getting to my feet was a struggle. The floor, walls, and ceiling were each made of the same rectangular stones. It was obvious from the rubble and debris covering the floor that this place was ancient. I shuffled to the only door in the room, a rotted piece of wood, pushed it open, and emerged into a hallway. Checking left and right, I sucked in a breath to call out for my kidnapper, but someone else beat me to it.

A man's voice that I didn't recognize asked, "Quaren?"

I slipped back into the room, listening as the man's footsteps drew closer. If I hadn't been tipped off by the sound of his voice, I don't think I would have heard him coming.

"Quaren, is that you?" whispered the man.

The tip of a sword entered the room. A short man with a slow pace followed. I didn't want to get stabbed, so I spoke up. "I was about to ask you the same question."

The man faced me, pointing his sword at me. A ray of moonlight lit up a pair of tinted glasses on his face. "How do you know Quaren?" he asked, watching me as if I were some kind of difficult math problem.

"He's the freak who sent me here!" I snapped.

"How?" the man asked.

"He drugged me with that stuff," I said, pointing to the circle of sand, "and this," I exclaimed, pulling out the dim, red stone from my pocket.

The man's eyes widened. "Why did he send you?"

I'm not sure why I was answering all his questions. I suppose it's because he reminded me so much of my grandfather. "He said he'd searched a long time for me, and that someone wanted me here," I explained.

The old man sheathed his sword, which had no rounded edges. Stepping towards me, he said, "I saw flashes of red lights erupting through this place upon my arrival. It was the same bright light that happened three years ago when Quaren left."

I replaced the red stone in my pocket, and asked, "So, you do know Quaren?"

He nodded. "He's a friend of mine. Will he arrive here as well?"

I shrugged. "Quaren made it sound like he was coming with me."

"Quaren's timing couldn't be better," he said. "But what I want to know is why he sent *you* instead of your father?"

"He couldn't have sent my dad, even if he wanted to," I mumbled.

"Why's that?"

"He died when I was two," I added, getting tired of having to explain this to people.

He ran his hand through his peppery-gray hair. "I'm sorry to hear that."

"You knew my father?" I asked, deciding it was my turn for some information.

He shook his head. "I knew *of* him."

"What did you need him for anyway?" I asked.

He stroked his graying beard. "Your father was our best shot at preventing a threat to Altrea."

"Oh," I said, turning to the door, expecting the faceless man to enter the room any moment. "What was that about a bright light?"

"It's what happens when someone uses a ley line," he answered.

I had a feeling this wasn't some kind of airline for kidnappers.

He continued, "Ley lines are what connect our worlds."

Goose bumps broke out over my forearms. "Our worlds?"

"Yes," he said, "Earth and Altrea."

"You mean like flight paths that airplanes use to get from one place to another?" I prodded.

"What's an *airplane?*" he asked, caulking his head to the side.

"They carry people through the air, over long distances," I said, making a flying motion with my hand.

"There are things in your world that can do that?" he asked.

I nodded. "Didn't I fly in one to get here?"

"No, you traveled here by ley line with the help of Quaren's red stone," he said. "It's called a verve stone. It's what broke you down into life-energy, stored you inside itself, thrust you through a ley line, and rematerialized you here," he said, pointing to the center of the white circle. "Don't you remember?"

I had a vivid memory of my body turning into the red embers and blowing away. That's not something I will ever forget. "This has to be some kind of joke. Where are the cameras? I want to see my mom, now!"

One of his bushy eyebrows arched. "I have no idea what you're talking about. But I can promise you that this is no joke. And your mother is not here."

My knees wobbled and my head spun. I placed my hand against the wall to keep my balance. "I feel terrible."

"Your trip took a lot out of you, but I have something that can help," he said, removing a saddlebag from his shoulder. He pulled out a wooden box. Inside were thin, dried leaves. He handed two to me. "These will help to restore your lost energy."

I looked at the leaves and at the sand circle, shaking my head. "No way."

"They're perfectly safe," he said, taking a bite of one of the leaves, chewing, and swallowing. "See."

I waited three minutes for him to pass out. He never did. "Fine."

He stuck out his hand and I took the leaves.

"Chew them up and place what you have left between your bottom lip and gums," he explained.

I did as he said. A warm sensation washed over me. I continued to suck on the stuff while waiting for Quaren to show up. But he didn't.

"My name is Melik," he said. "What's your name?"

The guy seemed trustworthy, like a kindly, old grandfather, but there was no way I was telling a stranger my real name. So I told him, "Spoon."

"It's nice to meet you, Spoon, son of Kalven," said Melik, bowing slightly.

"Right," I said.

Over the next ten minutes I was able to remove my hands from the wall and limp around the room without feeling like the floor was tilting. Those dried leaves were like packs of caffeine. The whole time Melik kept still as a statue. I had the feeling that he was a man who appreciated patience.

"Quaren told me that he knew I was my father's son because I spoke perfect Lyosian."

"He's a smart man to recognize that gift in you," said Melik.

"You aren't making any sense," I said.

"It's simple; your father's people have the gift of speaking, writing, and reading in any language. They also have violet-colored eyes. Though, it appears you didn't inherit that trait."

"My dad could understand other languages, too?" I asked, sounding surprised.

Melik nodded. "All languages to be exact."

"How can you be so sure?" I asked.

"What language am I speaking right now?"

"English."

Melik shook his head. "I'm speaking an old Byroc dialect from under the Domegal Mountains."

Either he was prepared to go to extremes to keep this joke alive or I was going crazy. I was leaning towards the second.

The two of us sat on the stone floor facing the white circle. I got up and paced around the room trying to burn off the buzz from the leaves. My stomach rumbled.

"Great idea," Melik said, grunting as he got to his feet. "I've been riding hard for the past two days. Let's eat."

"What about Quaren?" I asked.

"Remember the bright lights when you slipped through the ley line? They lit up the sky. I'm sure everyone in Tarboo saw it," Melik exclaimed, adjusting his tinted glasses on the end of his stout nose. "When he arrives, we will know."

Melik led me across the decaying ruins in the darkness, with only slivers of moonlight to light our way. I followed close behind, tripping on crumbling stones and roots. He took a right and two lefts without slowing his pace.

The further we walked the more of a tour guide Melik became. He told me that we were in an ancient castle ruin, set at the northern base of the Hollow Mountain, in the Gravsted Mountains. They'd been abandoned for hundreds of year. It was originally built as a summer getaway for the royal Androia family. But the family fell on hard times, and it was left to the harsh mountain weather.

We emerged onto a tilted balcony. Its former shape was that of a semicircle, but now trees grew up from the cracks in the stones, and the outer edge had fallen off in large clumps.

"Wow," I exclaimed.

The view was spectacular. The clear night allowed me to see the knifed peak of the mountain behind me. Snowy spikes, like jagged teeth, connected the east to the west. The scent of tree sap and wet soil filled the air. It all paled in comparison to what hung in the sky though. Three gigantic moons bathed the mountains in silver light. I tried to speak, but I just stared at them with my mouth open.

"You don't have moons back home?" Melik asked.

I shook my head. "Just one," I mumbled. Half my brain wanted this place to be a hoax. The other half screamed that they don't have three moons in London! "What did you call this place again?"

Melik patted me on the shoulder. "Altrea."

Chapter 6

I WATCHED THE SKY UNTIL my stomach growled from hunger again. Melik told me that he had some food in his pack. He led us off the balcony, across the ruins, and onto a courtyard covered in skinny trees. He whistled a tune I didn't recognize. It had a calming effect on me. A horse faced us, its reins wrapped around a curled branch.

"This is Bomber," Melik said, rubbing the horse's nose.

I've never spent much time around horses, unless you count seeing them at the fair. Bomber seemed nice enough. Melik wanted me to pet the horse's nose.

"You won't bite, will you, boy?" Melik asked his horse.

I stuck my hand out, trying to keep if from trembling. Bomber eyed my fingers with his big black eyes. I was ready to pull my arm away at the slightest danger. "Hello," I said, rubbing the patch of white on his forehead with my hand. It was soft.

Melik gave his horse one last pat on the neck. "Now that we all know each other..." he said, digging into one of the two bags secured to his horse's saddle. Bomber's ears flickered before he removed the food. The animal turned to face the largest gap in the rock wall that encircled the courtyard.

Melik's hand went to the pommel of his sword. "What is it, boy?" he whispered, turning to the gap, too.

I spun around, but there was nothing to see except shadows. I tried to ask Melik what had him so worried, but he shushed me. The horse stomped its feet on the hard earth. Gesturing for me to step behind with his free hand, Melik drew his sword.

My heart pounded in my ears. Melik was steady as a rock. We waited for what felt like days, but it might have been only a handful of minutes. At last, Bomber's ears stopped swiveling around.

Melik kept his eyes glued to the gap in the wall. "False alarm," he said, sheathing his sword. He removed a few parcels from his bag, and we returned inside.

We ate in a vast room in the center of the ruins. It seemed large enough to entertain a couple thousand noble men and women in its day. Through, the butler had definitely let the place go. Three of the four arched doorways had crumbled, and all the carved beams had rotted and fallen. The most noticeable portion of the ballroom was the vast hole in the ceiling. It reached up for two more levels, and acted as a skylight, letting in a column of moonlight thirty feet across.

Melik gave me another of his dried leaves to chew on. It was a good thing because the walk from the courtyard had me feeling sore and winded. Our snack was three stringy strips of salted meat, an apple, a handful of nuts, and some very sharp cheese. I didn't think anything less than two double-bacon cheeseburgers would fill me up, but I was thankful for Melik's snack.

"How are you feeling?" he asked.

"I haven't felt this tired since I went snowboarding with Alex for three days straight," I answered.

Melik furrowed his eyebrows. It turns out they don't have snowboarding on Altrea. I spent the next half hour explaining my favorite sport to him. He asked a lot of questions. I got the feeling he thought the act of strapping a piece of wood to one's feet and sliding down the side of a mountain was crazy.

"Your fatigue is to be expected," explained Melik. "Slipping through a ley line takes an enormous amount of life-energy. To be honest, from what I know about the process, you're lucky to be alive."

I rubbed my puffy eyes. "Have you ever slipped through a ley line?"

Melik chuckled. "No, I have not."

"What's so funny?"

"For one thing, you have to be able to access a verve stone," he said.

I glanced at the pocket where Quaren's little red stone rested. "They can't be used by anyone?"

"No," answered Melik. "The gift is most uncommon."

"That means my dad could use one, too," I wondered aloud.

Melik nodded. "Very observant. It is the only way to travel between worlds."

I picked up a piece of broken stone from the ground and tossed it into the darkness. "How many people have made the trip?"

He looked up, while touching each of his fingers to his thumb. "Four, that I know of. Besides your father, there were three scholars from Yont: Elven, Dwarvish, and Tollock. It's said that they filled several books with their time on your world."

"No one else?"

"Quaren was the latest to make the trip. He used notes that your father compiled during his studies of the scholars' combined texts," explained Melik, packing up the leftovers and stuffing them into his saddlebag.

"I've been… thinking," I said. "If slipping through a ley line is so dangerous, what made my dad do it?"

Melik took a deep breath, but he never got a chance to answer me.

A strange man in black stepped into the column of moonlight. His footsteps made no sound. He was wrapped in black from head to toe, with a thin opening across his eyes, allowing him to see. In each hand he gripped what looked like police batons that ran the length of his forearms. The ends of each nightstick flashed a serrated blade. Two more were strapped to his back.

"Hand them over," he commanded with a harsh voice.

Melik got to his feet, removing his sword from its sheath in one fluid motion. He pointed it at the newcomer. He didn't waver as he put himself between the man in black and me. I held my breath, a bead of sweat rolling down my back.

"Who is this guy?" I whispered.

"A Marzzoe," Melik breathed, widening his stance. "I hope the others are all right," he added, more to himself than to me. He grabbed my forearm. "We're leaving!" We made it three steps in the opposite direction when a second man in black stepped into the column of moonlight, blocking our escape. Melik shoved me behind him and pointed his sword at the new guy. I held my bleeding nose.

Turning my back to Melik, I faced the first Marzzoe. "Your friends won't be able to meet you here," he said.

"And you two can join them as soon as you tell us where the blueprints are," the second Marzzoe hissed.

Chapter
7

"What blueprints?" Melik asked, never lowering the tip of his sword.

"No games!" insisted the first guy. "We will not ask again."

"Good, because we don't have them," Melik said.

"Lies," he spat.

The Marzzoe twisted his wrist, spinning out his blades at Melik. Melik turned aside the attack with a flick of his sword. Metal clanged against metal. The Marzzoe somersaulted to his left, then leapt for Melik. He sent three slices aimed at Melik's head. He deflected two, but the third caught him in the shoulder. Not glancing at the red spot growing on his shirt, he set his feet.

Bouncing and flipping, the Marzzoe didn't let up. He spun his blades in devastating arches, coming at him from impossible angles. Melik was able to use his enemy's momentum against him. With the slightest touch of his sword, Melik altered each swing. The harder the Marzzoe tried, the more off balance he became.

"Spoon," Melik blurted between attacks, "you need to run!"

The other Marzzoe laughed, watching his friend. "No one leaves until we have what we came for." Raising his serrated blades, he walked towards me.

What I would've given to wake up from this nightmare. I prayed for this over and over, concentrating so much that I gave myself a headache. The sharp end of a serrated blade spun around in the Marzzoe's hand. Another step and it would skewer me. I held up my hands, as if they would help me.

Something hard rammed into my side. I hit the ground and rolled to my feet. Standing in my place, with his back to Melik, was a new person. He must have shoved me out of the way. The man had messy black hair. He wore a blood-red shirt and dark pants. His dense eyebrows were pressed into a V shape, and his top lip was snarling. He carried a long, thin-blade sword made of a black metal. The only nonlethal part of the weapon was the glowing, blue stone set in the base of its pommel. Where had this guy come from?

"Roban," said Melik, as if they were catching up at a coffee shop.

"Sorry we're late," the mystery man grumbled, not taking his eyes off his enemy.

"Right on time, if you ask me," Melik said, keeping his guard up.

The new guy shook his head. "And who's the brat?"

"Kalven's son," Melik answered.

Roban growled, "Why?"

"Don't know."

Both Marzzoe attacked. They got in a flip or two before I heard a jingling sound in the distance. It was followed by two twangs, seconds apart. Out of the darkness came two blurs – arrows I'd guess – each hissing for a Marzzoe. I thought they'd be goners, but the Marzzoe bent their bodies to escape injury.

Running feet echoed across the ruins. Two more people stepped into the column of moonlight. One was a woman, about my mom's age, with copper-red hair that cascaded over her shoulders. She had a round face, wore a leather vest, and held a short sword in her hands. She positioned herself behind the Marzzoe facing Melik.

A man wearing a green shirt with no sleeves was right behind her. He had chocolate-colored skin, wore a green headband, and had long arms that looked cut from stone. He was also showing off a set of white teeth, as if he'd walked into his own surprise party. "We can't let you hog all the fun," he said, waving a double-edged sword from side to side.

I discovered where the jingling sounds came from. A collection of beads, trinkets, and bracelets jingled on the wrist of the guy with the green headband. He wore a quiver on his back, and had a bow slung over his right shoulder.

"Vadin," Melik shouted, "take Spoon somewhere safe!"

Roban roared, "We're not here to babysit!"

"We are now," Melik corrected.

Vadin nodded and ran straight for me. "Time to go, Fork," he said with a wink, grabbing me by the forearm.

Chapter
8

VADIN AND I RACED through the darkness as a thunderstorm of swords clashed behind us. I wanted to check over my shoulder, but I never gave me the chance. We passed the room with the white circle, hung a left, and two more rights. I had the feeling Vadin was choosing his turns at random. He yanked me into a hallway with doors on either side.

We stopped at a door with one working hinge. "This'll have to do," he said, catching his breath. He took something off his shoulder. I thought it was his quiver of arrows. I was wrong. "Take this," he said, handing me a leather tube. It was tied at both ends with buckled straps. "Don't let it out of your sight."

"Okay," I said as I brought the leather tube close to my chest.

Vadin told me to get behind a pile of rubble on the far side of the room. I found a place to sit, while remaining unseen from the doorway. "Keep your head down, and don't make a sound. I'll return as soon as I can."

I nodded.

Vadin winked. He jogged out of the door, his bracelets jingling as he went.

I placed the leather tube on my lap, brought my knees to my chin, and hunched forward as far as I could. The room was silent, the kind of quiet you can feel pressing in around you. A tear streaked down my cheek as my mom popped into my head. I shook the image away. I was too scared to be sad.

My eyes refocused on the leather tube that Vadin gave me. I had a sinking suspicion that the blueprints the Marzzoe wanted were inside, which meant they'd be coming for me.

Swords clanged together in the distance. They seemed to be getting closer. With my head between my knees, I rocked back and forth. My heart felt like it was beating in my throat. Every muscle in my body tensed up, making it difficult to breathe.

An explosion of wood echoed from down the hallway. I held my breath. More wood shattered a minute later, even closer. The last sound of wood splintering was the closest. I had a bad feeling that my door would be next. I wished I could've been wrong.

The single hinge on the door never stood a chance. It exploded into the room. Pieces of the rotten wood landed on me. Fighting the urge to peek, I crammed my head between my knees. I strained to hear who was in my room when something sharp pressed against my throat.

"The blueprints," he said.

I looked up. A Marzzoe was standing on the pile of rubble, pointing a serrated blade at my neck. I never heard him cross the room. I held very still. I wanted to keep my head attached to my body. Somehow, I didn't shriek like a two-year-old. My fingers wrapped around the leather tube. A part of my brain was screaming for me to fight back or run away. All I was good for was another nosebleed.

I hadn't asked for this. Quaren was the one who was acting all mysterious about me coming to Altrea. I'd rather be home with my mom right now, not about to be murdered. Blood trickled from where the serrated blade pressed into my throat. Would Quaren ever learn that I wasn't special?

Roban stepped into the room. He wore his red shirt, and carried his thin sword. He was backlight by a dozen rays of moonlight, and his forearms were covered in weaving black tattoos. I would've thought them cool, if I weren't about to lose my head.

"Roban," I whispered, a trace of hope entering my voice.

Removing the blade from my neck, the Marzzoe faced Roban.

Neither figure wasted their breaths on words. Both shifted around the cramped room. Roban stopped between the Marzzoe and me, or at least between the Marzzoe and the blueprints.

Roban made the first move, his sword jabbing out in a fury. Contorting his body to evade each blow, the Marzzoe remained unharmed. He landed, planted his feet, and swung his serrated blades with an overhand chop. Roban blocked the assault with the flat side of his sword. He countered with a kick, but failed to make contact.

Taking advantage of the mistake, the Marzzoe cut Roban on the knee. Roban would not be outdone. He sent a number of rotating slices. One caught the Marzzoe on the upper arm. The fight went this way for some time, each person finding an opening with the other, but never anything too devastating.

Roban and the Marzzoe came together in the center of the room. They exchanged a stream of strikes, knocking each other to opposite sides of the room. With heaving chests, they glared at one another.

I ran my finger over the cut on my neck. It had stopped bleeding and felt sticky.

The Marzzoe mumbled to himself. He sounded like he was talking to Roban, but something seemed odd about the rhythm of his words. Finally, it hit me. He was chanting.

"Oh, no you don't!" barked Roban, charging with his sword raised.

The chanting grew louder and faster. The eyes of the Marzzoe flicked to life like a pair of yellow flashlights. Roban sprinted forward, the tip of his sword leading his charge. With only one step between Roban and his attacker, the outline of the Marzzoe vibrated like a hummingbird's wing.

I gasped. The assassin's silhouette pulled apart from the middle, but not in two halves. The man in the center remained, while additional bodies appeared out of black smoke and shadow. Now there were three.

The clone on the right hadn't materialized for more than a heartbeat when Roban stuck his black sword into his chest. He knew what the Marzzoe was planning all along.

With a blade in his chest, and no blood to be seen, the clone hissed furiously. The Marzzoe transformed into an inky mass, corkscrewing around the thin blade of Roban's sword until it disappeared with a pop.

The second clone grabbed both weapons from the original's back. Now it was two against one. Together the Marzzoe surrounded Roban. Roban positioned his sword to the spot between his opponents. He widened his stance, took a deep breath, and blinked.

If I hadn't seen the Marzzoe's eyes glowing yellow for myself, I'd never have believed Roban's eyes could glow, too. That's exactly what happened. Two blue lights cut through the darkness like a pair of high beams. And he wasn't done yet. The blade of his sword changed from black metal to what I can best describe as a whitish-blue hue of pure energy.

Chapter 9

THE ROOM LIT UP with the radiance of Roban's sword. Both Marzzoe stepped back. But Roban's new weapon didn't keep them away for long.

Working as one, the original and his clone flipped over, rolled under, and spun around each other. It was impossible to tell the clone from the original. Roban stayed in the center of the room. He was so fast with his humming blade that it blurred through the air with every swing.

The Marzzoe fought from a distance, only attacking his blind side. They failed to land a hand or blade on him. Roban was intense. He slashed with enough force to cut a tree in half. He was also precise. He knew how to move enough so the Marzzoe would miss him by inches.

Roban charged the closest Marzzoe, sending a stream of slices his way. Roban's combo missed, ending with a horizontal cut that should have smashed his sword against the stone wall, but not this sword. It slid through the rock like a hot knife through butter.

Roban continued his assault, while the gash in the wall glowed red. Could it be an energy sword?

Roban found himself on top of my pile of rubble. He used the height advantage to take control of the fight. Coming together in the doorway, the Marzzoe appeared to regroup. Without saying a word, they went head to head with Roban. They traded dizzying flips with an overpowering barrage of quick hits to the body.

Every time Roban made one of the Marzzoe dodge his incredible sword, the other came inside his swing to deliver a kick to his torso. Roban dropped one hand from his sword to block the body blows. But he wasn't able to stop them all.

One Marzzoe shoved him off the mound of rubble towards the doorway. The second Marzzoe attacked with a serrated blade aimed at Roban's neck. Roban somersaulted as he landed, planted his feet, and dove out of the reach of the Marzzoe's blade.

The first Marzzoe kicked a hunk of the door at Roban. He had no trouble slicing through the decayed wood. Using this as a distraction, the second Marzzoe came at Roban from the above. The first Marzzoe then went for Roban's legs.

Roban's glowing-blue eyes flared as he jumped over the blade whizzing towards his ankles. But he was not able to stop the batons that came at his outstretched elbow. The sound of that impact turned my stomach. Roban was knocked to his back.

The first Marzzoe landed on him. Both men wrestled to gain the upper hand, without getting stabbed. Roban won. He got both his feet underneath the Marzzoe's stomach and thrust him across the room.

Flipping from his back to his feet, Roban charged the second Marzzoe. He retaliated with three sweeping strikes of his glowing sword. His enemy used fast footwork to dodge the blows. With the Marzzoe backed against the pile of rubble, Roban swung with his left hand and punched the guy in the face.

The yellow lights in his eyes blinked off. He dropped on top of the pile of rubble, unmoving. Roban held his blade over the Marzzoe. But the first Marzzoe threw himself at Roban, saving his clone. These two battled each other towards the door.

I was no longer focused on the fight. Creeping over my hiding place, I peered at the unconscious Marzzoe. He smelled of soot and sour meat. A single beam of moonlight was glowing across his face. His eyes were closed, and the wrapping over his mouth had opened enough to see fine lips and teeth sharpened to a point. Being so close to him made my palms sweat. Could he be dead?

The assassin's chest heaved with life, as if to answer my question. Scurrying to the other side of the pile of rubble, I saw the Marzzoe taking in a few more gulps of air. I tucked my head between my knees. Wiping the blood from my nose on my pants, I chanced a sideways glance.

The Marzzoe rubbed his forehead, picked up his weapons, and stood up. The guy had a full view of Roban's back. It didn't take a rocket scientist to figure out Roban was in trouble. With a serrated blade in one hand, the Marzzoe sprinted for Roban.

I should have been screaming for Roban to turn around. I couldn't breathe, let alone speak. One more step and the Marzzoe would be on top of him. I finally stammered, "Behind you!"

Roban turned toward my warning, but it was too late. The sickening sound of the blade going into his side filled the room. Roban's body froze, his glowing-blue eyes switched off, and his blade turned back to metal. He and his sword fell to the floor.

"No!" I yelled, realizing too late that I was supposed to be hiding.

Both the original and his clone snapped their necks around. In unison they rushed me. I closed my eyes, tucked the leather tube behind me, and cringed. The Marzzoe never reached me.

Stab wound and all, the man with the weaving tattoos came to my rescue, again. His eyes glowed blue, his sword hummed with energy, and he used his last bit of strength to chop the head off the closest Marzzoe. This sounds like a disturbing sight, but there was no blood. The instant the sword passed clean through, the body of the Marzzoe transformed into a cloud of angry smoke before disappearing with a pop.

The glowing-yellow eyes of the remaining Marzzoe flared as he watched his final clone was destroyed. Roban pointed his sword at his enemy, daring him to continue the fight. The Marzzoe spun his serrated blades with his wrist.

Round three.

Releasing one hand from the handle of his sword, Roban pressed his palm against his side. Blood seeped out from between his fingers. His eyes and blade continued to light up the room.

The Marzzoe let two diagonal slashes fly at Roban with his serrated blades. Roban dodged the attack with a backwards step, but even the smallest movements caused him to cringe. He countered with swipes of his sword that left a trail of blue light. The Marzzoe avoided these strikes by bending his body at strange angles, not once using his blades to block the humming sword.

The two men came apart, chest rising and falling with swords at the ready. Neither man said a word as they circled each other. The Marzzoe made the next move with a serrated blade uppercut. Roban spun to his left, keeping his enemy at a distance by rotating his blade clockwise. Then he let go of his injured side and held his sword with both hands.

Roban went on the offensive. He chopped his way towards the Marzzoe. He sliced through rocks, the floor, and rotten beams, but like a ninja monkey the Marzzoe stayed one step ahead. He ended his assault by stabbing at the Marzzoe from across the room. Face cringing, Roban's front leg wobbled. Stretching out like that must have pulled at his stab wound. He stumbled.

In the fraction of a second that it took Roban to regain his balance, the Marzzoe drove the wooden end of his baton into the side of Roban's head. It wasn't a direct hit, but the impact still knocked Roban to the ground. Somehow, he rolled with the blow, got his feet under him, and kept the Marzzoe away with the tip of his sword moving in a figure eight pattern.

With clenched teeth, Roban removed one hand from the handle of his sword to draw a dagger from his belt. Pointing it at the Marzzoe, Roban transformed its silver blade to match his sword.

The Marzzoe tried to step back, but Roban wouldn't let him. He attacked with a combination of slashes that left parallel streams of whitish-blue light hanging in the air. He followed this up with a volley of slices aimed for the Marzzoe's stomach. The Marzzoe managed to stay alive, though his black clothes had been shredded to ribbons.

The Marzzoe closed the distance with a forward roll, which he came out of with a perfectly placed knee to Roban's gut. Wheezing, Roban spun out of striking distance. He reset his feet and held his blades over his head in an aggressive-looking stance. His dagger had left a gash on the Marzzoe's shoulder, and his sword had bit into his thigh. Neither wound bled.

Slivers of moonlight cut through a cloud of dust that the two men had kicked up. All of a sudden Roban went into overdrive. Spinning right, he avoided a serrated blade across his calves, and spinning left, he almost took the head off the Marzzoe with scissoring swipes of his blades. Roban was scary good. I had no idea that he could move so fast after fighting this freak for so long.

The Marzzoe scrambled away from the whirlwind of glowing blades. He leaped to his left, bouncing off a wall. He dashed right, and got pinned between a glowing sword and another wall. Roban had managed to corral the Marzzoe into a corner. Closed in on both sides, and without enough room to dance out of the way, the Marzzoe thrust the tip of his blade at Roban's heart, and then the other.

Roban was ready. He brought his sword down in a flash, severing the first serrated blade in half. The sword met no resistance. The dagger did the same effect on the Marzzoe's second serrated blade. Two clangs rang out as the top halves of the Marzzoe's weapons clattered to the floor.

A dull orange glow faded away as the cut ends of the weapons cooled. The Marzzoe's batons might have lost their fangs, but they could still do some damage. Setting his feet, the Marzzoe feinted to his right, and swung the wooden ends of his batons at Roban's ribs from his left. Both hit their mark.

Roban crumpled to his knees, but he did not fall.

The Marzzoe licked his lips as he spread his arms wide, bringing what was left of his serrated blades level with Roban's neck. Then he brought his hands together.

"Watch out!" I screamed.

In one fluid motion Roban's eyes opened, he dove forward, and he stuck the Marzzoe in the chest with both of his blades. The man in black crumpled to the floor. Roban pulled his sword and dagger free of the man's chest. The Marzzoe's wounds didn't bleed.

Roban watched the Marzzoe's unmoving body. I did too. He must have felt convinced the Marzzoe was dead because his sword and dagger turned back to metal, his glowing-blue eyes went dark, and he fell next to the Marzzoe.

Chapter 10

I SKIDDED TO A STOP at Roban's side. I kneaded my hands together, too afraid to touch him. A pause of silence magnified the pulse in my ears, which was followed by clashing swords in the distance. I prayed that meant Melik and the others were still alive.

My body twitched to run away. I imagined myself sprinting across the ruins, finding the room with the white circle, and beaming home. But with the other Marzzoe still lurking about, I couldn't leave Roban behind.

"You have to get up," I whispered.

With a jolt, Roban coughed up some blood. I waved my hands around like a lunatic, but I didn't know what to do. His eyes stayed shut. I heard a few raspy breaths. He choked out, "Get something to stop the bleeding."

"Right," I mumbled, searching around the room, but only finding rocks and rubble.

Roban squinted his eyes and through gritted teeth said, "Use your shirt, you fool."

I was wearing an orange hoodie over a white t-shirt. I removed the hoodie and pressed it onto his wound. He winced. I thought I'd done something wrong so I let up the pressure until Roban yelled at me to push harder. The orange fabric of my sweatshirt quickly turned red. Guilt burned in my chest. I should have done something to prevent this from happening.

A whisper from Roban brought me back. "Get Melik."

"What about you?" I asked.

Roban lifted his right arm up, grabbed my stained hoodie, and applied pressure to his own wound. "I'm fine," he spat, along with a few more choice words that I don't care to repeat. "Melik can stop the bleeding. Go!"

"I won't be long," I said, faking optimism. I set the blueprints at his side and left the room.

My shoes slapped against the stone floor as I ran to find Melik. I followed the sound of swords crashing together. In the ballroom, Melik was fighting a Marzzoe in the center of the column of moonlight.

He was an exact replica of the one Roban fought. His eyes glowed yellow, and he sent his serrated blades at Melik from the most impossible angles. I couldn't fathom how Melik had stayed alive for so long. He fought like a statue, except for his wrist, which deflected everything the Marzzoe threw at him with a flick of his sword.

A loud crash boomed like an avalanche. Looking up, I saw a shower of stones falling straight for my face. I jumped backwards, putting my arms up. A rush of air whizzed by my forearms as the debris missed me by inches. The stones hit the floor in a plume of dust and shards.

Vadin, with a heel over the edge of the hole in the ceiling, was standing on the floor above me. He was waving his sword at a Marzzoe of his own. My best guess was the other Marzzoe must have cloned himself as well. I wanted to look around for the clone, figuring it to be fighting with Jana, but I couldn't pull my attention off the battle above me.

Vadin jumped, spun, and cartwheeled around the edge of the hole, matching the Marzzoe move for move. And he did it with a grin on his face. He feinted to his left, flipped head-over-heels, and broke away to his right. I thought his tactic was suicidal, seeing as there was a wall three feet in front of him. Vadin knew what he was doing though.

As Vadin reached the wall, he jumped towards it, feet first. He landed with bent knees, absorbed the impact, and catapulted himself, sword extended, at the Marzzoe. Defying gravity, Vadin slashed as he collided with the man in black. A shower of sparks rained down from above. The man with the glowing-yellow eyes was knocked back.

I wanted to keep watching the epic clash, but an intense white light, or flare, pulsed throughout the ballroom in front of me. Squeezing my eyes shut, I covered my face with both hands. Finally, the burst of light went out.

I stood there, rubbing my eyes. I felt like someone had put hot coals under my eyelids. I looked around as water poured from my eyes. The light must have burned my retinas.

I saw the fuzzy silhouette of Melik, on his knees, groping around on the ground. His tinted glasses rested two inches out of his reach. The Marzzoe had both serrated blades raised above his head. He was heading straight for Melik.

My throat tensed up, and my hands shook. I felt rooted to the floor with fear. It was the same feeling of dread I experienced when Roban got stabbed in the side. I couldn't let anyone else get hurt, or die, because of me. I had to act.

A tingling sensation in my muscles coursed through my body. Every dark wall, chunk of stone, and shaft of moonlight suddenly appeared bathed in a red hue. It was as if I'd put on a pair of glasses with scarlet lenses.

I picked up a hunk of rock Vadin had kicked down from above and charged the Marzzoe. The ballroom glowed brighter in the strange red light. I brought the softball-sized piece of rubble behind my head. The Marzzoe, so focused on killing Melik, never saw me coming.

Chapter 11

I OPENED MY EYES SLOWLY, no longer seeing everything through red lenses. Lying on my back, I rubbed a grain of stone between my fingers and thumb. It was all that remained of the rock I'd hit the Marzzoe with.

Melik's head popped into my view. He peered down at me, once again wearing his tinted glasses and said, "Thank you."

I rolled over. The Marzzoe was nowhere to be seen. "Where is he?" I asked.

"Gone," Melik answered. "And because of you, I am not."

"I don't understand," I said.

"He transformed into a pulsing, black mist and vanished with a loud pop," explained Melik.

My legs felt like they were filled with sand, similar to the way they'd felt after I woke up in the room with the white circle.

Vadin jumped down from the hole in the ceiling and joined us, his bracelets jingling as he landed. He had a deep cut on his bare shoulder, but nothing that would kill him. Jana wasn't far behind. She came from the opposite part of the castle. She had bruises on her arms and a cut over her eye.

"What happened to your attackers?" Melik asked his two friends.

"Mine ran away shortly after the flash of white light," reported Vadin.

"Mine vanished in a puff of smoke that I didn't have anything to do with," said Jana.

Vadin arched an eyebrow at Melik. "What about you?"

"He destroyed the clone all by himself," Melik answered, gesturing at me with an open hand.

"But he's just a boy," said Jana.

"I'm fourteen, thank you very much," I blurted out.

"What's your name, kid?" Vadin asked, rubbing his crooked nose.

I understood their shock. Compared to them, I looked about as tough as a puppy. "Spoon," I answered.

"Way to go, buddy!" cheered Vadin, grabbing me by the shoulders and giving me a shake.

"Are you injured?" Vadin asked, staring at the blood on my hands.

"No," I said, trying to wipe them off on my jeans. How could I have forgotten? "It's Roban's blood!"

Melik put his hand on my elbow. "What happened?" he asked.

"A Marzzoe stabbed him in the back; he's in the room where Vadin hid me."

"What happened to the Marzzoe?" Jana asked.

"I pretty sure Roban killed him," I said.

"Where's the shoulder bag I gave you?" Vadin asked.

"I left it with Roban," I answered.

"Let's go," said Melik.

Roban had lost consciousness, and my blood-soaked hoodie was on the ground. It was hard to tell in the moonlight, but Roban's skin was almost gray. Jana bent over him, checking for a pulse with her hand at the base of his neck. "He's alive," she declared.

Melik picked the leather tube up off the floor and slung it over his shoulder. He opened his satchel. Bringing out two dried leaves, he placed them inside Roban's mouth. "You're going to be alright," he assured Roban.

Vadin checked for a pulse on the Marzzoe. "He's dead."

Melik dug into his bag and produced a tan shirt. He handed it to Jana, who used it to clear away the blood from Roban's wound. "It's deep," she said, inspecting the Marzzoe's work. "I'll clean it as best I can, but we need to stop the bleeding."

"I've got that covered," said Melik, reaching into his satchel again. He pulled out a glass bottle, no bigger than my pinky finger. The glass itself was tinted a dark purple, or black; it was difficult to tell. Turning towards his injured friend, Melik said, "Roban, we're going to use ulmaroo extract."

Roban didn't move, moan, or even grunt.

"All right," Melik said, taking out a knife from his bag. He handed it to Jana. "He can bite down on the handle."

Jana grabbed the knife and placed its handle between Roban's teeth.

"Listen carefully," Melik explained. "The extract will stop the bleeding, but it comes with a price. Roban will experience a great deal of pain as it works. Our job is to prevent further tearing as the extract closes the wound."

Melik went on to instruct Vadin and Jana to restrain Roban's arms and chest. I was told to keep his head still. Melik would take the legs. Everyone got into position.

Melik addressed the wound. He poured three drops of the tangy-smelling liquid onto each side of the gash. The extract fizzed like bacon fat in a frying pan. The skin around his cut burned and melted together. A cloud of purple smoke soon followed.

Roban's body rebelled. His arms and legs shook under our combined weights. It was all I could do to keep his head still. The only thing Roban didn't do was cry out in pain. It took ten minutes for the wound to close, and another five for Roban to stop squirming. My arms felt numb from the effort. Melik and Jana cleaned and wrapped the wound, while Vadin went to check on the horses. I stayed with Melik, too tired to move.

We huddled around Roban once our tasks were complete.

"How is he?" Vadin asked, adjusting his green headband.

"He's obviously lost a lot of blood, and now he's running a fever," answered Jana.

Vadin rubbed his chin, causing the bracelets on his wrist to jingle. "Can we move him?"

"We have to," Melik said. "We don't have enough supplies to keep an infection away, or treat his fever."

"Tarboo?" Jana asked.

Melik nodded.

"The Marzzoe I fought could return at any moment to finish his job," Vadin argued.

Melik tugged on his beard. "Spoon destroyed one of his clones, which should slow him down. The Marzzoe will certainly return to fulfill his mission and avenge his comrade's death. However, keeping Roban alive is paramount to fighting off a depleted Marzzoe. I believe Roban stands the best chance in Tarboo."

"We'll be fish in a barrel in that tiny village," Jana protested.

"It should take that Marzzoe a day to recuperate his lost life-energy," Melik explained. "That should give Roban a fighting chance."

Jana nodded and relented. "You're right. Roban is our priority."

"Roban's injury is as serious as it gets," said Melik. "The best thing we can do is get him to Tarboo without injuring him further."

"Agreed," said Vadin.

Jana nodded, too.

Vadin turned his head towards me and asked, "What about Spoon?"

Melik and Jana turned towards me, too.

"Quaren is his only chance of getting home," said Melik. "Since we have Roban, and the Marzzoe, to worry about, we no longer have the luxury of waiting for Quaren."

"You're telling me Quaren sent him?" Vadin asked.

"Yes," said Melik. "He's Kalven's son."

"From the other world?" Jana asked.

"Earth," I interjected.

"But why?" she asked.

Melik answered, "Quaren told Spoon that someone in Altrea thought him special."

"Who?" Vadin asked.

"I have no idea," answered Melik.

"What do you think, Spoon? You coming with us?" Jana asked.

I wasn't going to stay behind in this creepy castle. Not after everything we just went through. "Yes, I'm coming with you. There's no way I'm staying in this place."

Jana put her hand on my forearm. "Don't worry," she said. "Quaren will go straight to Fey's place when he returns."

"Which is precisely where we'll take Roban after Tarboo," said Vadin.

Melik and Jana nodded in agreement.

With a plan in place, everyone prepared for our departure. Jana was in charge of Roban. Melik found materials to make a stretcher. Vadin and I walked out to get the horses ready in the courtyard, and to find some Altrean clothes for me to wear.

The happy-go-lucky man made small-talk as we walked. He asked me if there were any vegetarians where I come from, if everyone dressed in such strange clothes, and about my home. I told him there were vegetarians, that yes, people dressed this way back home, and that I lived in a little, yellow house with a tiny backyard. My first two answers seemed to please him, but he frowned when I told him about my house.

"If you have a yard, does that mean your house is on the ground?" he asked.

"Yeah," I said, arching an eyebrow. "Where else would it be?"

"In the braches of trees, of course," he said.

"You live in a tree house?" I asked, my voice a notch higher than normal.

Vadin nodded, smiling. "My village is entirely off the ground, connected by rope bridges. My family farms, and our crops hang from the branches of the Locke tree. The entire forest is actually one tree, interconnected beneath the rich soil."

"I have to see that," I said, daydreaming about living in a tree house and using a *real* zip line to get to school.

"I'd love to show you Locke someday," said Vadin.

We emerged onto the courtyard, walking at a brisk pace. The sun began to rise over the horizon. Nothing had changed since Melik and I came out for a snack, except for the three new horses beside Bomber.

Vadin rubbed the neck of each animal. He talked to them like they were his children, and kissed them all on their noses. Jana had a white horse named Isabel with a long neck and a braided tail. Vadin's horse was the smallest, with shaggy, brown hair and a bushy mane. His name was Cow. Yes, like a cow. The final horse was the largest, with legs the size of tree trunks. He had a jet-black coat, and a snarl on his lips. His name was Knight.

"Let me guess," I said, pointing. "Roban's horse?"

Vadin flashed his white teeth. "How'd you know?"

"They have the same personality," I said, as if it were obvious.

Vadin laughed. His laugh had a deep, throaty texture to it. It was the type that made you want to join in. "Roban can be abrasive. But I've never met anyone who cares for Altrea more than him."

As we worked, I asked Vadin if he knew anything about the ulmaroo extract. He told me that it's a rare root that grows deep within the Domegal Mountains. It requires four years of precise preparations before it can be used to close wounds. After his explanation, he asked me what had happened to Roban and me. I told him everything. The hardest part was admitting that Roban's injury was my fault.

"You can't blame yourself," he said.

"That's easier said than done."

Vadin found me clothes to wear next. I would have kept wearing my jeans and t-shirt, but seeing as they were stained in Roban's blood, I figured it was a good idea to have a new outfit. I got a blue, long-sleeved shirt, a vest, brown pants with deep pockets (where I kept Quaren's verve stone), and a pair of boots. They were more comfortable than I would have expected, but they were made for someone larger. The only thing I didn't give up was my underwear, which Vadin promised we'd wash in Tarboo.

We headed back to the room were Jana and Roban were waiting. The ancient ruins, which had appeared in bad condition already, looked worse in the daylight.

Melik returned with all the materials needed to build a stretcher. He had four thin saplings, rope, and a number of blankets. Vadin and I helped. I was surprised at how easily it was to put a stretcher together. I had the feeling this wasn't Melik's first time building a stretcher.

With the stretcher finished, everyone lifted Roban onto it. The injured man, and his black sword, were secured to the stretcher with rope. The four of us each took a corner and carried Roban out of the room. Careful not to roll an ankle on all the rubble, we made our way through many decaying hallways. We took a lot of breaks, mostly because of me. We eventually emerged onto the courtyard.

Outside, Melik and Jana attached their end of the stretcher to Bomber's saddle. Vadin and I held up the other end, keeping Roban from sliding off the stretcher, feet first.

"Isn't this going to be a problem?" I asked Melik, gesturing with my head at the edge of the stretcher that would drag along the ground all the way to Tarboo.

Melik winked at me. He fished into his satchel and pulled out a spool of cord and a suede bag. The bag contained a flat golden stone the size of a dime.

Melik walked between Vadin and me. He used the cord to secure the stone to the frame of the stretcher, right between Roban's feet. The golden stone glowed slightly beneath its many wrappings. Clapping his hands together, Melik said, "You can let go now."

Vadin let go. Holding onto my corner with one hand, I quickly reached over and grabbed Vadin's corner with my other. Vadin attempted to hold back a laugh, but one sputtered out. I eased up my grip.

Something felt off. The weight of the stretcher, and Roban, had vanished.

I let go of the stretcher, and for the first time in my life, gravity didn't work. I blinked in disbelief. The end of the stretcher, along with Roban's feet, hovered three feet above the ground.

Chapter 12

"HOW'D YOU DO THAT?" I whispered, just in case my voice might cause the floating stretcher to fall.

Melik winked, making it clear I'd have to wait to learn his secret another time.

Unable to keep myself away, I walked over and slowly felt the air around the glowing, golden stone with my hands. There were no strings holding the stretcher up, at least none that I could see or feel. I got up the courage to touch the stone beneath the cords. It made my muscles tingle like they had with Quaren's red stone. Were the stones similar? They had to be. I looked up at Roban. His eyes were closed, and he appeared to be sleeping. But I could see a faint golden glow behind his eyelids.

With Roban secured, Melik got onto Bomber, Jana got on Isabel, and Vadin got on Cow. Melik reached a hand to me and said, "You're with me."

The only horse without a rider was Knight, which Vadin tethered to his own saddle. I gave the ancient ruins one last glance. As we headed away from the courtyard, I couldn't help wondering if I was making a mistake.

We rode, rested, and ate in the saddle. Unless it was a bathroom break, we didn't stop. No one spoke. I tried to ask Vadin a question about Altrea, but he shushed me before I got two words out of my mouth.

"Not now, Spoon," he whispered. "We're being followed."

I don't know how Vadin knew, but I believed him. After his announcement, every shadow, flapping wing, or funny-shaped cloud made me flinch. I tried to think positively.

I imagined myself fighting the Marzzoe in front of Melik and his friends. I saw myself taking him down with a kick to the head, and an elbow-drop to the chest. Everyone would cheer for me, and Jana would shed a single tear. Coming back to my senses, I realized that I couldn't do anything, even if I wanted to. I had no skills, no courage, and no pointy object.

We found a place off the main path to sleep after the sun set. My back ached, my butt was soar, and I walked bowlegged. I wasn't built to ride a horse. Everyone helped lift Roban off the stretcher. Melik removed his golden stone and returned it to his satchel, while Jana cleaned Roban's wound. Vadin prepared the horses for the night and scouted the perimeter. I didn't like the idea of him being alone with the Marzzoe around, but I guess he's already proven he can take care of himself. Finally, I helped gather wood for a fire, which Melik taught me how to light with a flint, steel, and some tinder he carried in his satchel.

With our chores done, we sat around the fire and ate. I told them about Roban's fight with his Marzzoe. They listened intently, but didn't ask a lot of follow up questions. I guess they're tired from the long ride. The rest of the night was a bore. Everyone turned in early.

It took me some time to get used to sleeping outside thanks to the lumpy ground, cold breeze, and curious animals.

The days and nights that followed were more of the same. Our elevation decreased as we zigzagged down the foothills, and we started seeing other travelers. One man in a fur-lined coat, who smelled like he used soil and manure for deodorant, offered us mushrooms. A pair of men rode on a donkey-drawn cart filled with root vegetables. They wore brimmed hats and were missing teeth.

Trotting along the single path, we entered a valley. My back might've been killing me from the ride, but the views were worth the pain. I counted four waterfalls pouring over sheer cliffs with snowcapped peaks rising behind them. These were much bigger than the ones I'd seen on a hike with Alex's family. A cluster of rooftops next to a bend in a river sent up puffs of smoke like a nest of baby dragons.

I eventually lost track of the houses as we traveled deeper into the valley. Up ahead I saw a few farms notched out of the forest that were no larger than a football field. Two boys in patched clothes, each coated in a layer of dirt, manned them. Melik offered the boys a head nod as we passed. The oldest returned the greeting without a smile. I couldn't help wondering if he was related to Roban.

Tarboo was dingy and small. It didn't look like it got a lot of visitors. One dusty path led us to the center of the village, with a few buildings on either side. The place was empty. "Not exactly a tourist destination," I said.

"People out here cherish the simple life," defended Melik.

The last building on the right was a pub called The Goat and Teacup. Vadin tied up the horses out front and kept an eye on Roban. Jana went into the pub to get us some rooms. Together, Melik and I walked next door to shop for supplies.

A woman in a faded-pink apron met us inside. She was short, with a large midsection, and dirty-white hair tied into a bun. She greeted us with a warm smile and asked Melik what he wanted. He responded with a kind word, which brought a red hue to the woman's cheeks.

Melik rattled off a list of items and their quantities. The shop worker shuffled around the tables stacked with colored fabrics, bins of grain, and shelves of jars of all shapes and sizes. It surprised me to see such selection in the middle of nowhere.

It didn't take long for the lady to stack everything Melik requested on the counter. Melik paid his bill with three silver coins with trees etched on them. He told the woman to keep the change. As we walked out of the store, Melik handed me a piece of hard candy he'd bought without me noticing.

"Thanks," I said. The candy was thin, and it smelled like flowers. I licked it once, expecting it to taste bitter for some reason. To my surprise, it tasted like honey and brown sugar. "This is really good."

"They're called sweet twigs," he said.

With sticky fingers, we carried our bags over to The Goat and Teacup. The place wasn't much bigger than a classroom. It had an assortment of empty bottles that crowned the edge of the ceiling, high stools that were pulled up to a bar, and a few shabby tables and chairs scattered about the room. Behind the bar stood a young man with a rag hung over his shoulder.

"My name is Erran. Your friends have already paid for two rooms, as well as dinner."

"Thank you very much," said Melik.

Erran pointed us in the direction of our rooms. Our room was at the top of the stairs. It had two small beds, a window covered in white sheets, and a table with four chairs. Melik set his bags on the floor and returned to the hallway. I did the same.

The room next door was a mirror image of our own, except Roban was tucked into the bed on the right, without the golden glow from his eyes peeking out from underneath his eyelids. Jana and Vadin were seated at the table, arguing over the ingredients on the sandwiches they'd ordered. It became clear that Vadin didn't want anyone else's meat touching his food. Jana just wanted him to drop the issue. Melik and I joined them and ate.

"Melik, who were those Marzzoe?" I asked, chewing on my sandwich.

He leaned forward, resting his elbows on the table. "They're assassins, trained in the Enfergate Chasm. They're experts in poisons, hand-to-hand combat, and getting into the most guarded places without being detected. But their trump card is the ability to clone themselves."

"Why didn't they just show up cloned from the start?" I asked.

Jana answered, "Three trained killers is a formidable weapon. But everything comes at a cost. Making clones divides each individual's life-energy."

"Like Roban has proved, your best chance at fighting a Marzzoe who cloned himself is to separate them, and take them out one at a time," Vadin explained.

"It's not much of an advantage," I said.

"I agree," said Jana. "It shows you how strong Roban is, though, for taking out two clones and their original so quickly."

Everyone nodded, and I couldn't help glancing at the injured guy on the bed.

"The way I see it," said Vadin, pointing his thumb at me. "If it weren't for old Spoony here and his big rock, we might all be dead."

I hadn't considered my part in the fight much. It all happened so fast. I was so scared that I didn't remember much. "Thanks," I said, tracing a finger around a knot in the table. I asked another question to change the subject. "Why are assassins hunting you guys down?"

Chapter 13

MELIK MADE EYE CONTACT with Vadin and Jana. They nodded at Melik. "It's so ill-fated that you were sent here at a time like this. You see, we're in the middle of a task to liberate these," said Melik, taking the leather tube off his back and setting it on the table.

I asked, "The blueprints, right?"

"That's right," said Jana.

"To make a long story short," said Vadin, "we belong to the Guild of the Three Moons. A group dedicated to defending the peace in Altrea. We're currently working to prevent Baracus from conquering all the lands that surround the Lake of Tilvera for himself."

"Is he the bad guy?" I asked.

"The worst," said Melik. "Most call him the Soul Stealer. He's said to be able to kill a hundred men without spilling a drop of blood, and he's the reigning king of Gramhammer."

"But what can your guild hope to do to stop a king?" I asked.

"We can be creative," Vadin said, bouncing his eyebrows. "But our current task had been to acquire these blueprints from Baracus."

"Which we've obviously done," said Jana.

"Though not without paying a heavy price," added Melik.

"What do you mean?" I asked.

"Seven of us went to Vald, the capital of Gramhammer, to acquire these," said Melik, patting the leather tube on the table. "Only four of us returned."

"I think it's safe to say that the Marzzoe got to them first," said Jana.

"Or they never made it out of Vald," said Melik.

None of the guild members talked for the next few minutes, as if giving their lost friends a moment of silence. Finally, Vadin continued the conversation. "Spoon, I've been dying to know how you ended up on Altrea."

Taking a deep breath, I answered, "It all started with Quaren sneaking into my bedroom and scaring me half to death," I admitted. "What's wrong with that guy anyway?"

"What do you mean?" Melik asked.

"His face," I huffed.

"Oh, that," said Melik, grinning. "I can see how it might surprise someone who isn't used to his kind. Quaren is a Lyosian, and they're all faceless."

"He's not the only one?" I asked.

Melik shook his head.

"How does he, uhhh… how do they, speak without mouths?" I asked.

"With their minds" Melik answered.

"Can he read minds?" I asked.

"No," he said. "But it has been said that some Lyosians have developed that ability."

I rubbed my head. Things were getting even weirder.

"Spoon. You were saying," Jana asked, trying to get me back to the story.

"Right," I said, interlocking my fingers. "Quaren said he knew that I was my father's son because I was speaking perfect Lyosian."

Both Jana and Vadin nodded their heads as if this made sense to them.

"I thought he was looking for my dad," I continued. "After I told Quaren my dad had died when I was two, he said he'd been searching for me, and that he'd planned for us to return in order to meet up with his friends."

"That wasn't the original plan," Melik said, sitting up in his chair. "He traveled to your world to retrieve Kalven, and we had planned a yearly meeting at the ruins until he returned, or three years passed."

Jana turned her eyes back to me. "Did Quaren say anything else to you?"

"Yes. He said that it was because someone over here thought I was special," I explained, glancing at the faces around the table.

"I wonder who told him that?" said Vadin.

No one answered. Finally, Jana asked, "What happened next?"

"Quaren made the white circle and had me stand inside. Then he gave me his glowing-red stone." I shuddered at the memory of breaking down into red particles and getting sucked into the verve stone. "Before I knew it, I was talking to Melik."

"It's hard to believe that Quaren could be on Altrea as we speak," Vadin said.

Melik nodded. "At least we know that he'll head to Gaelwallia whenever he arrives. We can ask him about his changes to the plan then."

Everyone around the table had dark bags under their eyes and kept yawning. Melik sent us all to bed. Jana slept in the spare bed in Roban's room. Melik, Vadin, and I slept in the other room. Melik and I got beds, while Vadin slept on the floor. Melik also said that he'd take the first watch.

Vadin and I went to bed. He was snoring in about five minutes, while I rolled around on the squeaky bed. I couldn't turn my brain off. I just kept thinking about my mom, how she was stuck at home, alone, crying her eyes out. Sleep didn't come easily.

I woke up to the smell of eggs and bacon. "Sleep well?" Melik asked.

"Not really," I said, rubbing my eyes.

Melik wasn't alone in the room. He sat at the table with Jana and Vadin. The guild members were busy heaping spoonfuls of eggs and bacon from two steaming plates. "You'd better hurry before everything is gone," warned Melik.

I shuffled to the table, but stopped at the mirror on the wall. I hunched over a little to see my face, which was common for me because I was always one of the taller kids in my class. My hair was sticking out at funny angles, and my eyes were bloodshot. I tested for morning breath. Yup. What I would've given for a toothbrush and some toothpaste.

"How's Roban?" I asked, sitting at the table.

"His wound stayed closed," Jana said between bites. "But his fever hasn't broken."

"What does that mean?" I asked.

Melik folded his hands together. "If the fever doesn't break, Roban will not make it," he said.

I must have had a worried expression on my face because Vadin said, "Don't worry, Spoon, Roban is too stubborn to die."

Jana forced a smile in agreement.

We ate the rest of breakfast without saying much else. Melik went back to get some more sleep. So did Jana. Vadin and I checked on the horses.

Walking downstairs, and out the back of The Goat and Teacup, we arrived at the stalls. I wanted to plug my nose from the manure stench. Vadin didn't seem to mind, and I pretended that I didn't either.

Each animal had its own tiny stall, with water and hay hung on the gates, but there wasn't much room for them to move. Vadin talked in baby talk to Cow, who jumped up and down. He rubbed Cow's nose, and then removed an apple from a bag in his hand. The shaggy horse chomped at the piece of fruit, spraying pieces of apple out of his mouth. Vadin did the same thing with Bomber.

"Would you like to feed Isabel?" Vadin asked.

"Okay," I said, without much confidence.

Vadin showed me how to put out my hand, flat like a tabletop. He set a bright-green apple on my palm. "Now, hold it out for Isabel, and don't curl your fingers," he instructed.

I tried to do as he instructed. Jana's horse stretched out its neck and snatched the apple. "Thanks," I said, wiping horse slobber onto my pants.

"Do you want to feed Knight next?" he asked me.

The jet-black horse was staring a whole through my forehead. "No, thank you," I said.

"There's no reason to be afraid of Knight," said Vadin, rubbing the mammoth horse's nose. "He might act all mean and tough on the outside, but he's really a big softy."

I nodded, but I didn't buy it one bit. Vadin fed Knight an apple and refilled all the feedbags as we talked. His asked me if I had any siblings. "No, I'm an only child. My parents had planned on having a bigger family, but that obviously changed when my dad died."

Vadin began to brush the horses.

"What about you, do you have any brothers or sisters?" I asked.

"I do," he said, running a comb over Bomber. "I'm the youngest of four sons and three daughters, although my oldest brother, Shadin, died years ago."

I felt like a moron. I was always doing things like this, asking friends about their dogs or grandparents, and then learning that they passed away that weekend. "Sorry," I said quickly, worrying that my stupid question ended our conversation.

A few moments passed before Vadin spoke again. "My brother was murdered."

Chapter 14

VADIN STOPPED COMBING his horse as he told me about his brother. "I was about your age, and he was twenty. We grew up together on our family's farm. And, I'm telling you, we grew the best produce you've ever tasted," he declared proudly.

"In the treetops?" I asked.

"That's right," said Vadin. "That fall, Shadin and I were to sell our harvest in the local village, Bura. We needed the money to survive the winter. It was something my family had done for generations. But only this time there were rumors of Gramhammer soldiers lurking around the village. My parents were uneasy about us going, but in the end Shadin insisted, and I tagged along.

"The day we were there, Bura was teeming with soldiers. Shadin's plan was to sell our goods, buy what we needed from the merchants, and leave as soon as possible. It was pretty easy to sell our produce; it was the biggest and best in the village. We made more money than we had in ten years. Everything had gone according to plan up to that point. As I prepared our horses to leave, though, Shadin decided we should celebrate our success with a meal. I begged him to stick to the plan, but he had his mind made up, and there was no changing it.

"We found an inn near the barn where we'd tied up our horses and carts. The place was packed with people. We were lucky enough to come in just as a group of merchants were leaving in their colorful hats.

"Soldiers arrived soon after us. They demanded the people seated in the center of the inn give up their tables. Everyone agreed, except for my brother. The commander was the last man to enter the inn. He had a hooked nose, beady eyes, and pointed chin. But what I most remember about him was how he talked to himself, ever so quietly, as if he were conversing with an invisible friend. I thought him mad.

"Shadin just sat there eating a bowl of steaming stew refusing to move. I begged him to leave. Just as we made eye contact, the tip of a blade emerged from his chest. Shadin gasped for breath, then toppled face first into his bowl, unmoving. The commander had run his sword right through Shadin. As he shoved my brother out of his chair, he laughed to himself like a hyena.

"I leapt to my feet to avenge my brother's death. I couldn't live without my brother. The soldiers had other ideas though. I tried to make them kill me, but they wouldn't let me die. They left me broken and bloodied out front of the inn."

I gawked at Vadin, my mouth hanging open. It's not like there's anything I could say anyway. Vadin retreated into himself as he finished with the horses. Patting me on the shoulder, we returned to our rooms.

The afternoon sun shone into the window of our room at The Goat and Teacup. Melik said it was spring, and that it didn't get much warmer up in the mountains this time of year.

With Melik and Jana up from their naps, everyone packed in preparation of Roban's fever breaking. Melik organized his effects into his own bag. Everything had its own pocket, or was folded and placed in the ideal spot. This was a far cry from Vadin's throw-it-in method.

We went downstairs for dinner. Erran, the bartender, told us to sit where we wanted. With only one other group eating, we had several places to choose from. We went with a table closest to the window because Melik wanted to be out of earshot of Erran. Jana ordered drinks for everyone. Vadin kept glancing around the room, and out the window. I asked him why, and he said that he was still keeping an eye out for the Marzzoe.

"So, Spoon," said Melik, trying to change the subject. "What do you do back home?"

I told them about being an eighth grader, and going to middle school. My answer led Melik to ask me a lot of questions about the different levels of school. He said that they didn't have anything like that around here. In Altrea, the average teenager has the option of learning a trade through an apprenticeship, while the wealthier families send their children to the Annals in Yont.

"Did you know your dad went to the Annals?" Jana asked.

I shook my head.

"Quaren said your dad was a genius," Melik explained.

"Did Quaren go to school with my dad or something?"

"No, but Quaren's brother, Roon, shared a room with your dad," said Melik.

"My dad's roommate didn't have a face either?"

"I guess that's right," Vadin said, chuckling.

Erran walked over to our table and told us what food choices he could offer us. Melik, Jana, and I ordered the ham sandwich. Vadin got a salad. As we waited for our meal, Jana asked me, "Did your dad ever tell you why he hid on your world?"

I shook my head. "He never mentioned that he was from Altrea, let alone why he left," I explained. "Do you know why?"

Jana sipped at a mug of magenta liquid. "It's kind of a long story," she said, setting her mug on the table.

"I really don't mind," I said, leaning forward.

"Alright," Jana said, taking a deep breath. "According to Quaren, Roon and Kalven spent countless hours in the belly of the Annals running experiments. They only came out for food and water. Most nights they slept on the floor. Eventually, Roon sent Quaren a letter asking his brother to rush to Yont. Quaren came, but his brother never showed up."

Erran brought out four plates of food. As we each ate our meals, I worried Jana might forget about what she'd just been telling me. Thankfully, Melik continued the story from where Jana left off.

"Quaren spent years searching for his brother. It was just recently, though, that he'd gotten a real lead," Melik explained. "It turned out that one of the Twelve Generals of Gramhammer had learned of Roon and Kalven's experiments. No doubt through his network of spies, I'm sure. Roon was kidnapped and forced to divulge his discovery to the general, while Kalven managed to escape to Earth."

Vadin finished his last bit of salad, pushed his plate to the middle of the table, and turned his attention to me. "A year later a Guild spy in Vald reported that the king of Gramhammer, and eight of his generals, had been murdered."

"It turned out that the old king of Gramhammer had called a meeting of his generals. Nine obeyed their king's request. At the start of the meeting, the youngest general stepped onto the table in the center of the room: He informed the leaders of Gramhammer that their reign had come to an end.

"The old king, his personal guard, and the remaining generals reached for their weapons, but none were fast enough. Tentacles of green energy shot out of the youngest general's tri-bladed sword. They connected to the chest of every man seated at the table. All that was left of the king, the guards, and the eight generals were shriveled husks of skin."

"Let me guess," I said. "The youngest general is Baracus?"

Melik nodded. "It requires an elite level of skill to become a general of Gramhammer. But the amount that Baracus improved is unimaginable. Roon is our best answer to Baracus' spike in life-energy."

Jana interlocked her fingers on the table. "He is a monster."

"The worst kind," Vadin said. "If we don't stop him, no one will."

Erran cleared off our empty plates. He offered to bring out something sweet to eat, but Melik declined.

The four of us didn't stay in the inn much longer. Jana wanted to check on Roban, and Melik decided to help her. Vadin went and busied himself with cleaning his bow. I was feeling kind of tired, so I opted for a nap.

"Wake up," Melik said, shaking my shoulder. "It's time to go."

I pulled myself off the bed, feeling woozy. I must have fallen into a pretty deep sleep because I felt as if I'd been pressed into the bed by a heavy weight. I rubbed my eyes and saw Vadin throwing his things into a pile on his bed. "What happened?" I asked, fearing the worst.

"Nothing bad," said Melik. "Roban's fever broke about an hour ago."

I let out a sigh of relief.

"It never ceases to amaze me what that man's stubbornness can overcome," Vadin said.

"We leave within the hour," said Melik.

I helped Vadin carry his bag to the other room. Jana had already prepared the injured guildsman for the trip. Roban's skin was a pasty white, and his eyes were sunken and closed. He looked half dead. Jana tried to give him something to help him sleep, but he refused to drink it. The four of us lifted carried Roban downstairs.

Out back, Melik, Jana, and Vadin buckled their saddles onto their horses. Melik reattached his stone to the stretcher, causing Roban's eyes to glow golden from beneath his eyelids. How was that possible? Roban's stretcher was secured to Bomber's saddle as it floated off the ground like before. It was no less incredible the second time.

With Roban taken care of, Vadin turned to me and said, "Spoon, I'm afraid none of the horses can ride all the way to Gaelwallia fast enough with two riders. You'll have to ride Knight."

Vadin guided Roban's horse out of his stall and onto the patch of grass behind the inn. He tossed on a black saddle and buckled it. I stood fifteen feet from the monster horse. Knight's deep breaths sounded more like a jet engine than an animal's lungs. How would Vadin even get me on top of that towering beast?

Knight turned his head, gave me an evil horsey glare, and stomped the dirt. "I'm not getting on that thing," I protested, gesturing towards the angry beast. "He looks like he wants to kill me."

"You'll be fine," assured Vadin.

Knight snorted, as if disagreeing with Vadin.

"You're just a big, old softy, aren't you," said Vadin, fastening the final strap on the saddle.

Vadin helped me onto Knight's back. I swayed there, feeling dizzy, and felt a bead of sweat trickle between my shoulder blades. Vadin showed me how to put my feet in the stirrups and use the reins. He told me to tap my heels on Knight's sides if I wanted him to go forward, and to pull on the reins if I wanted him to stop.

I pressed my thighs together as hard as I could because it felt like I was going to fall at any moment. Vadin could have at least gotten me a helmet or something. I tapped the sides of Knight with my heels but nothing happened. The monster horse didn't move, unless you count bending forward and eating grass.

"Is he broken?" I hollered.

At the sound of my voice, every muscle in the horse contracted. Sidestepping, Knight rotated and kicked out his back legs, and launched me right out of the saddle.

Chapter 15

I LANDED ON MY BACK, sucking in great gulps of air. Wheezing for a breath, I opened my eyes. I was nose to nose with Knight. The evil horse sneezed in my face and glared at me.

"Spoon!" Vadin cried, rushing to my side. "Is anything broken?"

"No, I'm fine," I breathed, wiping horse snot from eyes.

"He's never done that before," said Vadin. He helped me to my feet. "You sure you're alright?"

I patted the dust from my new Altrean clothes. "Yes."

"Good," said Vadin. "Then we can get you back into the saddle."

"You're kidding, right?" I asked, my voice getting louder.

"We don't have any other choice," he said. "Roban won't make it unless we can get him to Gaelwallia as soon as possible."

The memory of Roban getting stabbed in the side flashed through my mind. "Fine," I sighed.

Vadin joined his hands together in a cradle and lifted me onto Knight's back. "This time," he advised, "don't squeeze so tight with your thighs."

I nodded.

The beast of a horse stepped forward. This would have been amazing if I'd actually tapped my heels on his side. "How about the two of us be friends?" I whispered.

"Great job, Spoon," Vadin encouraged. "Now, get him to stop."

I pulled back the reins. Knight took two more steps before coming to a stop and bending forward to chomp on grass. "It worked. I can't believe it," I said, in shock.

It was at his this moment that Knight hit the eject button. The massive horse didn't get me with his first buck. I held on to the reins with a death grip and locked my legs. He didn't get me on the second buck either, if you call dangling from his neck as holding on. But he made certain to shake me loose with his third buck.

I belly flopped on the ground.

I rolled over, pain shooting across my lower back. Does Knight know it's my fault that his master's on his deathbed? Can a horse take revenge?

Vadin hustled over to help me to my feet. Jana and Melik were on their horses, waiting on me. "It looks like this isn't going to work," he said, holding up a rope.

I smiled, hoping that I'd be riding on Cow with Vadin, and that Knight would be tethered behind us. I was wrong. Vadin attached a rope from Cow to Knight, but I still had to ride the evil horse.

We were finally on our way. Vadin said that we'd be heading northeast until we reached a place called the Forest of Anco. Then we'd veer north to Gaelwallia. But the way Vadin talked about the forest gave me the impression he wasn't looking forward to that part of the trip.

The three guildsmen never grew tired of scanning our surroundings. The Marzzoe was out there, according to Vadin, but keeping his distance.

Riding should have been easy for me. I didn't have to do anything to keep Knight behind Cow. But that didn't stop the evil horse from making my life miserable. With every bump, dip, and root, Knight slammed each hoof into the path, sending vibrations up my spine, numbing my legs. I decided to keep my mouth shut about my discomfort. I couldn't let that animal get the better of me.

We ate lunch in the saddle, only stopping to give Roban more medicine. Melik and Vadin didn't like these delays, but Jana insisted.

Later that night we camped under a billion unfamiliar stars. All the while Roban had beads of sweat on his brow, and his tattoos appeared washed out. Jana got Roban ready for bed, while Vadin tended to and fed the horses. Melik and I worked together to make a fire.

Struggling to keep our eyes open, we ate around the flickering flames. Vadin offered to take the first watch. The rest of us quickly slipped into our blankets and tried to sleep on the rocks. Despite how tired I was, I couldn't help but wonder if Alex noticed I was missing. Boy, what I wouldn't give to be back in the woods with him and his brothers playing, having fun, and enjoying summer vacation.

At dusk the next day, after another ten hours in the saddle, we staggered underneath a tree that would have put a redwood to shame. Jana, again, got Roban prepared for bed and even offered to make the fire, while Melik cared for the horses and unpacked. Vadin checked the perimeter.

At last we gathered around the campfire once our nightly routines were completed. Everyone looked weary and ready for sleep, but yet here we all were not in bed. Roban had his place by to the fire. He seemed to be speaking more with Jana, but always with his jaw clenched. For the millionth time, I prayed he'd be okay.

"How are you holding up?" Melik asked me.

His question got me thinking about waking up on a different world, and trying not to get my head chopped off by a cloning assassin. I should be freaking out. But I wasn't. Everything felt normal, like any other day of the week.

"I'm tired," I said, choosing not to say what was really going through my mind.

"Me too," agreed Melik.

Jana called the first watch that night. Melik took the second watch, and Vadin the third. Somehow I fell asleep in record time, dreaming of my comfy bed back home.

The next few days were pretty much all the same. I got up at the crack of dawn, rode until my spinal cord went numb, and slept on the ground. This dullness stopped at the Durlonemor Mine. Vadin said that it was a verve stone mine that he'd worked at when he was younger.

"It's off the beaten path, but it will provide us with a roof over our heads when it rains this evening," he explained.

Knight stomped down the path as it twisted and turned. At the moment, the sun was out, and there were even puffy clouds in the sky. We must have walked for half an hour. It was a good thing Vadin knew where we were going because the trailhead to the mine was hidden beneath overgrown bushes and vines.

Vadin finally found the way after getting off Cow and slicing through the dense vegetation with his sword. We heard a loud twang with his next slice. Pausing, he pulled his sword behind his head. He slashed at the same spot once more. He was rewarded with another twang. Vadin hopped off Cow to continue his assault on the shrubs from the ground. He cut down everything in the three-foot radius of a small statue.

"What is that thing?" I asked.

"It's a moondoggy," he replied.

Chapter 16

THE STATUE WAS MADE OF a greenish-gray stone. It was covered in vines, roots, and moss. Its head resembled a dog, except its ears and tail, which had the most in common with a panther. Its body was the size of a ferret, and there was a curious look in its eyes. The statue was cute in its own unique kind of way.

"We don't have those where I come from," I said.

Vadin turned to me, tilting his head, and said, "A moondoggy is a mythological creature. It's said if one finds you, you'll have extraordinary luck. But no one has seen one in a thousand years."

He used his hands to clear the statue of leaves. "The boss of this mine was always drawn to the moondoggy legend, which is why he marked the turnoff for the mine with his favorite creature."

After a few more whacks, Vadin made the path passable. He got on his horse and the rest of us followed him single file down the trail. We emerged onto a hill that was covered with yellow grasses and sprinkled with flat rocks. To the east, a creek cut across the clearing. Beside it was a skeleton of a building made out of flat stones. The most striking features were the rusting tools littered around. In the fading light the place looked spooky.

"When was the last time you were here, Vadin?" Jana asked.

He ran a hand over his shaved head and answered, "I lived and worked here until I was eighteen. This place used to mine red verve stone."

We approached the mine as if it were a five-star hotel. We dismounted next to a patch of tree saplings at the creek's edge. As I hopped off, my feet crunched on the rocks. My back popped as I arched my aching spine and stretched my sore legs. The guild members tied their horses to the thicker trees near the bubbling water. Cow, Bomber, and Isabel sucked up a few gallons of creek water before coming up for air.

"Time to drink, horsey," I announced, tugging at the massive horse's reins, with my back to the water.

Knight gave me an evil horsey eye, unmoving.

"Don't you want some yummy water?" I asked, trying to mimic Vadin's baby voice.

I might as well have been talking to a statue.

I heaved on Knight's reins harder. "Come on you blasted horse," I mumbled.

Again, nothing.

"Please," I begged, yanking with both hands.

Knight didn't budge.

I was so mad that I leaned back, dug my heels into the rocks, and gave the reins a strong jerk. At that instant Knight stepped forward. The change in momentum propelled me backwards. I lost my grip of the reins and fell in the creek.

The shock of glacier water shorted out my nervous system. My skin prickled all over as if a thousand needles were jabbing me. Splashing and coughing, I stood up in the knee-deep water.

"Stupid horse," I declared.

As I ran my fingers through my hair, Knight stooped down and drank from the creek. It was as if he understood my insult. He raised his glossy head and shot me in my face with water and horse spit.

"Spoon," hollered Vadin, grabbing Knight's reins. "What're you doing?"

"I slipped on the rocks," I lied, finding it hard to form the words because my teeth were chattering.

Vadin wrapped Knight's reins around a branch, and the horse drank as if nothing had happened. "You're mean," I mumbled to Knight.

Defeated, I hung my head, grabbed my bag, and squished after Vadin. We crossed the hill and approached the stone building.

"This is where everyone slept and ate," said Vadin, pointing to the rectangular building. "And that's where the red verve stone was brought up from underground," he added, pointing to a circular structure. "Durlonemor produced double the amount of most mines. It was said that the vein of verve would last another fifty years. I wonder what went wrong."

"What do you mean?" I asked, dripping.

Vadin scratched his head. "Durmat, the boss of this mine, was not known to make a miscalculation of that magnitude."

Everyone else was unpacking in the rectangular building, which was missing all its windows.

"What happened to you?" asked Jana, glancing up after changing Roban's bandages.

"The rocks are slippery," I grumbled, crossing my arms over my chest.

Jana patted me on the shoulder and made me something hot to drink. I sipped at my wooden cup as Jana stoked the fire. From his stretcher, I swear I saw Roban crack a smile.

As everyone but me made preparations for the night, Vadin shared how he ended up living here at the mine. "I'd been pursued here by four Slatmor guards," he said, winking at me. "After my brother's death, I moved to Slatmor. The guards were under the impression that I'd stolen Cow, which was a lie. I'd won him in a game of Talakic. But the guards didn't believe me.

"Cow and I left Slatmor immediately, but those people are crazy about their horses. We rode west, making our way around the southern edge of Anco. The guards chased us all the way to Tarboo, to this mine. Cow and I barreled down the trail, and turned onto the path to this mine. We hid here as the guards continued north. My plan was to return to the trail when the coast was clear, but Durmat found us.

"He questioned me about being at his mine. I told him how I'd buried my brother two years earlier, wandered from place to place with no money, and got chased out of Slatmor. Durmat listened, without moving. When I finished my story, he told me that I could work at Durlonemor as an errand boy, and sleep with the miners. It was a turning point in my life."

Shivering next to the fire, Melik let me borrow a shirt and pair of pants. My clothes dried next to me. As our meal cooked, Vadin went out to check the perimeter, while Melik and I set out to bring the horses up from the creek.

"Spoon, have you ever ridden a horse?" Melik asked, untying Bomber's reins from the branch.

"No," I said. "We have horses, but most people drive a car when they want to get around."

Melik grabbed Isabel's reins, and I grabbed Cow's reins. We marched the horses towards the rectangular building where we were going to sleep for the night, out of the rain.

"Tell me about these *cars*," said Melik.

I answered his question, but it wasn't easy. He kept asking me about how the engines worked, and why they had wheels and not legs. I did the best I could, and filled in the rest with educated guesses. Somehow, the conversation rolled into motorboats and airplanes. I'm sure I just confused him.

"The Byroc have been trying to make a one-person people-mover for some time," he explained. "But not with an engine like your cars."

The possibility of not riding Knight made me grin. "When do I get to ride one of those?" I asked.

"Later rather than sooner," said Melik. "But the Byroc will make one. It's simply a matter of time."

I imagined myself flying through the trees on one of these people-movers. But my daydream was interrupted when a question popped into my head. "What's a Byroc?"

Melik smiled. "Well, I am."

"You?"

Melik nodded. "Yes. I'm a Byroc from the Domegal Mountains."

"Are they, or should I say you; are you human?" I asked, mumbling the last half of my question.

"Yes," said Melik. "Every race in Altrea is human. But some are more or less than others."

We reached the building and found a safe place to tie the horses up for the night.

"Do you want the long story or the short one?"

"The long one," I answered without hesitation.

Back at the fire, Jana got Roban ready for bed, and Vadin hadn't returned yet. Roban grumbled every once in a while, but other than that he was quiet. Melik and I sat around the fire.

"Byrocs have lived under the mountains since the beginning. It's where we worked, married, and raised our young. We never desired to leave our dark sanctuary. Our race has never been one to make friends, or expand our lands. We care for our families and villages, and take pride in our skills to work the materials we cut from the heart of our world.

"As far as we were concerned, there was nothing above ground that outweighed the benefits of life below. We only troubled ourselves with mining, forging, and hording our fortunes. Most in Altrea forgot about us, and we were happy to drift into myth. But that all changed about five hundred years ago with The War Under the Mountain."

I leaned in closer, nodding for him to tell me more.

Melik continued, "It was the first of many wars between the Byrocs and Gramhammer. At the time, we thought everyone had forgotten about us. As it turned out, Gramhammer hadn't forgotten. They found bits of truths of our existence over the generations before putting them all together. The Gramhammer leaders were desperate to find alternative ways to fund their wars - same old Gramhammer - and they were prepared to do anything to achieve their goal. We were taken by surprise when Gramhammer attacked. We are a strong people, both physically and mentally, but it took some time for us to counter.

"Countless battles later, the Byroc were pinned into their last stronghold, deep within the Domegal Mountains. With defeat immanent, Prince Rocmarex snuck off the battlefield and traveled to Midnight, the capital city of Silverwood. He knew that the Essenzians were the Byroc's last chance of survival. And he was willing to risk banishment, and the loss of his crown, to save his people."

Chapter 17

MELIK CONTINUED, "Prince Rocmarex reached Midnight and asked King Tomardue and Queen Amoria for their people's support in the war. In the history of Altrea, the Essenzians and Byrocs seem to interact like oil and water. But Prince Rocmarex's courage changed their hearts. King Tomardue and Queen Amoria agreed to come to the aid of the Byroc, but on one condition: Rocmarex was to bring his people out from under their mountains when he became king. Rocmarex knew this was no small task. None of that would matter if Gramhammer conquered his people and put them into slavery. So he agreed to Silverwood's request.

"Returning to battle, Prince Rocmarex found his people all but defeated. However, all of that changed when the legion of warriors from Silverwood entered the fight. It was the turning point in the war. Gramhammer retreated to their black desert, but not before the king of the Byroc's was killed.

"Following the battle, and his father's funeral, Prince Rocmarex became king, and at his coronation ceremony he addressed his people. He told them of his agreement with the King and Queen of Silverwood. They were furious, but a Byroc never breaks his word, and by next spring the first of my people came into the light.

"Most of the top dwellers treated us like a primitive race. But we had long become students of our surroundings. We excelled in science and mathematics, and invented devices to aid in our endeavors. Over time, our scholars were considered some of the greatest minds in Altrea.

"The only physical drawback my people faced under the sun was sensitive eyes. This is why a Byroc wears tinted glasses. Too many lifetimes underground will do that to you," said Melik, taking a breath. "And although we miss our subterranean homes, most feel that King Rocmarex's decision was positive for our people. Some even compare his wisdom to the Larrabee."

"Are all Byroc good like you, Melik?" I asked.

Melik shook his head. "I wish that were true. But we do all have a strong love for Altrea, and maybe that's because we know it from the inside out."

The wind howled, and the weather changed for the worst. Melik and I joined the others. Everyone appeared happy to be out of the elements. Though the threat of the Marzzoe was real, these guild members never showed it. I sure wish I had their strength. Jana made tea that tasted like dirt. She'd used one of those dried leaves from Melik's bag, which made my knees bounce as I sat around the fire.

A single raindrop turned into a downpour in a matter of seconds. Heavy patters on the roof echoed throughout the leaky building and pulled at my heartstrings. It reminded me of home. Growing up in Washington state, rain was always in the forecast. I became accustomed to its drumming sounds and fresh smell. But in Altrea it felt different.

"You feeling okay, Spoon?" Jana asked, putting her hand on my shoulder.

"Yeah, it rains a lot where I come from," I said, thinking how I might as well have a *homesick* sticker on my forehead.

"A great deal has happened; it can't have been easy," said Jana.

"I've been feeling guilty about not missing home as much as I should. Maybe I'm in denial, or maybe I'm good at blocking it out."

Vadin poked the fire, sending a shower of sparks into the air. Melik removed a pipe from his bag and puffed it. Jana and I sat in silence as the flames flickered. Everyone seemed lost in thought until the downpour turned into a mist. I'm not sure any of them would have spoken the rest of the night if I hadn't asked a question.

"You mentioned earlier that Essenzians and Byrocs interacted like oil and water," I said, looking at Melik. "So, what's an Essenzian?"

Melik sucked in a breath, but Vadin beat him to an answer. "They're the oldest inhabitants in Altrea, and the region of Silverwood is their home," he said. His explanation was simple enough, but the way he said it had us all leaning back and laughing. Vadin had done a near perfect impersonation of Melik. "They're a proud race. Essenzians need little sleep, they never get sick, and they have the eyesight of hawks. Some say they even live forever. But my favorite characteristic is that they can speak, read, and write in any language." Vadin paused as everyone laughed. He pretended to push up a pair of imaginary glasses to the top of his crooked nose. "That about wraps it up for Essenzians."

"I do not sound like that," Melik said.

I laughed harder, my eyes watering. Catching my breath, I said, "My dad is an Essenzian?"

Melik answered, "Yes."

"I wish I could see like a hawk, or not get sick, too," I said.

Vadin poked at the fire as another question came to my mind. "Your Essenzians sound like elves from fairytales and folktales on Earth. And the Byroc sound like dwarves."

Jana asked, "What do you mean?"

"Elves and dwarves are creatures in very old myths and folktales. Elves have been described in many ways, but my favorite were the ones with heightened senses, immortality, and pointy ears. The dwarves were described in stories as very short, stubborn, and in love with treasure," I explained.

Jana laughed. "The similarities are startling, except the pointy ears and short stature."

Melik rubbed at his beard. Taking a deep breath, Melik spoke in his best impersonation of Vadin. "You know, I believe these similarities are proof that the three explores from the Annals influenced those who they talked with on your world, Spoon. Elven was an Essenzian, Dwarvish a Byroc, and Tollock a man from Yont. These scholars must have passed on pieces of Altrean cultures as they interviewed the people of Earth."

Melik's impression had us all grabbing our sides with laughter, but mostly because it was so bad. My side hurt from laughing so hard.

After all the laughing finally died down, and a calm and quiet descended over the campfire, I found myself watching the coals of the fire. I couldn't help but wonder what other connections I might find between the worlds.

One by one we all slowly went to bed.

The light rain on the roof had lulled me to sleep. I might have slept all night if I hadn't had to use the restroom. Smoldering coals were all that was left of the fire. Vadin was in his roll next to me, and Melik snored on the other side of him. Jana was missing from her bedroll. It must be her turn on watch.

I shuffled over to the horses to find a tree. A minute later and I was on my way back. I heard someone talking in a hushed voice. I stopped in the building's entryway, turning my right ear to the sound. The voice sounded upset, and it was coming from behind a broken mining cart on its side. It didn't sound like the Marzzoe. I was about to go and wake up the guys when I heard someone crying in the same direction.

"Thank goodness it's you," I said, relief washing over me as Jana walked out from behind a rusty cart.

Jana's green eyes were puffy and red. How long had she been crying? "What are you doing up so late, Spoon?" she asked, wiping her damp cheeks.

"Bathroom," I said, yawning. "You?"

"It's my time to be on watch."

"Is everything alright?"

Jana smiled, but it appeared to be forced. "I'm missing my family more than ever right now," she said, choking up.

She frowned. I wanted to give her a hug, but she kept whatever was bugging her to herself. "I know how you feel. I'd do just about anything to be home with my mom and grandparents right now," I said, touching Quaren's verve stone at the bottom of my pocket.

Jana nodded as tears streaked down her cheeks.

I left Jana peering into the night. She had stopped crying, but I had a feeling she needed more time to compose herself. I tossed a few branches on the fire before snuggling under my blankets. Feeling sad for Jana, I fell asleep.

We left the mine at sunup. We rode beneath rock ledges, around fields of snow, and between trees that blocked out the sun. The views were spectacular. The best part was the forest floor was bare and gently sloped. This meant we could move faster without further injuring Roban.

We traveled all day, and then slept near a mountain spring. The next morning, and the one after that, drug on the same way. It might've been an enjoyable trip if Knight hadn't continued to punish me with every step he took.

The countryside changed the farther northeast we traveled. The towering trees were replaced with thin ones that bent with the wind. The underbrush grew thicker and thicker. In a matter of days we were completely out of the foothills.

The land was flat for as far as I could see. Vadin said this was the plateau we had to cross in order to reach the Forest of Anco. A sea of grass covered the ground and reached up to the soles of my feet in Knight's stirrups. The wind rippled over the grass tips, making me feel seasick.

Ten minutes into our trek and Roban was almost knocked off his stretcher. Roban let out a painful groan, accompanied by some choice words. A large boulder had been hidden beneath the tall grass like icebergs. Melik's golden stone hadn't raised the stretcher high enough to pass over the rocks below. We had to slow our pace to avoid any other landmines.

The countryside wasn't the only thing to change. The temperature went up the farther we got out of the mountains. It got warm enough for me to shed my vest.

We passed our first tree that afternoon. It was a gnarled thing with diamond-shaped leaves and peeling bark. We ate lunch under the tree's sickly branches.

I tripped over a rock hidden beneath the grasses while looking for a place to sit down. I fell face first into the grass. I popped up as fast as I could, but it wasn't fast enough. Vadin saw me fall when he was cutting firewood for tonight's fire. He enjoyed pointing out my klutziness for the rest of the evening.

Sitting and eating on my rock, I couldn't shake the feeling that the Marzzoe was watching us. To make matters worse, I thought I heard something over my left shoulder. Knight's ears turned in the same direction as a patch of grasses suddenly quivered.

"What was that?" I asked, pointing.

Vadin was closest to me. He stood on top of his rock and faced the direction I'd instructed. The cluster of trembling grass moved towards us.

"Whatever it is," said Vadin. "It's moving."

"Could it be the Marzzoe?" I asked.

Jana and Melik had joined us, staring over the tall grass, too. "The assassin is out there," said Vadin, squinting. "He has probably made it to the edge of the plateau at best." He faced the grass ahead of us. "But this new threat is different."

The guildsmen's horse whinnied and stomped in place.

"What is it?" I asked.

Melik put his right hand on his shoulder bag. "Let's not wait around to find out."

We got on the horses and left the ancient tree without another word. As we pushed through the sea of grass, we kept checking for whatever was following us. I don't know what was worse, seeing it keeping pace in the distance, or when it disappeared.

We made camp later that night. Roban's wounds had torn when he hit the boulder. Jana and Melik changed out his bandages and discussed keeping a close eye on them. Our fire was small, made with branches from the gnarled tree Vadin had brought. I couldn't sleep that night; I was too worried that our new friend would visit.

We saw our first sign of the Forest of Anco that evening. It rose from the dull plateau with an unnatural darkness. It was hard to believe that anything grew up through this suffocating grass. But Anco did just that. The black mass grew larger with every passing hour. We reached it as the setting sun covered the forest in golden-pink light.

Anco seemed like a sleeping giant, lying in the middle of the grassland, waiting to wake up and walk away. It was weaved together with crooked trees, knotted branches, and tangled vines. It gave the impression that it ate little kids for breakfast. A slight breeze came across my face and I smelled the aroma of musty undergrowth and wet dirt – it was overpowering. Everyone stared, lost in thought. Even Knight remained alert and unmoving.

A dozen birds exploded from the grasses behind us, breaking our trance. I spun around, my heart pounding in my chest. Marzzoe? I saw no sign of the assassin. An earsplitting screech exploded from the same direction as the birds. I'm talking about a noise so intense that it could shatter a window. Knight jerked his head back, stepping to the side. I clung to his back and held on tight. The scream sounded like it came from an animal with sirens for lungs.

"Uhm, what was that?" I asked nervously.

"Nothing cute and cuddly," Vadin said, rubbing his horse's neck.

"Nygar," Roban groaned from his stretcher.

My mouth hung open at the sound of his voice. The guild members looked at their injured friend. Roban's eyes glowed with a golden light.

"He's right," said Melik. "The call belongs to a nygar. They're plains lizards that hunt the birds perched in the tall grass. They can get rather large."

The lizard didn't sound much better than the assassin to me.

"Do you think the nygar is what was following us yesterday?" I asked.

Melik and Vadin nodded.

"But why would an animal that eats birds do that?" said Jana.

"Because of me," Roban grumbled, pulling out a bloodied hand from his side.

Melik leapt from his saddle and rushed to the floating side of the stretcher. He removed the layers of blankets from around Roban, dabbing at the bandages underneath with the palm of his hand. "Roban's wound is still seeping blood from yesterday," he said, holding up his hand and showing us his red fingertips.

Chapter 18

As if on cue, a second ear-shattering screech rang across the plateau.

"We must hold here and change Roban's bandages," Melik ordered.

"Why don't we lose the lizard in the forest?" I asked.

"No," Jana snapped. "If we entered that place with fresh blood, we'd have far worse creatures at our heels."

As I peeked at Anco, a third screech blasted out from the gray-green grasses. The sound set my teeth on edge, like someone running their nails down a chalkboard.

"Jana's right," Vadin said. "If we stay here with that lizard, we can track its movements and take care of Roban."

"Tonight we hold our ground and tend to Roban," said Melik. "Tomorrow, with no blood and the sun in the sky, we can enter Anco."

"We'll have two sets of eyes on watch throughout the night," said Vadin. "Spoon and I can take the first watch, while Melik and Jana fix up Roban and get some sleep."

Everyone nodded.

Roban's bandages were changed, and the bloodied ones were burned. Vadin and I kept a constant lookout for our nygar stalker. Jana brought us dinner and some of her tea that tasted like dirt before her and Melik got some shuteye. The added energy from the meal kept me awake for the next hour, but the one that followed was much harder to stay alert. At least the nygar was a no-show.

My turn to sleep and Melik's turn to be on watch finally arrived. I slid off Knight's saddle and untied my blankets. I waddled my bowed legs over to the fire and laid down on the opposite side of Jana. I stared up at the starry sky. I fell asleep to the sounds of calling birds, howling beasts, and buzzing insects within the forest.

I dreamt about a camping trip to the Columbia River. I played all day on the sandy beach and swam in the cold water. When I went to bed in my tent, I found it impossible to sleep because of all the sports equipment my cousins had hidden underneath my sleeping pad. I got my revenge the next night when a family of raccoons woke up my cousin because of the trail of tortilla chips I'd left around his tent.

"Spoon, Spoon," a voice called. I rolled over, trying to go back to sleep, but someone kept shaking me. "Sorry kid, but it's time to get up."

Blurry-eyed, I sat up. Melik was kindly trying to wake me. It was his turn to get a few hours of shuteye. I saw Vadin asleep in his bedroll near the fire. I stood and rolled up my blankets. Melik cuddled in my spot with the leather tube under his blankets.

"How did you manage to sleep with all these rocks here?" Melik asked, rolling over. "I'm too old for this."

As he stretched his back, I heard his joints crack and pop.

I said goodnight as he wiggled over to a more level spot. As I made my way to Knight, I noticed his eyes were closed. I must admit, startling that evil horse sounded like a wonderful idea. I slowly tiptoed towards the horse. Carefully sucking in a breath to scare him… Knight's eyes popped open. I jumped and squealed. He had managed to scare me!

"What was that?" Melik asked, jumping out from under his blankets, and grabbing his sword.

"Nothing," I assured him, thinking how thankful I was that it was too dark to see my face turning red. "It was only Knight. He scared me."

"Good," said Melik, slipping under his blankets. I worried that he might not fall back asleep, but he was snoring before I reached Knight.

I attempted to get up on Knight's saddle, but every time I went to swing my leg over his back, the evil horse stepped to the side, causing me to do the splits in the air.

"You need some help?" Jana asked.

"I guess so," I said, slightly embarrassed.

The guild woman jumped off Isabel. "Here," she said, interlocking her fingers. I placed my foot in her hands, and she lifted me onto Knight's saddle. Of course, Knight stayed still like a perfect gentleman while Jana was there.

"Thanks," I said, wanting to say something rude to Knight. I held my tongue for fear of being bucked off.

I sat there, scanning the plateau for any signs of lizards, or assassins, just in case. In our dwindling firelight, I could see about fifteen feet in any direction. Jana rotated her neck, searching the grasses, too.

We should have been able to make a bonfire with the forest next door, but Anco didn't let anything outside its borders. Vadin had attempted to hack a few branches down earlier, but his sword couldn't even scratch the trees. It was as if the outside wall of Anco was petrified. I feared our small fire wouldn't last another hour, let alone until morning.

Our shadows stretched out over the grass. If they were our real size, we'd be twenty feet tall. No hungry lizard would mess with us.

A memory of Alex's eleventh birthday came to mind. He had a slumber party, and there were seven of us. We'd each downed a two-liter of soda, and then couldn't fall asleep because of all the caffeine. After a pillow fight and wrestling match, two of my buddies put on a shadow puppet show. Its main characters were Frank the farting ferret, and Bob the barfing bunny. We rolled around in our sleeping bags for an hour, laughing so hard that our ribs hurt.

I made my hand into a shadow-ferret, opening and closing my fingers to make its tongue stick out. I used my other hand to make a shadow-bunny, which of course attacked the ferret. I even used sound effects as the animals fought to the death. The bunny ended the ferret with a devastating head-butt.

"You're pretty good at that," said Jana.

I let my hands drop to my lap, feeling like an idiot for forgetting that Jana was right next to me. "Thanks," I said, the tops of my ears burning up. "I'm going to nationals in the fall."

Jana may not have understood my joke, but she still smiled at my sarcasm. "You remind me of my son," she said, rolling her eyes, as if she was mad at her statement.

"What's his name?"

The guild woman kneaded her hands together. "Keyat," she said, keeping her eyes on the back of Isabel's neck. "He's a year older than you. I also have two younger daughters named Karian and Paley. We used to live in Garus, where my husband, Hoaltmare, worked as a fisherman."

"Where are they now?" I asked, remembering how she'd said earlier that she missed her family very much.

Jana breathed unsteadily. "They're in a Gramhammer slave camp," she explained. "I'd been helping a friend with her new baby the day slave traders kidnapped my family. I tracked them into Gramhammer, but I was unable to get them out."

"Is that why you're in the Guild?"

Jana nodded. "I'd hoped the Guild would've been able to help me, but so far the Guild has come up with nothing but dead ends."

"That's terrible," I said, shaking my head.

Jana didn't say anything else for the rest of our watch. When it was time for her to wake Vadin up, I said goodnight to her. She forced a smile, bowed, and went to tag in Vadin. It didn't take long for Vadin to appear, rubbing some sleep from his eyes.

"Good morning, sunshine," I said with fake enthusiasm.

"Morning, Spoony," mumbled Vadin, putting the last branch onto the fire. "I sure could use a warm bath and a soft bed if you know what I mean," he said, getting into his saddle. "See anything?"

"No."

"Good."

"And the fire?" he asked.

"This little wind is burning it too quickly."

We had no choice but to turn and watch for nygar, but I couldn't stop taking peeps at the sputtering flames. In an attempt to focus on something else, I turned toward Anco. I heard creaking trees and rustling branches. The place felt alive, as if it were breathing. It gave me goose bumps.

"What's it like in there?" I asked, turning to Vadin.

"Trouble," he said. "I've gone through Anco a few times, and that's all we've ever come across." Vadin rubbed his shaved head. "There are no advantages in Anco, only disadvantages lurking behind every corner; disadvantages with too many teeth to count."

Vadin's pep talk acted like a shot of caffeine. I readjusted myself in the saddle and ran my eyes over the grasses lit up by our fading firelight. I settled in for the last shift. But it didn't take long for the firelight to grow weaker.

A cluster of rippling grass tips appeared.

"It's back!" I said, pointing.

Vadin groaned. "Wake the others."

I jumped off Knight. "The fire is going out," I said, waking up the sleeping guild members. "And our friend is back."

Melik and Jana woke up. They folded their blankets and tied them to their horses.

"Get me off this stretcher!" Roban barked. "I can help!"

"You're in no position to fight right now," Melik said.

"I'm a liability, and you know it," he shot back.

"We will deal with this lizard," said Melik, securing the golden stone to the stretcher, and securing it to the back of Bomber's saddle. "And we will do so without your help."

Roban eyes glowed with a golden light, and his stretcher hovered off the ground, as he complained.

Together, the three guild members reached for their weapons. Melik unsheathed his straight-bladed sword, Jana a short sword with a round pommel, and Vadin a bow and arrow. I didn't even have a rock to defend myself.

A drop of blood fell from my nostril. I wiped it away as best I could without getting it onto my clothes. To be honest, I had bigger problems to worry about.

"Spoon," Vadin said, reaching a hand towards me. "Take this, just in case," he winked.

Vadin handed me his medium-sized sword. It had a tree etched into its leaf shaped-blade with roots growing over the guard. I bounced it in my hands, feeling its worn wooden handle and testing its weight. It felt heavier than I'd expected. But what did I know. The only swords I've ever held were made of foam. "Whatever you do," Jana said. "Don't get off your horse."

My hands were sweaty, and I feared losing my grip. I adjusted my grasp on Vadin's sword.

Back in the saddle, I strained my eyes to see in the dim light. The nygar must've moved into the surrounding darkness. The fire burned to a single flame, and the ring of light that cast over the grasses shrunk by half. A soft breeze blew over the coals, breathing new life into the fire. It blazed for about ten seconds, as if it were counting down, before it went out.

Chapter 19

IT GOT SO DARK, SO FAST, that I would've thought we'd been buried alive. A high-pitched screech rang out. Would the nygar snatch me off Knight without anyone noticing? After a few panicked minutes my eyes adjusted, and that's when I noticed an amazing blanket of stars and three moons hanging in the night's sky.

Melik pointed. "There," he said, his tinted glasses set on top of his head.

My gut turned to stone. "I see it, too."

The cluster of rippling grass tips passed in front of Knight. It stopped twenty feet to our right.

"I don't see anything," said Vadin.

"Me neither," Jana said.

"I wish I had the eyes of a Byroc to see in the dark," Vadin whined.

"Or the eyes of half an Essenzian," said Jana.

A second patch of grass tips rippled to life on the opposite side of the lizard. "Melik," I said.

He answered, "It's another nygar."

"I can see that one," said Vadin.

"Me too," said Jana.

The nygar on the right still hadn't moved. The new lizard inched closer.

"They're surrounding us," said Melik, squinting at the tall grasses.

Sword outstretched, I said, "There's a third one. And it's twice as big as the first two."

We all peered into the darkness. The third cluster of grass tips rippled in front of us. We could hear the large lizard's feet slap against the hard earth as it shoved its body through the thick stalks.

Knight's ears flickered back and forth. He bounced around, whining. Bomber and Isabel were acting the same way. Cow kept his calm with the nygar closing in.

The largest cluster of vibrating grass went still just ten feet in front us. I held my breath, waiting for a sign of movement. I couldn't blink. Praying for it to go away, I heard hissing under the grass. With all my senses locked onto the hidden lizard, I'd forgotten about the other two.

Melik raised his sword. "Here they come."

A nygar burst out of the grass from our right, and another from our left. Each one had a spade-shaped head, a long body, and a mouthful of needle-sharp teeth. They had short legs that catapulted their bodies over the grass, straight for us.

Jana and Vadin brought their horses in front of Melik and me. Roban and his stretcher were attached to Bomber's saddle; complete with the verve stones keeping it afloat.

Vadin shot an arrow into the shoulder of the nygar closest to him before I could blink. The impact knocked the creature off course. The lizard shrieked as it crashed, flattening a large section of tall grass. Digging its claws into the soil, it regained its feet.

At the same time, Jana jutted out her sword to block the nygar's attack. She let gravity do all the work. The tip of her blade stabbed into the lizard's shoulder. The nygar fell like a rock, but not without taking a piece of the guildswoman. Jana was left with a nasty cut across her forearm.

Together, the nygars screeched in pain before disappearing beneath the grass.

"Don't let them pull you away from Roban," Melik ordered.

"Let me fight," Roban growled. Nobody responded to him because we were too busy fighting.

Jana called out, "Does anyone see them?"

"There," I said, pointing. "The smaller ones are joining up ahead. But I don't see the big one yet."

The two lizards came together and stopped moving. I turned my head from side to side, searching for the third one. A cluster of grass tips burst to life. The largest nygar rushed towards the gap between Bomber and Knight.

Launching itself above the grass, the lizard attacked with its mouth open and drool flying. Melik lashed out at the massive creature. Vadin let loose an arrow. Melik cried out as the lizard managed to claw a chunk of skin from his forearm. Before the lizard disappeared below the grass, I noticed an arrow in its hind leg. Vadin had found his mark.

A new cluster of grass tips vibrated to our right. A nygar catapulted out of the grass. Jana blocked the lizard's path to Roban with quick jabs of her sword. She might've been the smallest of the guild members, but her size didn't hold her back. The lizard countered by diving under the grass and then leaping at her from another direction. Jana did what she could to hold her position. But the nygar was able to draw her away from the other guild members.

The largest lizard reappeared and it dashed for the growing gap between Jana and Melik. Melik couldn't reach the nygar. Vadin shot the creature again. Now the nygar had two arrows sticking out of it. Melik managed to turn Bomber enough to stab the lizard in the back right before it reached Roban. Vadin urged Cow in behind the nygar. He fired another arrow into the neck of the creature. The nygar's scales must be tough because it didn't fall.

With Melik and Vadin fighting the big lizard, and Jana battling a smaller one, Knight and I were left pressed between Cow and Bomber. I scanned the area for the third nygar. Could Vadin's arrow have killed it? I doubted it.

Rotating to see behind me, I spotted a cluster of grass tips vibrating towards Knight's back. The third nygar was joining the party. I held up my borrowed sword, ready to protect Roban. Knight sensed the lizard. The evil horse wanted to face the nygar, but his tether to Vadin's saddle wouldn't let him turn all the way around.

The nygar bounded through the grass like a dolphin in water. Knight kicked out at the oncoming lizard, whinnying, but he couldn't break free of Cow. As the top of the nygar's head emerged from the center of the rippling grass tips, I did the only thing I could think of; I cut the rope.

Chapter
20

WITH HIS FREEDOM, Knight jumped to the side and filled the line. He reared back and kicked the nygar in the head. The lizard let out a screech as it spun through the air. I might've cheered if I hadn't been tossed off Knight's saddle myself.

The tall grass did nothing to cushion my fall. I hit the ground so hard it knocked the breath out of me. Sucking in gulps of air, I looked around. Knight stomped and snorted, daring the lizard to try again. Surprisingly, the nygar didn't emerge from the grass for a second attack.

To my left, Melik and Vadin fought the big nygar from horseback, driving the creature back. Sword in hand, Jana fended off her lizard from Roban. I had no idea where my nygar was, and, oh yeah, I was off my horse.

I stood up, wanting to fix this problem as fast as possible, but Knight wouldn't stop bucking and kicking. Getting close enough to climb into his saddle was not an option. I opted for my next best option and decided to run towards Jana. I'd taken about five steps when suddenly a nygar sprang out of the tall grass, soaring straight for the guildswoman.

"Jana, watch out!" I screamed.

She didn't need the warning. Her blade bit into the nose of the lizard. The blow dropped the creature right in front of Isabel. Its sides twitched as it took in a few uneven breaths and then it lurched back to its feet. I watched as the lizard licked its lips with a forked tongue. It had a nasty, oozing gash across its nose. Turning towards Jana, its muscles tensed, but it kept its distance.

"Spoon!" I heard Jana cry out without taking her eyes off her lizard. "Where's Knight?"

That was a great question! I spun around on my heels, searching the plateau. Finding the black horse at night should've been impossible. With the light from the three moons, I could see Knight was kicking and running across the grassland with a scaly lizard attached to his back.

Knight whinnied and sprinted for Anco. The evil horse lowered his head and bolted through the wall of the forest. My best guess was he wanted to use the branches to scrape the nygar off his back.

"Knight!" I screamed. I squinted at the hole where Knight and the nygar had made, waiting for them to come out again. "Come out. Come out. Come out," I chanted to myself. He never came.

With sword in hand, I burst through the tall grass, heading for the forest. I struggled to shove myself between the stalks. Eventually, I reached the wall of Anco.

Squinting, I tried to see inside the forest, but all I saw were shadows. My throat felt dry and scratchy, and I had the feeling that some bloodthirsty creature would bite my head off the moment I set foot in Anco. I glanced over my shoulder and saw Melik and Vadin fighting off the large nygar, and Jana slashing at the other smaller one.

"Stupid horse," I spat.

Pushing through the gap Knight had made, I used the sword to clear a path for myself. Overhead, sheets of moss hung off the branches like flying wraiths. It was a good thing I wasn't claustrophobic. This place would have been the end of me.

I stepped over a jumble of roots, around a tangle of vines, and underneath a fallen tree. It felt like I was on an obstacle course. With my shoulder, I shoved my way into the unyielding forest, cutting my arms and face on the numerous barbs and thorns, and snapping twigs as I went. It got so dense that I almost lost my grip on the sword.

With every step I feared the nygar had eaten Knight, and was coming for me next. My heart boomed in my chest. At last I came to a clearing about the size of two basketball courts and at least four stories tall. Shafts of moonlight made it to the forest floor, allowing me to see that I wasn't alone.

Knight had deep gashes running down his back and side. He wobbled, twisting his large ears at me. His reins dangled over his head. The nygar was here, too. The lizard's head hung low, spotting me out of the corner of its large reflective eye. It still had an arrow sticking out from its left shoulder.

Rearing back, Knight kicked his front hooves. The lizard accepted his challenge. It charged, going airborne. Knight's hooves hit nothing but air. But his reins were a whole other story. Arching through the air, his reins looped around the lizard's neck, acting as a noose. The nygar hung there, strung up from Knight's neck in the reins, unable to touch the ground.

Thrashing and hissing, the nygar snapped at the reins. Knight bucked around the clearing, kicking up moldy leaves. The lizard shook violently trying to escape while Knight struggled to keep his legs under him.

The animals fought for their lives. It was only a matter of time before the "disadvantages with too many teeth to count" in this creepy, dark forest would smell the bleeding horse or hear the screaming lizard.

The clearing was empty, and it was too dark to see much. What I would have given for a flashlight right about now. I did the only thing I could do. I gripped the handle of the sword and stepped into the clearing.

The longer it hung from the reins the less of a fight the lizard put up. As soon it saw me advance through the clearing, though, the nygar lashed about even harder. I quickly backpedaled, feeling terrible for the pain this caused Knight.

As I reached the edge of the clearing again, the nygar calmed down. I rocked from side to side on the balls of my feet, praying that one of the guild members would come and save Knight. The glossy horse turned to me, his eyes watering and legs wobbling.

He fell to his knees.

Close enough for its rear feet to claw into the dirt, the nygar screeched with new-found leverage. Knight stopped moving. His spirit, and body, were both shredded. The horse that had made my life miserable had given up.

The nygar worked at the reins with its needle-like teeth. If it broke free now, it would be him and me; killer lizard verses a kid with a utensil for a name. I wasn't about to let that happen. I might not know how to fight, but I do know what to do with the pointy end of a sword.

I charged over the uneven clearing. The lizard saw me coming and lashed out at Knight's side. My muscles tingled as I raced forward. I jerked the sword behind me for the final blow. With eyes flashing red, I plunged the sword into the nygar's shoulder.

Chapter
21

THE NYGAR'S LIMP, MOTIONLESS BODY laid across Knight's legs. I slowly removed the sword. My stomach lurched at the sound it made. Then I used the blade to cut Knight's reins, and struggled to roll the lizard away with my shoulder.

"You dead?" I asked.

The horse didn't reply.

I waited for Knight to move, but nothing happened. "Please don't die, Knight," I pleaded, pressing my ear to the horse's side. "Breathe," I demanded. "BREATHE!" I listened for a heartbeat, or air filling Knight's lungs. Nothing. "Wake up you stupid horse!" I cried.

A faint thud vibrated within Knight. It was accompanied by a wheeze of air. I watched Knight's side rise and fall. "That's what I'm talking about!"

Knight lifted his head off the leaf-covered ground.

"Hey, horse," I said, kneeling. "I killed that thing."

Knight blinked. He looked like someone had attacked him with a cheese grader. "You're going to be alright," I lied.

I rested my eyes. I wanted nothing more than to crawl into my own bed back home and wake up from this nightmare. I was on another world, separated from the only people I knew, and stuck with a dying horse in a creepy forest. "Let's get out of here," I said, standing up.

Knight turned his head, but not at me. "What's the matter?" I asked, checking behind me. "Oh, that!" I said.

The nygar wasn't where I'd left it.

I moved in a slow circle, searching for the dead lizard. I found its silhouette on the opposite side of the clearing. The creature couldn't put its full weight on its front right leg. In the moonlight, I saw blood and mucus dripping from its quivering lip. My nose started to bleed as the nygar limped toward me.

I lifted the sword and pointed it at the nygar. "Bring it on, tripod."

The lizard charged. In one fluid motion, the nygar jumped for my face. I ducked, and slid to the side. Tripod missed. It landed, spun around, and faced me. The nygar dug its claws into the ground and licked its lips. I got my feet under me and held up the sword.

Keeping its body level, the nygar charged me. My right hand, which held the blade, was too slow. The lizard hit me with a claw, spinning me around. I crumbled to the forest floor.

Pain exploded in my right arm, leaving me dizzy. I pressed my left hand to where it hurt the most. A warm liquid covered my fingers. I felt three parallel gashes across my bicep.

On three legs, the nygar circled me. I let go of my injured arm and grasped the sword with both hands, struggling to hold the slippery handle. The nygar was almost behind me, on the other side of Knight. Rushing over to the dying horse, I met the lizard.

The lizard screeched at me, almost slowing to a stop. I wanted to cover my ears, but letting go of the sword didn't seem like the best idea. We stared at each other for what felt like hours. I thought about how this nygar had almost killed Knight, how we were stuck in this forest because of it, and how the lizard's friends were trying to eat my friends.

A spark ignited inside me.

Adrenalin pulsed deep within my body. My muscles tingled, and the clearing became painted in a red hue. The lizard stepped backwards, hissing. I took a step forward, closing the gap between us. I surprised myself at my recklessness, but at that instant I felt that I could run through a brick wall.

The creature turned its head at the perfect angle for me to see myself in its bowl-sized eye. I held the sword out in front of me, and my eyes were glowing red.

Without thinking, I attacked. My muscles blasted me forward. The lizard sent out an earsplitting shriek before springing at me. It lunged for my left arm. I jumped to the nygar's right side with the bad leg. The lizard swiped at me with its good claw, missing me by inches. I landed on two feet, bent my knees, rotated my hips, and swung the blade in an uppercut motion. The sword found the unprotected belly of the lizard.

Chapter 22

I STOOD THERE, drenched in sweat, pointing Vadin's sword at the sky. Beams of moonlight revealed the top half of the nygar's body on my right, and the bottom half on my left. Turning towards Knight, my red vision faded and disappeared.

"Did you see that?" I asked the horse.

The horse blinked. At least he was alive.

I knelt next to Knight, setting the sword down. I ripped off my shirtsleeves to wrap around the three gashes on my arm. It helped to stop the bleeding, but it also felt like I was pressing hot pokers against my skin.

I'd seen red before. When Quaren's verve stone broke me down for the trip through the ley line. The time I destroyed the Marzzoe clone with the rock. And I saw a flash of red before I stabbed the nygar, and again when I sliced it in two. But how can a skinny kid like me cut such a large animal? It shouldn't be possible.

I turned my attention to Knight. Roban's horse had stopped bleeding, but he had lost so much blood. Blood. The stress of it gnawed away at my insides. We didn't go into this place because of it, and now I had a chopped up lizard, a shredded horse, and three holes in my arm all oozing the stuff. I couldn't have been in a worse situation if I'd planned it. Knight and I might as well have neon signs above our heads that read, FRESH MEAT! COME AND EAT US!

I spent the next few minutes trying to move Knight. I pushed, pulled, and shoved on the horse anywhere he wasn't injured. I huffed and complained that we'd be eaten if we didn't find the others. Knight just wouldn't budge.

Fed up, I declared, "I'm going for help."

Saving Knight was my highest priority, but unless I carried him, the horse was too mangled to move. I needed to find Melik and the others. Shuffling across the clearing, I forced my way into the hole Knight had made getting here. The opening felt more compact for some reason. It was as if the vines themselves were holding me back. I struggled to squeeze through for fifteen minutes before I could go no further. With no other choice, I returned to the clearing.

Knight hadn't moved. Sitting next to him, I rested my head against one of the few spots where he wasn't injured. Birds cawed from far-off branches. My eyelids started to feel heavy. I feared of falling asleep, but that changed when a kitten entered the clearing.

Unlike any cat on Earth, it had big black eyes with bright green slights, a flat nose, and wide ears. Its back was covered with black fur. Its belly and ankles might've been red. It was hard to tell in the dark. The biggest difference was the three tails that swooshed around its head.

The animal went straight for a half of the nygar. The little critter wasn't strong enough to bite off a hunk of meat. If I hadn't been sitting in a murderous forest on another planet, the kitten might've been cute.

"Hey, kitty, kitty," I called out. "Where'd you come from?"

The kitten let out a unique meow. It tried to eat more of the nygar, but failed. Growing frustrated, it cried louder, which scared me. I couldn't imagine what that little fuzz-ball could call in.

My answer came in the form of two cats the size of grizzly bears. They dropped from the branches above without a sound. Both had black fur covering their backs, and dark reddish fur everywhere else. They also had the same three tails. The difference was that they had muscles, on top of muscles, knife-sized fangs pointing towards the sky, and curved claws made for tearing. Compared to mom and dad, the kitten looked like a stuffed toy.

The cat family ate half the nygar. Their crunching made me feel sick. The kitten squeaked with delight as its mamma helped it eat, while Daddy inspected the other tasty treats in the area. Us.

The three-tailed cat swayed from side to side. Licking its lips and sniffling, it headed our way. I had the sword in my hand, but at my side. Everything in me wanted to raise it up and defend myself, but I didn't want to spook the cat. Its paws were large enough to take my head clean off my shoulders.

I stood between Knight and Mr. Cat. My heart pounded. I thought about playing dead. Last summer, I read about a person surviving a bear attack by playing dead. Before I could try, Knight got to his knees.

Mr. Cat backed away from the large animal.

Roban's horse stumbled to his feet. Expecting Knight to make a break for it, I turned around. The evil horse snorted and stamped his front foot. He gave the cat an evil horsey glare.

"Knight?!" I exclaimed, somewhere in between a question and a statement.

The horse didn't stand a chance. Mr. Cat responded with a growl that I felt more than heard.

Knight responded with a loud snort. Licking his lips, the cat crouched, ready to pounce.

The stubborn horse stood his ground. Covering my eyes, I waited for the cat to attack. It never happened. The clearing was bombarded with the howls of dogs. With their backs arched, the three-tailed cats snarled at the newcomers.

Four animals crashed the party. Scarred, missing tuffs of pale fur, and with ribcages pushing up through their skin, these fox-wolf creatures appeared vicious. They yelped and barked at the cat family. Mr. and Mrs. Cat responded by showing off all their sharp teeth.

Knight and I were behind the cat family, and in front of what remained of the dead nygar. The real fight began when two of the dogs tried to take the remaining half of the lizard.

The three-tailed cats swatted at the dogs with their claws. Mrs. Cat made contact with the ear of the dog on the left, sending it toppling sideways. It yelped for a while, pawing at its missing lobe. It retreated to its friends with its tail between its legs.

The mutt on the right, however, managed to take a quarter of the nygar away from the cat family. The four canines snapped at each other to get a meal. The carcass was gone in a matter of minutes.

The cat family might've been outnumbered, but they didn't budge. The dogs fanned out in the clearing, surrounding the cats. This meant they were circling Knight and me, too.

I found myself rooting for the Mr. and Mrs. Cat, though I knew that once the immediate threat was over, Knight and I would be their next meal. The dogs' foamed at the mouths, but each one got swatted away.

Squawks rained down from overhead. The trees had filled with hundreds of birds. In the moonlight, I caught glimpses of featherless heads and jagged beaks. I had a sick feeling that these birds didn't care who won or lost the fight, as long as there was food to eat.

The cat family paid no attention to the audience in the treetops. Biting and clawing at anything that got too close, they held their ground. The dogs finally found a gap in the cats' defense when all four rushed the cat family.

In the chaos, a dog squeezed between Mr. and Mrs. Cat. I held out the sword in time to stop the canine a foot in front of me. Its muscles rippled as it licked its lips. It was missing most of its ear.

"Get back!" I shouted.

The dog didn't get the hint. It inched closer.

"Stay back!" I demanded.

The dog stepped forward.

"Don't come any closer!" I said, not sounding as intimidating as I needed to.

To my relief, the dog stayed put. Strings of drool hung from its curled lips. I was close enough to taste its rancid breath. I struggled not to gag.

The dog stepped backwards, and it was then that I realized the dog wasn't looking at me. Its eyes were staring up and over my left shoulder, and its tail was tucked between its legs. Why was this dog so freaked out?

During my next breath the dog turned and ran. It didn't get far. A creature sailed clear over Knight and me. It landed behind the escaping canine, stepped forward, and wrapped its massive hands around the hips of the dog. Picking up the mutt, it tossed the dog against a tree on the other side of the clearing.

Chapter 23

A NINE-FOOT-TALL CREATURE roared at the pack of dogs, beating its chest. My best description for the monster was Bigfoot on steroids. It walked on its hind legs, was covered in thick brown hair, and leaned forward on account of its colossal shoulders and chest.

Even with its immense form, the beast was incredibly agile. Bigfoot lunged to the side, wrapped a bear-like claw around the thigh of another dog, and then hurled it across the clearing. Two of the other mutts jumped onto Bigfoot's back. He easily tossed them away.

Mr. and Mrs. Cat attacked without warning. They hit the creature hard. Mamma cat attacked the chest, and daddy cat went for the back of one leg. Bigfoot fell. It scrambled around on the ground, with his amber eyes enraged. Reaching over its shoulder, Bigfoot searched for a cat to grasp.

The cats' sank their teeth into the creature's thick hide. Bigfoot snarled. Rolling to its knees, the creature was able to wrap its hairy knuckles around Mr. Cat's leg. The cat dug its claws deeper into the monster, but it wasn't strong enough. Mr. Cat was smashed into the ground.

With three of her four claws digging into the monster's back, Mrs. Cat was not going anywhere. Snapping a branch from a tree, Bigfoot attempted to swat the cat away. It didn't work. Bigfoot tried a back flop. That didn't work. But when Bigfoot ran towards a tree trunk, spun around and jumped, and the cat was smashed against the bark, Mrs. Cat finally let go.

Though its parents were unconscious, the kitten ran up to Bigfoot and chomped on its toe. The monster looked at the fuzz-ball and growled. Wide-eyed, the kitten retreated to its mom.

Bigfoot turned to Knight and me, its chest heaving. My throat felt filled with sand. I couldn't take my eyes off its fangs. The monster never reached us. Squawking and cawing, birds rained down. Overhead, they swirled together like an angry storm and darted for Bigfoot, talons out.

The monster swatted and roared at his airborne attackers. The birds kept coming in waves of black. Covered in flapping feathers, and pecking beaks, the monster yanked bird after bird off its body. Unable to do any real damage, the flock cried out in frustration and retreated.

Crossing to the center of the clearing, Bigfoot faced us. It had a single gash over its right eye. I couldn't break eye contact with the monster. It lumbered closer to Knight and me. Did it want to eat us?

Bigfoot stopped ten feet from us. My hands shook, listening to the monster's deep breaths. It looked twice as big up close. Bigfoot snorted, turned to its right, and walked until the forest swallowed it up.

Every part of me hurt, and my head felt filled with cotton balls. Flies buzzed around what was left of the nygar. I had a feeling those birds would return if Bigfoot stayed out of the way.

On wobbling legs, Knight closed the distance between us. I put my hand on his side. He shook his mane, taking a step. Using my hand to steady him, we walked to where Knight had entered the clearing, but the hole was gone. The forest had changed and a new path had opened.

Opposite from where we stood, a tunnel appeared. It was walled with leaves, vines, and moss. With nowhere else to go, Knight and I limped our way to the clearing's only exit, getting farther and farther away from Melik and his guild friends.

The tunnel was wide enough for us to walk side by side, and Knight didn't have to slouch. With no signs of life, besides a swarm of bloodsucking insects, we snaked our way across Anco.

I don't know how Knight managed to walk for so long, but he'd never left my side. With a rumbling stomach, itching skin, and a pounding headache, Knight and I reached the end of the tunnel. We emerged into a labyrinth of trials that snaked beneath the towering trees.

"We're so lost," I said, hanging my head.

After surviving the three-tailed cat family, the pack of dogs, angry birds, and Bigfoot, I was beginning to believe our luck had run out. The tunnel had destroyed any sense of direction I'd had. Melik and the others would have moved on for Gaelwallia by now, and we needed food, water, and medical attention.

During my pity party, an animal tiptoed along a nearby game trail. With the face of a dog, it walked on all fours and didn't slow down at the sight of Knight or me. Like the statue that marked Vadin's verve stone mine, this creature had curious eyes and a long, waving tail.

"A moondoggy," I said, wiping my hand over my face.

The animal was small enough to fit into a bag or purse. It had sleek brown fur, and a cut over its left eye.

"Hello," I said.

The moondoggy stopped right in front of me, barked once, and then tiptoed down the game trail. Its tail wagged as it disappeared behind a tree. I stood next to Knight, praying that Vadin was correct about this little creature.

We had no difficulty keeping up with the moondoggy. I tried to keep track of all the turns, but there were too many to count. It was almost like the moondoggy didn't want us to know where it was headed, or how to find our way back.

Rays of sunlight began to light the forest floor. We saw a family of white monkeys swinging through the canopy, and a small deer with twisted horns dart across the trail. At least we didn't see the pack of wild dogs, three-tailed cats, and bloodsucking bugs. Maybe the rumors about the moondoggy were true?

The moondoggy came to the edge of a small stream. With a pink tongue, it drank from the running water. Knight and I were not so polite. We dunked our faces beneath the water, sucking in mouthfuls at a time.

Coming up for air, my stomach rumbled. The moondoggy turned to me, barked, and bounded along the edge of the gurgling water. It took me a moment to understand what I was supposed to do. Knight couldn't follow the moondoggy because of the tree branches that hung over the stream, but I could if I hunched over.

"I won't be long," I said, patting Knight on the neck.

The injured horse huffed, staying behind. I caught up to the moondoggy. She sat on a flat rock, licking her front paw. Barking, she hopped between tangled roots. The moondoggy continued to the base of a tree with orange crusty bark. She pawed at the trunk before barking once more.

I tilted my neck back and saw fruit hanging above my head. It was an ivory color, and shaped like a pear. High in the branches, dozens hung down. Maybe it was because I was starving, or because the fruit smelled sweet like pineapple, but my mouth began to water.

"Can I eat it?" I asked, pretending to chew.

The moondoggy barked, swishing her tail back and forth.

Taking the answer as a yes, I reached up and picked the ivory fruit, feeling the bumps that covered its skin. Lifting the fruit to my mouth, I took a bite. Its flesh was hard and surprisingly filling. It tasted like a jawbreaker. With sticky juice running down my chin, I ate the rest of the fruit.

I picked six more for Knight. "Breakfast," I called out.

The horse ate greedily. I returned three more times until he had his fill. With a full belly, I wanted nothing more than to curl up next to the stream and fall asleep.

The following two days were the same as this one. The moondoggy would lead us along game trails, show us where to find food, and locate safe places for us to sleep. But everything changed on the third night when I heard the voice.

Chapter 24

MY EARS PERKED UP at the sound on the wind. I strained my neck to catch the voice. It was difficult to pinpoint. I was curled up next to Knight under the weeping branches of a tree. Closing my eyes, I tried to block out the chirping birds and the rustling leaves.

The voice sounded female, and far away. I couldn't understand what was being said, but I was pretty sure I knew who it belonged to.

"Jana!" I called. "Is that you?"

The voice responded, but it was too mumbled to understand.

"Let's go," I said, urging Knight and the moondoggy up. "Jana, we're over here!" I shouted into the darkness, hearing her again.

The farther I went, the more words I recognized. I heard my father's name, stones, and something about potential. But I'd lost track of Knight and the moondoggy. Guided by rays of moonlight, I skidded to a stop in front of a tree so tall that its leaves swayed in the canopy.

"Jana!" I yelled.

The voice returned, but it came in the direction where no game trail led. I shoved between bushes without checking over my shoulder. It was tough going without a trail. The trees grew so close together that they blocked out almost all of the moonlight, but the voice was getting louder.

Emerging from the suffocating plant life, my shortcut stopped at the edge of a fog-covered ground. No tree grew through the fog, letting Altrea's three moons shine down like cosmic spotlights.

Tendrils of mist, shaped like the fingers of a witch, pulled the fog away, revealing a small lake. Its black water reflected the trunks of twelve trees that surrounded the lake like sentinels. Each one had moss that dangled to within an inch of the surface of the water. The place gave me the impression of sacred ground.

Knight caught up to me at the sandy edge of the lake, but the moondoggy was nowhere to be found. I looked out over the mirrored water. Was I the first to see this place?

"No," rang her voice, crystal clear, in my mind.

"What?" I asked, spinning around.

"You're not the first," she said. "But you are of a few."

"Oh," I said, pretending to understand. "Is that a good thing?"

"It depends," she said, her voice sounding different now. It had a musical ring to it.

"Who are you?" I asked.

"We are a Larrabee. But you may call us Luna."

"And what exactly is a Larrabee?"

A small figure, no longer than my forearm, fluttered down from a branch over the lake. She had long arms and legs, pointed ears, and curved wings that flickered and radiated a rich bluish light. Her face was refreshing, with an ageless quality, but not quite human. She wore a wrap of gold and was barefoot.

"You're a fairy," I said.

"No," said Luna, crossing her arms across her chest. "Why do men always need to be told things more than once?" she huffed. "I believe we told you that we are a Larrabee."

"I didn't mean to upset you," I apologized. "Where I come, you're a fairy."

"You didn't upset us, Ethan," said Luna. "We're only making sure you know the truth."

Hearing her call me by my real name sent a chill down my spine. "How do you know my name? I haven't told anyone my real name since I arrived in Altrea."

"The answer to your question is complex," said Luna, hovering over the middle of the lake.

"I have all night."

"Very well," the Larrabee said, nodding. "We Larrabee have the ability to see all potential future outcomes, and in most of them a boy named Ethan Spooner, from Earth, arrives at our lake this very night. Am I to presume that you are him?"

I nodded.

"We also can assume that you're the son of the Essenzian, Kalven Spooner?"

"Yes," I answered. "And you know these thing because you can see into the future?"

She shook her head. "We see possible futures," Luna said. "All of them to be precise. There are millions upon millions of possible futures that are ever changing. But we have met your father as well."

"He was one of the few who have been to your lake, too?" I asked.

Luna nodded. "We allowed him to visit us because he held the key that could put a stop to the future that posed the greatest danger to Altrea. Kalven arrived at our lake after his friend Roon had been kidnapped.

Kalven needed a place to hide from Baracus' agents. We informed him that in most of his futures a woman with mismatching eyes would kill him within ten weeks. In a handful of futures, though, she didn't murder him for many years. We also told Kalven that those handful of futures all occurred on Earth; the same place he'd become a father."

I paced along the edge of the lake. It was too hard to believe that this little fairy is responsible for my birth. I asked, "What does this have to do with me?"

"Everything."

The way she said *everything* gave me goose bumps. "Does this have anything to do with my futures?"

Luna smiled. "Of course," she sang. "Some of your futures have you staying on Earth. Others have you dying in the ancient ruins at the hands of the Marzzoe. Another has you not following Knight into Anco. More have you getting eaten by the three-tailed cats, or the pack of dogs. But there are a few that captured our attention."

Leaning forward, I said, "Please, go on."

The Larrabee fluttered to within two feet of my nose. "They show you living up to your potential."

I rolled my eyes. "What's that supposed to mean?"

"Do you know how you defeated the Marzzoe?" she asked.

"With a rock," I said, gripping the sword in my hand.

"And the nygar?"

"A sword."

The corners of Luna's mouth turned up. "Did you see red?"

I thought back to the time I whacked the assassin with my rock, or cut the nygar in two. "Yes, both times."

"Seeing red is natural for someone with your talents," said Luna. "It means that you're among the few who can use a verve stone."

"The stone that brought me through the ley lines?" I asked.

"Yes."

I reached into my pocket and pulled out Quaren's glowing stone.

"Jumping between worlds is an exceptionally rare job for a verve stone," she explained. "Its main function is to give its user an ability. The red verve stone gives its users added physical strength."

I remembered how my muscles tingled every time I touched Quaren's stone, and how I'd killed the assassin with one blow, and cut the nygar in half. "It gives me a superpower?" I asked.

"That's one way to look at it."

A grin spread across my face. "No way," I breathed.

"You must realize that any human who can use a verve stone would also acquire added strength from Quaren's stone," said the Larrabee. "However, you are not a normal human."

I looked up from my palm, furrowing my brow.

"I'm not insulting you," Luna insisted. "I'm stating a fact. You have the blood of men flowing through your veins, thanks to your mother. You also have Essenzian blood inside of you."

"Is that a good thing?"

"Yes," said Luna. "You see, verve stones work differently for an Essenzian. To those who can use a red stone, physical speed is given."

"Why is it different for men?" I asked.

"We're not sure," said the Larrabee. "For some reason nature has given the verve stones a kind of check-and-balance system; strength and speed in the red stone's case."

"You said that I have human and Essenzian blood in me, so why didn't I get faster when I killed the assassin and the lizard?" I asked.

Luna brushed a strand of hair behind her ear. "In a number of your futures, you do acquire both increased strength and speed from Quaren's verve stone," Luna explained. "It is worth stating that you'll never have full power over either verve stone ability, not like someone with pure blood, but there will be advantages, should your dual abilities manifest."

I closed my fist around the glowing stone in my palm. "Two superpowers!" I cheered, pumping my arm.

"You have the *potential* for two," said the Larrabee. "The odds are less than one hundred million to one."

There was that word again.

"After all, you're not the only half-blood Altrea has seen," said Luna. "Through being half-blooded, and able to use a verve stone is uncommon in our history." The Larrabee added, "We'll have to be patient to learn which of your futures your present becomes."

"What are my possible futures?" I asked.

Luna fluttered so close to my face that I felt little puffs of air with each beat of her wings. "Most of these futures have you returning to Earth and living a long life. However, the futures that caught our attention involved you using both your Essenzian and human abilities. Some have you falling to the same woman that killed your father. Others have you dying at the hands of Baracus the Soul Stealer."

"The evil king?" I asked.

"Yes," said Luna, nodding. "One set of futures has you being murdered by one of the Twelve Generals of Gramhammer. Another a Marzzoe. In the next bunch you join forces with Baracus and help him conquer Altrea, then stab him the back and take over Gramhammer. Yet another future has your eyes glowing like the sun as you fall off a high cliff. In your final future, we found what we've spent a lifetime searching for – the defeat of the Soul Stealer."

"You said, *defeat?*"

Luna nodded.

I rubbed my jaw. "How do you know which future will come true?"

"We don't," Luna said. "We can see possible outcomes. Your decisions will determine which future you choose; nothing more."

Thinking about the few futures that didn't end with me dying, I said, "This sounds crazy."

"We understand," said Luna. "It is a lot to process."

My pacing made a trail in the sand. Knight followed, never leaving my side. Finally, I said, "If I can't turn in my homework on time, how do you expect me to defeat Baracus?"

"With the help of your friends," she said.

"Do you at least have some unbreakable sword that I can use on Baracus?" I asked.

Luna smiled with her blue lips. "No, but we can offer you Moka. She is our most trusted ally." Hovering over the water, she whistled.

A moondoggy emerged from behind a tree, looking like the same creature that brought us to the Larrabee, right down to the cut over her eye.

"Please keep Ethan safe, Moka," Luna ordered.

The moondoggy barked once.

I stood there, thinking about what Vadin had said about the moondoggy being good luck. Watching the creature, and thinking about beating a king who can kill a hundred men without spilling a drop of blood, I couldn't help wishing I had an unbreakable sword instead.

Luna rose towards the sky. "Our time is done for now, Ethan," she said. "We will be watching." With that the fairy, or Larrabee, flew to the branches of the closest tree that overlooked the small lake.

The moondoggy escorted us away from the mirrored lake, underneath walls of moss, and between golden-leafed trees with nothing more than moonlight to guide us. Knight's heavy hooves clomped beside me. He hadn't left my side. Moka weaved over the dead leaves on the game trail, not making a sound. A small part of my brain kept me from tripping over roots and vines, while the rest chewed on everything Luna had told me. It gave me a headache.

We came to a river, which sounded much larger than the stream from before. Moka stopped at a lush patch of grass. I dropped the sword, unable to carry it a step further. Drinking the cool water, and eating a few nuts that the moondoggy had discovered, we made beds of leaves at the river's edge. We fell asleep to the sound of gurgling waters, without a worry in the world that a hungry creature would eat us.

I woke up to the sound of Moka's barks. I had a crick in my neck and my hollow stomach rumbled. The moondoggy lead me to a bush with orange berries, and a tree with nuts. Knight and I ate as much of it as we could for breakfast, and then made our way down the right side of the river.

It didn't take long for Knight to fall behind. The horse was so chewed up from the lizard that I couldn't believe he could stand, let alone walk. We were forced to slow our pace.

Lunch included three roots and a mouthful of river water. We walked the trail until the light of Anco had faded. We slept by the river once more. Never seeing a creature that wanted to do us harm, and always along the side of the river.

Two mornings later, we came to a dead end. The river went underneath a thick wall of trees, vines, and moss. Moka sat up and barked, her tail swishing from side to side. I walked beside her, unable to see through the mass of gnarled plants.

One by one, vines and roots and branches pulled themselves away from the area in front of Moka. It was like she had a garage door opener that caused the plants to part ways. With my jaw hanging open, beams of sunlight broke through the wall. I covered my eyes. The journey through Anco had made me forget how bright the sun was. More light poured over us as the hole in the forest opened enough to pass through.

Moka exited Anco, and Knight and I gladly did the same.

Outside, the sun was low on the horizon with blue sky for as far as my eyes could see. The river rushed out of the forest and cut over some rolling hills. My nose was assaulted with the aroma of fresh grass and wet earth. It was such a perfect moment that even Knight appeared happy.

The landscape in front of me was covered with the plushest grass, and the best part was it was just high enough to only cover my ankles. I ran my fingers over the green stuff. Knight celebrated by chomping away at the thin blades in great mouthfuls. Moka even cleaned her front paws.

The moondoggy continued to guide us in the same direction as she had in the forest. We trudged along the river's edge all day. We had all the water we could drink, and Moka found us some sour orange berries, but my stomach rumbled for meat. Each step was a struggle.

I'd looked forward to sleeping all day, but Moka didn't stop after sundown like normal. I had no doubt in Luna's moondoggy, but it would be dark soon. Then her motivation for our hard march showed itself as a flickering light at a bend in the river.

"Is that a campfire?" I whispered.

Moka didn't seem to mind the campers as she continued to stroll on ahead. Knight and I were left trying to keep up, but it was getting difficult to see Moka. Approaching the firelight, my stomach knotted at the smell of cooked meat. Moka had almost reached the campfire. The hairs on the back of my neck were standing up. Should we be doing this?

A jingling sound came from behind me, which was accompanied by a whinny from Knight. "Spoon, is that you?"

Chapter 25

VADIN LED US TO THE FIRELIGHT. He rode Cow, who skipped under him. The closer we got to the campfire, the more my stomach rumbled. The smell of cooked meat almost knocked me to the ground with hunger. The fire was built in the center of a circle of river rocks. Roban rested on his stretcher nearby. Melik and Jana eyed a skinned and feathered bird roasting over orange flames, heads hanging low.

"Look who I found," Vadin said, unable to hold back a toothy grin.

Melik and Jana turned, locking eyes with Knight and me.

"We thought you were lost in Anco," said Jana, dabbing at the corners of her eyes.

"Never to return," Melik added, a smile splitting his face.

"You're not dead," Roban grunted, as if it were a bad thing.

It felt good to be with friends again. Having real people to talk with was a bonus, too.

Vadin and Jana had their fair share of bumps and bruises, but it was Melik's forearm, dressed in a fresh bandage, that caught my attention. "Nygar?" I asked, pointing.

"Yes," he replied. He glanced over my bruised, sliced, and bug-bitten body. "You look terrible." Then he turned to face Roban's horse. "And Knight looks even worse."

"What did you do to my horse?" Roban groaned.

"I didn't do anything," I stammered. "Between the nygar and the forest, he never stood a chance."

"This is all your fault," Roban spit. "It was bad enough that I got skewered for you, but you had to spread your bad luck onto Knight, too!"

"It's not like I wanted any of this to happen," I countered. "If you want to blame anyone, blame your faceless friend."

"The only reason Quaren went to your world is because of the mess your father left behind," Roban countered. "As far as I'm concerned, your entire family is a plague to us all."

"Enough," said Melik.

Roban huffed, but said no more.

I wanted to kick something over after Roban's tongue lashing, but Melik pulled me aside to scrub out the three gashes on my bicep. And scrub he did. I gritted my teeth and barred the pain, not wanting to embarrass myself in front of the guild members. It was more than enough to help me forget how upset I was with Roban.

Vadin attended to Knight. He used the root extract on the deepest of the horse's wounds. Knight didn't squirm or cry out. While Vadin worked, he noticed Moka resting on Knight's back.

"You found a moondoggy?" he said in awe, jaw hanging open.

"No, she found us," I said.

Vadin was mesmerized at the sight of the mythological creature. It was all he talked about for the rest of the night. Moka appeared to enjoy the attention.

"This will leave a nasty scar, Spoon," said Melik, tying the last knot on my bandage.

"But the ladies will love it," Vadin added, winking at me.

Having done everything they could for Knight and me, the horse was left to heal with his friends, while I sat with the guildsmen around the campfire.

Jana hugged me, and began to fill me with food and water. As I ate, Melik told me what happened with the nygars, and how they got through Anco.

"Jana killed her lizard," he said. "However, Vadin and I had trouble with the big one. It always got up, no matter what we did to it. We slowed it down from horseback, but Roban was thrown around like a rag doll behind Bomber in the process. I was forced to cut the stretcher free from my saddle.

"I stabbed at the nygar, and Vadin put another arrow in it. The stubborn, old scale-back wouldn't fall or flee. The lizard stopped leaping at us with his attacks. We feared it would reach Roban by slipping undetected beneath Cow and Bomber. With no clear option, I dismounted to protect Roban. I did what I could to keep the lizard away from Roban, but I was at an obvious disadvantage on foot. Vadin joined me, despite his sword being with you, and his quiver down to one arrow, joined me.

"His timing couldn't have been better. The lizard shot out of the grass between Cow and Bomber. I blocked its path by my sword, and Vadin put his last arrow in its neck. Our attacks were ineffective, given the creature's thick scales. If we didn't find a spot on the nygar, we'd be done for.

"The lizard returned to its aerial assault. We knew we needed to meet the nygar in the air, but with no trees to climb, and Roban to defend on the ground, we needed to work together to gain altitude.

"Vadin jumped onto my shoulders. Wobbling like a leaf, I listened for the direction of the nygar's next attack. It came from our right. I had just enough time to face the lizard. It launched itself through the air. Somehow, Vadin blocked both its claws as it tried to take my head off.

"Vadin blocked the lizard's arms over his head as the creature's hind legs stretched to the ground, the belly of the nygar passed in front of my face. It was the first opening we were given. I took advantage of the opportunity and stabbed the lizard in the gut with my sword. When the dust settled, we had two dead lizards, and you and Knight were nowhere to be found," Melik finished.

"We searched everywhere for you," said Jana. "It was impossible to tell where you entered Anco. We stayed around, hoping you'd emerge sooner or later, but you didn't. Roban's injury kept us from being able to wait any longer. Reluctantly, we hiked to the trail that divides Anco."

"Did any creatures try to eat you?" I asked.

"We didn't see, hear, or meet anything but bugs on the trial," said Vadin. "It was the most boring trip I'd ever taken. I've never gone near that place, let alone inside, without facing one or two hungry creatures."

I had the feeling that a little blue fairy had something to do with the guild member's safe journey. "Do you think the Marzzoe made it through Anco?" I asked.

"Absolutely," Vadin said without pausing.

The coals of the fire breathed as a light wind rolled over them. "Now that you know how we got here, what happened to you and Knight?" Jana asked.

I put my hand over the bandage on my bicep, touching it with my fingertips. "I'd rather wait to tell you guys somewhere secure from listening ears."

"You're wise beyond your years," Melik said, nodding. "We'll wait until we reach Gaelwallia, where we can talk freely."

The sun peaked over the green hills. It burned off the morning fog that hung in the lowest spots of the flat land. Under my warm bedding, not wanting to get up, I heard the guild members preparing to leave. Moka had fallen asleep at my feet, curled above my toes.

The moondoggy moved before me. She preened herself, and walked to the river to get a drink. I sat up. Ruffling my hair, I realized that I didn't have a bag to pack like the others. It had been torn off Knight's back by the nygar and lost in the tall grass. Melik had found me a change of clothes that would get me to Gaelwallia. The pants needed rope to stay around my waist, but the shirt fit well enough.

While the others finished up, I walked over to where the horses were tied. Knight was able to hold his head a little higher than the previous night. He still had a lot of healing to do though.

We carried Roban over to the horses once everyone was ready. The wounded guildsman insisted on walking, but Jana refused, reminding him of the hole in his side. Roban didn't take her directive well, refusing to talk with anyone for the next hour.

Like the numerous times before, Melik floated one side of Roban's stretcher off the ground with a glowing, golden stone. "Is that a verve stone?" I asked.

Melik adjusted the leather tube on his back and then tilted his head and looked at me out of the corner of his eye. "Yes," he said.

"What exactly does it do?" I asked.

Melik took a breath. "It lets someone make things lighter."

The memory of Roban fighting the Marzzoe, his eyes blazing blue, popped into my mind. "Does Roban have one, too?"

"Yes," he answered. "His verve stone allows him to infuse any object with pure energy."

"Where's his stone?" I asked.

Melik pointed to the pummel of Roban's black sword. "Right there," he said.

I scratched my head. "How'd he use his stone when he was unconscious?"

Melik tapped his chin with a finger, probably figuring out the best way to answer my question. "Let me ask you this," said Melik. "Was Roban breathing when he was unconscious?"

"Yes."

"Was his heart beating?"

"Yes."

"Verve stones work the same way as those bodily functions," he explained, sounding like a college professor. "It's Roban's lifetime of training that allows him to use a verve stone without touching it."

With everything packed, and the fire doused, we left our riverside camp behind. I rode with Melik because Knight needed more time to heal. We traveled with the river on our left. In the chill of the morning, a gray bird with a hooked beak flew over the surface of the moving water, and a family of prairie dogs popped their heads out of various holes in the grass.

As we traveled northeast, Melik told me that Gaelwallia used to be two separate villages on adjacent shores of the Westland River, which happened to be the name of the river we'd been following. He explained that those villages held two different families; the Hayder and the Ahee. The families have always had strained relations with each other, but ten years ago a royal marriage brought the two sides together.

I passed the hours on horseback daydreaming about superpowers, and how I'd use them at school back home.

After sleeping on a carpet of grass each night, Gaelwallia emerged below us. The city rested on the shore of the Lake of Tilvera, stretching over the lake with hundreds of docks, and spilling out from both sides of the Westland River. Farmlands closed in around the outskirts of the city. What was really amazing about Gaelwallia were the two colossal walls that encircled every building, farm, and dock.

Arriving at the outer wall, I saw it was made of large stones that fit together so closely an ant couldn't squeeze between them. Men in uniform and armor patrolled the top of the wall with crossbows in hand. The wall had a guard tower every two hundred feet, and an iron gate. We waited in line to enter Gaelwallia. The guards appeared to be talking to each group, scowling at them with furrowed brows, and sending many people away.

"Are these guys going to let us in?" I asked Jana, who was riding on Melik's right.

"They should," she answered. "Gaelwallia is a peaceful place, but they guard their freedom well."

"We will be interrogated," Melik explained. "So let me do the talking."

"I've passed through this wall many times. The longest wait was three days," said Jana. "But Roban doesn't have time to wait."

"I agree," he said.

We only moved ten feet over the next half hour because the guards at the gate wanted to see in everyone's carts, barrels, and boxes. One guard yelled at an old lady for not opening her bag fast enough. A guy my mom's age was tossed out of line and handcuffed. I strained my neck to see what got him the rough treatment, but I never saw what set the guards off.

Melik positioned Bomber under the gatekeeper. "Here goes nothing," he mumbled.

"What business do you have in Gaelwallia?" called a guard in a silver helmet. He seemed like a guy who didn't say *yes* often.

"My name is Melik, and these are my friends," he said, gesturing to the other guild members on horseback. "We're here to get this man to a healer right away."

Roban had a scowl on his face, and his arms were crossed over his chest, but he kept his glowing eyes shut.

The guard glared down his oversized nose. "Very well, you may enter."

"Thank you," said Melik. He guided Bomber through the iron gate. Vadin and Jana hurried after us, probably worried that the guard would change his mind.

"Kind of anticlimactic, don't you think?" I asked, once we were out of earshot from the guard.

Vadin raised an eyebrow, grinning larger than usual. "I've been held up at this gate more times than I can count. It's never this easy."

"That was a first for me as well," Jana added.

"Let's hope our good fortune holds for the next wall of Gaelwallia," said Melik, leading the group single file.

The second wall was made of stone as well. Where the outer wall was eighty feet high, the inner wall had to be at least one hundred. Melik said the inner wall was designed so archers and catapults could fire over the outer wall without causing damage. I guessed the distance between the two walls to be about twenty-five feet. He also told me that the outer wall is newer because of the growing threat of Gramhammer.

We found the next gate and its gatekeeper. The line went faster, although not much. Twenty minutes later we approached the second gatekeeper. Melik said the same thing as he'd said at the outer gate, and this gatekeeper waved us past, too. Vadin and Jana's eyes widened at good news.

"I don't know what to say," Melik said, shaking his head from side to side. Moka, curled up between Melik and me, put her head up and yawned. He turned to look at the moondoggy. "Perhaps the stories about you are true after all?" he said as we hurried towards the city.

We passed into vast fields of farmland. They ran the perimeter of the inner wall, and had patches of every color imaginable growing. The sight was remarkable. Rutted paths connected the crops, aqueducts, towering silos, and barns to each other. On the side of the farms were hundreds of buildings all jumbled on top of each other like some big house of cards. The sweeping waters of the Westland River dissected the city. But it was what was in the center of the river that caught my attention. Glistening in the mists of foaming waters, two towers stood proudly.

"Those are the most important buildings in Gaelwallia," Melik explained as Bomber's hooves clopped on the path. "The skinnier, taller tower on the left is called the Yorkshire Tower. It's the main battlement of the city, as well as the home of the Hayder family. The shorter, thicker tower is called the Mul-dahee Tower. It's where laws are completed and judgments are made, as well as the residence of the Ahee family."

Both towers had their own unique architecture and decorations. They were linked together by two drawbridges that met in the middle, and to their own side of the river by a rope bridge.

Our next turn led us onto a busy street filled with merchants trying to sell their goods. The market smelled of baked bread with a side of rotten fish. It had tents on both sides of the street, complete with shoppers milling about. One woman had two very alive chickens in each of her wrinkled hands. She flung them over her head and screamed, "Chicken dinner! Chicken dinner!"

"I'll take my chicken in nugget form," I said to Melik. "That way they won't fly away when you try to dip them in sweat-and-sour sauce."

He had never eaten fast food in his life, but that didn't stop him from grinning at me.

We drifted the length of merchant row, passing shops, blacksmiths, inns, and pubs. It was apparent that Melik knew where he was going. He never slowed down, no matter how many times we turned onto a new street. My best guess on our direction was east, away from the Westland River. In our wake the stacks of buildings shrank.

Once at the edge of the city, we came to the seam between two buildings where a gray door hung. Melik and I dismounted Bomber. He handed Vadin his horse's reins. With his leather tube still strapped to his back, Melik knocked three times and waited. No one came. He knocked three more times and waited. Still nothing. Had we come all this way for nothing? Finally, a small hatch in the door creaked open.

A set of beady eyes peered out of the peephole. Rolling his sleeve to his elbow, Melik held his forearm up to the hatch. The eyes disappeared, but the peephole stayed open. Melik lowered his arm, but kept his sleeve rolled up.

The person behind the door returned a few minutes later. A lit silver candle was held up to the hatch's opening. He held up his arm once more without being asked. As soon as the silver light hit his forearm a tiny patch of skin came to life. On it appeared two crescents fitted together around a circle. They gleamed in silver ink.

The person behind the door slapped the small hatch shut. Melik stayed put, rolling down his sleeve. I heard the sound of metal scraping against metal from behind the door. Locks? The door swung out. A woman with graying hair, and wearing a black shawl, stepped into the doorway. She held a smoking, silver candle.

"Hello, Fey," said Melik.

Chapter 26

THE OLDER WOMAN SPOKE with a raspy voice. "What went wrong? You're early?"

"Roban I'm afraid," Melik answered. Stepping to the side, he gestured with his hand to the stretcher half floating behind his horse.

"I'm fine," Roban complained from his stretcher.

Melik exchanged a knowing glance with Fey.

"Vadin," she said, as if she were used to giving orders, "take the horses to the stables and get Roban ready to go inside."

"You got it," he answered.

Jana dismounted from Isabel, handing her reins to Vadin. She followed Fey, Melik, and me through the gray door. Two hanging lanterns marked the beginning of a circular room at the end of the hallway. Besides lantern light, the room was bathed in colors from a stained-glass skylight set in the ceiling.

I tilted my head up, gazing at the detailed artwork. A man with sun-filled eyes, holding a sword, stood atop a waterfall. He appeared to be about to jump off the falls.

"That's the Prince of Midnight," Melik said, not lowering his eyes. "He's the most famous warrior in Essenzian history, said to have defeated the first Gramhammer king after the king had changed his realm of peace to war."

The circular room was wrapped in bookshelves. Each one was stacked, piled, and stuffed with thousands of dust-covered books and scrolls. Sprinkled around the room were glass jars where the body parts of animals floated in yellow water. Three leather chairs faced a fireplace. A table with six wooden chairs rested in the center, and a long couch sat opposite two chairs under a wall of tiny numbered drawers.

Fey stopped in front of a shelving ladder. The rest of us gathered around. She swept her russet eyes over Melik and Jana, but they stopped on me.

"He's Kalven's son," said Melik.

She arched an eyebrow. "What happened to Kalven?"

"He passed away when Spoon was young," Jana answered.

"Has Quaren arrived?" Melik asked.

Fey shook her head. She took in a breath, but before she could do anything with it, Vadin entered the circular room. "Roban is ready," he said.

"We'll continue this when we've taken care of our injured friend," said Fey.

Everyone helped carry Roban in on his stretcher from the stables. We shifted him onto a bed, doing our best not to injure the guildsman further. Roban insisted that he didn't need to be babysat, but Fey hushed him up by saying, "I'll be the judge of that."

Vadin, Jana, and I huddled around Roban's bed as Fey and Melik removed the bandages. The strips of fabric closest to the stab wound were not bloody, but his skin had turned yellow, blue, purple, and dark red. It looked like an elephant had stepped on his side.

Fey clicked her tongue. "Ulmaroo root?" she asked.

Melik answered, "It was our best option."

"You're lucky you were carrying that stuff," said Fey, wadding the old bandages and throwing them into a woven basket behind her.

"It's saved me more than once," said Melik.

"Will you two stop prattling and tell me how long this is going to keep me off my feet?" Roban insisted.

Fey poked the spot where Roban's flesh had been melted together. Roban cringed. "You did that on purpose!" he spat.

"Your internal bleeding has internal bleeding," Fey said. "The only thing keeping you alive is shear stubbornness. Any regular person wouldn't be able to speak with this kind of injury."

"How long?" Roban grunted.

"I'll know more after I make a full examination," Fey declared. Turning her attention to Vadin, Jana, and I, she said, "You three go to the inn and fetch us some dinner. Melik and I should be done when you return."

"You got it," Vadin said.

The Krusty Dragon was marked with a battered sign hanging above a red door. It had a dragon carved on it with a foaming mug in one claw and a spoon in the other. The inn was old and weathered, and the neighboring buildings towered over its sagging roof and foggy windows.

Vadin pushed his way into the inn with Jana and me at his heels. I'd expected Moka to join us, but she'd curled up under Roban's bed and wouldn't budge. Maybe he needed some of her mojo?

A bell chimed as the three of use entered the bottom floor of the two-story inn. The place smelled like sour dishwater and smoke. It was packed full of worn-out tables and chairs. People ate, talked, and drank out of large mugs. I swear one guy in the corner even had three eyes.

The inn's ceiling was vaulted, and above the bar ran a railed balcony with doors. The bar itself had a cherry finish with dents and gouges from years of use. A skinny man stood behind the bar drying mugs with a wet towel. His graying hair was slicked back, he was clean-shaven, and his large hands reminded me of the paddle of an oar.

"Good evenin'," the innkeeper said, glancing up from his work. His accent made him sound like a pirate. "By glum, it's you, Master Vadin. It has been too long since you last graced my establishment. How's life treated yee?" he asked.

"Busy, Jarvis," said Vadin, leaning on the bar and giving the innkeeper a toothy smile. "How are you?"

"Well, t'is place keeps me happy it does," Jarvis whistled through the gap of his front teeth.

"You remember Jana?" Vadin asked.

"Of course, of course," the innkeeper said, bowing at the guild woman. "You look as radiant as the midday sun, milady."

"Thank you," said Jana, her cheeks turning a shade darker.

Jarvis lifted a wooden spoon out of the sink full of suds and dried it with his towel as Vadin introduced me.

"And this is a new member of our group. His name is Spoon," the guildsmen said, patting me on the shoulder.

Everyone looked at the spoon in Jarvis' hands, and back at me. "It's nice to meet you, Mr. Jarvis."

Vadin placed a hand over his mouth to hold back a laugh.

"Just Jarvis me boy," the innkeeper snorted.

Jarvis finished drying his spoon and placed it in a container with other utensils. He made his way to some large barrels on the side of his bar. He filled six of his clean mugs with a foamy liquid. "Gents, your ales," he called to three men. They left the bar with two mugs each.

With his order filled, Jarvis returned his attention to us. "I haves a nice oak barrel spirit if yee tongues need some entertainment," he said, putting extra emphasis on the syllables in entertainment. "This evening's special be mincemeat pie, same as always. I also have an open room if you needs a place for the night."

"No beds for us," Vadin said. "But we'd love five of your famous mincemeat pies, a salad, two mugs from the oak barrel, and a glass of juice for the young warrior."

"Coming right up," said the innkeeper. "Sit anywhere while you wait, and I'll have those drinks out to you shortly."

"Thank you," Vadin answered.

Vadin chose an empty table next to the bar, which looked as if a family of mice had chewed on it. Jarvis popped out from behind the bar and dropped off our drinks. I sipped my juice and listened to the conversations that swirled around the inn. The table behind me was talking about their potato crop, and some woman to my right kept gossiping about a friend who'd lost her mother. The skinny innkeeper brought out four parcels of delicious-smelling food wrapped in brown paper as soon as my cup was empty.

"Thanks again," said Vadin, paying Jarvis.

As the innkeeper pocketed the coins he leaned forward and Vadin asked, "Have you heard about Delgard?"

"No."

"Word is Gramhammer is marching towards them as we speak," Jarvis explained.

"Melik won't be happy about that," Jana said.

"Why?" I asked.

"It's the Byroc's largest castle," she said. "Gramhammer has tried to invade Del-gard for centuries, but it's said to be grown from the mountain itself. They have dragons that roam its caves, and creatures formed of magma that guard its walls. The Byroc scientists are also housed in Del-gard."

"Baracus is either crazy to attempt such an impossible feat, or a genius," Vadin admitted. "Whatever the case, if the king of Gramhammer succeeds he will bolster his army by two folds."

"What do you mean *bolster*?" I asked.

Vadin answered, "The scholars of Gramhammer have developed a soldier's brew. It's a potion that changes men into mindless zombies. Whoever drinks the brew will lose their memories and obey Baracus' every command."

"It's a fate worse than death," Jana added bitterly.

We arrived at Fey's and found her and Melik finishing with Roban. I sat across from Jana and Vadin in the circular room, leaning back in my chair. With time to kill, I asked the two guild members a question that had been bouncing around my head all day. "How does Fey fit into the Guild?"

"Fey Menandar is an elder of the Guild," Jana answered. "One of three. To be honest, I've only met her a few times. Melik knows her the best. He's worked out of Gaelwallia for the past ten years."

"How does someone get into the Guild to begin with?" I asked.

Vadin said, "I left Durlonemor Mine in search of the man who killed my brother. It was years before I got close enough to run a blade through the guy, though he beat me to it." Vadin rolled up his sleeveless shirt to reveal a disgusting scar over his shoulder blade. "He nearly killed me too," he said. "After healing, I received a letter to join the Guild. I didn't accept straight away, but I eventually did."

Jana said, "I got involved with the Guild while I searched for my family. I'd attempted to free them from the slave camp twice, but we were always thwarted. I didn't know at the time, but a guild member worked with me during my next breakout attempt. He invited me to meet Fey, and the rest is history."

"What about Melik?" I asked.

Jana and Vadin made eye contact, and from the looks they gave each other, I didn't think either of them wanted to answer my question.

"He lost his family," came a voice from behind me. It belonged to Melik, who'd just entered the room.

Chapter 27

"I DIDN'T MEAN TO GOSSIP," I apologized.

Melik scratched his beard.

"I'm sorry," I said, wishing I could take back the question.

"Don't worry about it," he insisted.

To my surprise, Melik sat in a chair and told me how he'd lost his family.

"I was hunting a ram off the cliffs of Mount Radnomar, which I killed on the third day. And when I finally returned to my village, I found it deserted. I ran between the buildings calling for my family and friends. To my horror, I found the butcher's body lay unmoving in front of his shop. Then I saw a childhood friend face-down on some stairs. Only one person answered my calls; an old man with a black arrow sticking out of his thigh. He said soldiers from Gramhammer had stormed the village, forced everyone into the streets, and loaded them into carts.

"I rushed to my home. Our things were tossed to the floor and broken. My wife was gone. The same was true for my parents and extended family. I grabbed what I thought I'd need on the road, then I hopped on my horse and followed the cart tracks south to Gramhammer, but I never found a single person from my village in all my years.

"To sustain my search, I became a mercenary for anyone who needed a hand against Gramhammer. These acts got me noticed by the Guild. A letter came for me to join soon after. But my story is the same a countless others."

Fey entered the circular room as soon as Melik finished his sad story. The four of us ate our mincemeat pies while Vadin enjoyed his salad. The name of the pies didn't sound appetizing, but I could've eaten four more.

Fey reported that Roban had no more blood to lose. His wound didn't get infected, and would heal faster now that he wasn't bouncing down mountain trails. She also told everyone that Melik had caught her up on everything that had happened since I joined the party.

It was finally time for me to fill everyone in on the trip through Anco. I was about to begin, but figured Roban wouldn't want to miss my story, even if he claimed that it would be dull and boring. So we all got up and went to Roban's room and squeezed around his bed. I spelled out everything that had happened to Knight and me.

I told them about cutting the nygar in two, being saved by Bigfoot, meeting the moondoggy, and having the Larrabee tell me about my futures.

Vadin and Jana were impressed with my fighting, while Fey and Melik gasped at meeting Luna. Roban kept quiet. Unless you count the choice words he called me every time his horse almost got eaten. Fey asked about my potential to have Essenzian and human abilities from verve stones. Melik focused on the future where the half-blooded boy from Earth defeats the Soul Stealer.

"Now we know where Kalven got his idea to hide on Earth," said Vadin. "All these possible futures are hard to wrap my mind around."

"You're telling me," I said.

"But none of this explains why Quaren sent Spoon to Altrea," grumbled Roban.

"He's right," agreed Fey.

Everyone mulled over the information overload. Melik broke the silence a few minutes later. "I guess the real question is what future do you want, Spoon?"

I could still hear Luna telling me about the futures where I went home and lived a long life, died on Altrea, or joined Baracus.

"I've given this question a lot of thought, and I decided that I want to fix the problem my dad left behind."

Melik nodded.

"As the Larrabee said, you will have our help," Melik said, patting me on the shoulder.

"So, what's our next move?" asked Jana.

Fey started with a rule. "Spoon is not to be left alone. If Baracus learns about his futures, he'll stop at nothing to make certain they benefit Gramhammer. These walls are strong, but they won't hinder a Marzzoe. We have to expect the assassin's return. To be honest, I can't fathom why he hasn't attacked already. We must be prepared."

"Next, Spoon will begin his training to fight under the three of you," said the guild elder, looking at Melik, Jana, and Vadin. "He will also carry a sword."

"He can keep mine," said Vadin, winking at me.

Fey nodded.

A smile spread across my face.

"Don't act like this is going to be some kind of vacation," warned Vadin. "When we're done with you, you may never want to hold a sword again."

Fey added, "Once Roban is well enough, he'll teach Spoon how to use a verve stone."

My gut felt like it dropped on the floor and rolled underneath the bed.

"You're not seriously putting all our eggs into *this* basket," scoffed Roban, gesturing to me with a flick of his thumb.

"You heard what the Larrabee saw," said Vadin. "Spoon is the only person on Altrea who has a shot at defeating Baracus."

Roban countered, "The Larrabee also said that those futures were ever-changing."

"To answer your question, Roban, we will continue with our original plan," Fey said "But we will assistant Spoon as well." Looking up, she nodded at Melik.

He released the leather tube from his back and set it on Roban's legs. With steady hands, he unbuckled the top and bottom of the tube and poured out its contents. A rolled up piece of gritty paper landed on the bed. Melik unrolled it. I saw the detailed drawing of an immense structure, shaped like a compass rose.

"Spoon," Melik said, "these blueprints are of Narbodonna, Gramhammer's most guarded structure, save for its capital, Vald."

Fey added, "Narbodonna is located in the Beyond, the harshest environment in Altrea. It's a black sand desert found in the borders of Gramhammer, a place where a sandstorm can peel the skin off a man, with sections of quicksand that can devour a horse, and no water for miles in any direction."

Melik took over. "Seven of us snuck into Vald for these blueprints. Our plan was to break into the records room, and make it appear that each of our three teams had the blueprints. We all planed to rendezvous in Tarboo. Only four of us made it back alive. Thankfully, we returned with our prize."

"What could be so important to lose your friends over?" I asked.

Fey answered, "Not what, but who."

Chapter 28

MY EARS PERKED UP.

Fey continued, "Baracus' most prized possession, the thing he keeps locked up in his most secure facility, and the reason he sent two Marzzoe to stop us from getting near it, is your father's friend Roon," explained Melik.

"A number of years ago, Quaren approached the Guild with a special request," said Fey. "He told us that his brother was responsible for Baracus' sudden increase in power. Quaren went on to claim that his brother had been forced to give Baracus the secret that Roon and Kalven had discovered.

"Quaren had searched for his brother, but found nothing. He scoured Gramhammer until he talked with a castle servant who'd seen a Lyosian sent to Narbodonna. The situation might not be that uncommon. Nevertheless, I had my spies in Gramhammer check it out.

"We learned from a cook that Baracus gets sick twice a year, like clockwork. We spoke to a carriage driver who had brought the same mysterious passenger into the Beyond twice a year, over the same times as Baracus' sicknesses. And the driver always gets paid handsomely," said Fey. "I would've liked more verification that Baracus was visiting Roon on these trips, but I couldn't let this opportunity slip through my fingers."

"Thus, the blueprints," said Vadin.

"What is so special about Roon if he has already made Baracus so powerful?" I asked.

"The boy isn't as dim as he looks," Roban rattled off.

I gritted my teeth at his insult.

"We asked the same question," said Jana. "Our best answer is the power that Roon and your father discovered isn't complete. It must require regular maintenance from someone who understands how it works."

I scratched my head.

"In other words," said Vadin, "Roon has stayed alive all this time because he keeps Baracus' power operational and functioning."

"Roon is our best chance at putting a stop to Baracus' increase in power," added Jana.

"But Luna never said anything about Baracus being defeated this way," I said.

"This outcome is more than possible," said Roban.

I guess he had a point, but I wasn't about to let him know it.

"At the very least, we'll be able to rescue Roon," said Fey, "and if we can hinder Baracus in the process, or assist a certain half-blood from Earth in defeating the Soul Stealer, then I'm all for it."

The next morning, I woke up to Vadin standing next to my bed with his hands on his hips. "GOOD MORNING, BEAUTIFUL!" he shouted at me. "Your training starts now," he laughed.

I had a foggy memory of Melik telling me that my training would begin in the morning. Maybe it was a Byroc thing, but my definition of *morning* and Melik's definition of *morning* were not the same.

The room's window let in no sunlight. I tried to roll over and pull my covers over my head, but Vadin just tore them off.

"You're not a nice person," I grumbled.

"I think we'll begin with a brisk run through Gaelwallia to get our blood pumping," he said a little too enthusiastically.

I couldn't think of anything more fun to do at dark-thirty in the morning.

We ran for an hour, if you don't count the half hour of breaks I took along the way. I struggled to keep my eyes open at breakfast. I hoped for a nap afterwards, but Vadin yanked me into Fey's backyard before I even finished my last strip of bacon.

Boxed in between the neighboring building's vine covered walls, and the stables opposite the house, the backyard had an outhouse, a teetering gazebo, and an overgrown garden with planter boxes filled with fragrant herbs, vegetables, and flowers. Adjacent to the outhouse was a diamond-shaped area made of flat stones; the perfect place to learn how to fight.

Vadin led me to the grassy area next to the planter boxes. He made me do pushups, sit-ups, and a variety of other exercises. My shirt was soaked with sweat when he gave me some wrestling tips. I devoured everything Vadin threw at me. He was all about constant movement and attacking first. He taught fighting stances next. These came easier to me than I'd expected. Amazingly, I could block a punch by lunch.

Melik was my trainer for the rest of the afternoon. He was the complete opposite of Vadin. He taught patience, and not wasting motions. Wait, watch, and use your opponent's movements against them. He sounded like some Altrean Kung Fu master.

I learned firsthand what Melik meant when he had me try and tackle him at a run. I lowered my shoulder and charged, but before I wrapped my arms around his waist, he stepped out of my way, touched my shoulder, and sent me sprawling into the wall. I worked on that move for the next forty minutes.

My body felt like mush by dinnertime. Roban complained that I ate enough for three grown men. All I wanted to do was watch a movie and sleep till noon. The only thing standing in my way was feeding the horses.

Moka and I made our way out to Fey's stables. The roof sagged in the middle, but there was hay, oats, and water where Vadin had described. Each horse had its own stall. Knight was in the furthest one from the house.

"How have you been?" I asked, scratching his nose.

Knight huffed and licked my hand. Moka found a comfortable spot on the top of the large horse. "I missed you, too."

I gave the glossy horse a once over, marveling at how fast his wounds were healing. "I would've been lunchmeat if it weren't for you," I said, handing him an apple. "And still lost in Anco without you," I said to Moka.

As Knight chomped, I realized that he was no longer the same evil horse I'd ridden out of Tarboo. Moka peered at me from her perch on Knight, and I had the distinct feeling that she understood what I was thinking.

"You know what," I said, looking from Moka to Knight, "my mom would've loved you both."

Knight held my gaze. I rubbed his nose. Bending forward, the horse drank from a bucket that hung from the door. Moka had to act fast before she slid into the water. The moondoggy hopped from the horse's head to the edge of the stall door, and then onto my shoulder. She curled into the hood of the long-sleeved shirt Fey had given me that morning.

My head swam with thoughts about my mom. I remembered her singing to me on my seventh birthday, teaching me how to ride my bike, and roasting marshmallows over a campfire. But each memory always transformed into a nightmare with my mom sitting in our empty house, crying her eyes out over a picture of me.

Feeling a sting of guilt, I made sure the rest of the horses had fresh water, oats, and an apple. Moka and I headed into Fey's. I planned to soak my sore muscles in a warm bath. Bed wouldn't be far behind.

A second before my covers were torn off me, Vadin yelled, "GOOD MORNING, BEAUTIFUL!" He was having too much fun torturing me.

So much for sleeping in. My body felt like a corpse. Every fiber of me hurt. Even a dozen new muscles I didn't know I had hurt.

"A little sore today, huh?" smiled Vadin.

"What makes you say that?" I asked, shuffling across the bedroom's floor like an elderly man. "I always walk like this."

It took me twice as long to get stretched out and warmed up for our predawn run. In Fey's backyard, I wrestled with Vadin as the sun rose over Gaelwallia, and learned how to throw punches before noon.

Melik showed up after lunch with Jana, both carrying a wooden sword. "These will assist you in learning the stances and techniques," he said, handing me a training sword.

"Without poking my eye out," I said, noting the dull tip at the end of the practice weapon.

"Or mine," added Jana.

I spent the afternoon working on three stances. Melik would call them out, I would move my body, and Jana would correct my mistakes. This shouldn't have made me so tired, but my muscles were shredded from yesterday, and the wooden sword felt like it weighed a hundred pounds by dinnertime. I was so far past exhausted that I went to bed without dessert.

"Good morning, beautiful," I heard Vadin whisper in my dream. He did it again, but in my dream I pressed my eyes shut and pretended not to be awake. "GOOD MORNING, BEAUTIFUL!" he sang loudly in my ears.

My eyelids shot open. I wasn't dreaming. I tried to roll out of bed, but my legs felt made of rubber. I guess I wasn't moving fast enough for Vadin. He splashed a cup of water on my face. Grumbling, I whacked Vadin with my pillow, but that made him laugh even harder at me.

I didn't think anything could be worse than my first two days of learning how to fight. But I was very wrong. After our warm-up run, which doubled in length, Vadin coached me through some strength training with heavy chains that were each a half-inch thick. We moved to punching a heavy bag filled with sand, and wrestling out of a headlock.

Melik wouldn't be outdone. He had me holding stances for three minutes with knees bent, wooden sword held above my head, and feet spread shoulder-width apart. I did three and my muscles burned so much I wanted to cry. We did thirty.

I finished the day working with Jana. Her style fit somewhere between Melik and Vadin. She wouldn't root herself to the ground like Melik and use all of her opponent's momentum against them, but she wasn't in constant motion like Vadin either. She was the best at analyzing her opponent's weaknesses, and capitalizing on them.

Today, Jana emphasized the importance of keeping my sword tip up. She would whack me with a training sword every time I let it fall below my eye level. Now I know what a piece of tenderized meat feels like.

I drug myself to the table for dinner. I ate without looking up.

Would old Ethan have survived this training? No way. But something here was different. I haven't minded how worn out I feel. It could be because of the single future Luna saw of me defeating Baracus. It could be that I want to fix the problem my dad left behind. Or it could be that I like training. Whatever the case, I feel as if I'm the only person on the planet that can do anything about the Soul Stealer. No pressure.

I woke up before Vadin on my fourth morning of training. My body didn't want to waste a second of sleep, but it was overwritten as a devious idea formed in my mind. Without making a sound, I slid out of bed, dressed for our morning run, and tiptoed out of the room. Moka, who'd been sleeping at my feet, padded beside me. We headed for Vadin's room. Placing my ear against the wooden door, I listened for about a minute, but no one woke up. I opened the door and snuck in.

Vadin and Melik snored in their separate beds, both breathing with a deep and even rhythm. I crept across the room where Vadin slept. I couldn't believe the guy was still wearing his headband. Come to think of it, I've never seen him without it. I wonder what he'd look like with it off?

I lost my train of thought when Moka jumped onto Vadin's chest. I sucked in a breath, certain he'd wake. He did not.

I reached out and grabbed his blanket with two hands. I ripped off his covers and shouted, "GOOD MORNING, BEAUTIFUL!"

Vadin sputtered and gasped as the chill of the morning bit at his skin. With puffy eyes, he saw me, and for a split second I thought he might pull a dagger from under his pillow and stab me. Instead, he burst out laughing.

"Good morning to you, too," said Vadin after he caught his breath.

"You deserved that," Melik said, rubbing his eyes with the backs of his hands.

"I suppose I did," said Vadin, yawning. "I assume this means you won't need a wakeup call anymore?"

I shook my head, unable to say anything because I was grinning so much.

"Melik, would you like to join us this morning?" Vadin asked.

"Absolutely not," he said, rolling over.

As the days passed, I overheard bits and pieces of random praises from my trainers. Melik mentioned to Jana how fast I'd picked up a move. Vadin told Roban how much stronger my punches had gotten. Jana and Fey talked about how much faster my reflexes had become.

My training routine shifted into more complex techniques. Vadin had me learning how to attack with flips and somersaults. Jana had me fighting against two opponents. Melik had me deflecting wooden sword strikes with the flick of my wrist.

I practiced each one over and over, like a difficult math problem, until one morning everything would click. I loved this about the training. No matter how much I struggled to learn something new, or how many hours I practiced, I would always master it.

Melik attributed my sudden increase in strength, speed, and agility, as well as my ability to learn new skills and heal quickly, to the Essenzian blood in my veins. Thanks, Dad!

Speaking of my Essenzian half, Melik wanted me to begin my trainings with Roban on how to use a verve stone. I was excited to learn how to use my superpowers, but I was just as afraid of Roban.

I got out of my first scheduled lesson with Roban by faking a stomachache. A sore throat got me out of the next lesson. A cough was enough for me to miss my third. Melik caught on to my little scheme. He threatened me with a run around Gaelwallia, and a fifty-pound bag of rocks over my head. I decided to walk over to Roban's door and knock.

Chapter 29

"WHO IS IT?" asked Roban.

I took a deep breath and stepped into the doorway.

"All the way in, boy!" barked his abrasive voice.

With two more steps, I entered the bedroom. Roban was propped up with fluffy pillows. He had a tinge of gray to his skin and his eyes were bloodshot. An uncomfortable silence hung over the room. I pictured Roban getting stabbed by the Marzzoe, with me unable to help him.

"I'm sorry," I blurted out.

"What are you whining about?" he growled.

"It's my fault you got hurt," I answered, my voice cracking.

"Don't be stupid," he said with a scowl.

"But it is."

Roban stared a hole into my forehead. "How can you expect to defeat Baracus if you're so spineless?" he asked. "No wonder the Larrabee only saw one future where you defeat him."

I clenched my hands together so hard that my fingers went cold. "What's that supposed to mean?"

"Exactly what it sounds like," Roban said. "You're more likely to grow wings on your butt than defeat the king of Gramhammer."

"Won't learning how to use a verve stone help?"

Roban shook his head. "Even if you knew everything I know about verve stones right now, Baracus would kill you as if you were a bug."

"So, you want me to just give up?" I asked, my voice rising.

"Yes, that would make my life much easier."

The back of my neck was red hot. "That is not going to happen," I declared.

"But you can't win," declared Roban.

"I have to try," I said, glaring at the angry man.

"Why?"

I rubbed my hands together. "Because no one else can," I declared.

Roban shrugged. "It's your funeral."

I stood next to the bed, unsure if Roban would train me or not. He reached over to a nightstand and drank from a wooden cup. "Most of what I'm about to tell you won't make sense to your juvenile mind. I'll do the best I can with what I've been given to work with," he explained.

I bit my tongue.

"Sit down," ordered Roban.

I sat on the stool in between Roban and Melik's beds. "Every living organism is connected, or linked, and it's this principle which allows a verve stone to function," said Roban. "Through these links, verve stones collect a small amount of life-energy from nearby organisms. When the verve stone is accessed, the stored energy is mixed with the user's life-energy. Any given ability is powered by this combination of energies; the same way that Quaren's verve stone made you stronger.

"A side effect of these mixed energies is called a *brasa*. It's the light that shines out of the eyes of the user while the verve stone is being used. This side effect also signifies which colored verve stone is being used."

I imagined Roban fighting the Marzzoe, his eyes blazing with blue light. Melik already told me Roban had a blue verve stone in the pummel of his sword. "Verve stones don't seem very uncommon if you and Melik have them," I said.

"You're wrong. The red verve stone is the most common. Pure verve is colorless, and the most rare. Different combinations of trace elements are responsible for the various colors of verve stones. Some of these combinations are extremely rare because their trace elements are practically nonexistent."

"Just how many colors are there?"

Roban sighed, shaking his head. It wasn't hard to tell that my extra questions were upsetting him. "At least eighteen that I've seen or heard of, undoubtedly more, but the rarest verve stones have long been hidden away, or lost, for centuries."

"And each color of stone gives two superpowers?" I asked.

Roban nodded. "One for a man. One for an Essenzian."

"What does yours do?" I asked.

"My blue stone allows me to infuse energy into objects," he explained. "It allows an Essenzian the ability to create an energy exoskeleton."

I remembered Melik's story of Baracus killing the old king of Gramhammer with tentacles of green energy that sucked the life out of his victim's chests. "What about Baracus' verve stone?"

Roban crossed his legs under his blanket. "It allows him to absorb life-energy from any organism," he said.

"And whatever your dad and Roon discovered made his ability unstoppable."

The thought of Roban calling someone unstoppable gave me goose bumps. "Have you ever fought him?" I whispered.

"No."

"When do you think I'll be able to use my Essenzian ability?"

"I don't."

It was the end of my sixth week of training, and to celebrate the six of us were preparing to go to the Krusty Dragon for dinner. I'd already fed Knight, and left Moka asleep on my bed. I stepped out of the shower. Drying myself off with a towel, I checked my reflection in the mirror above the basin. I had a hard time recognizing myself. My reddish-brown hair hung past my ears, I had a defined jaw line and rounder shoulders. I flexed my defined biceps like a bodybuilder. Even my scars from the nygar looked impressive.

Behind me someone whistled at me as if I were a pretty girl. Spinning around, I found Vadin standing in the bathroom doorway with green headband rocking back and forth. He was laughing hysterically. It took me another moment to realize that I'd frozen in place, both biceps still flexed.

"Hey there, tough guy," Vadin said. He laughed so hard that he had tears in his eyes. "Do you think you could squeeze those big muscles into a shirt and join us for dinner?"

The Krusty Dragon was packed with hungry customers. We sat at a table next to a group of farmers who smelled like fresh manure. Two women in dirty aprons carried plates of food and overflowing drinks out to tables. A third brought the empty ones into the kitchen.

Vadin made his way over to Jarvis and put in our order. When he returned, the guild members whispered about a report that Fey had received from a Gramhammer spy. "Baracus' army is moving north along the edge of the Enfergate Chasm," she said.

Vadin curled his lip, making him look as if he'd just drank a cup of sour milk. "That place gives me the creeps. I've never been inside it, thank goodness. But I've heard enough stories of people traveling near the chasm at night, and waking up a man or two short."

"I've heard it's full of all kinds of creepy crawlies," added Melik.

"Not a place you ever want to visit," said Vadin.

Jana cleared her throat to speak, but she closed her mouth.

"It appears that Gramhammer wants to take Delgard with overwhelming force," explained Fey. "The Byroc have a long-standing treaty with Aleawn. But even with the combined militaries of both armies, our people think Baracus' soldier-brewed army will be enough to tip the scale for a Gramhammer victory."

The news put a damper on the mood of the group. As we ate our dinner, and a berry pie, Fey asked me if Spoon was my real name, or if it was short for something. I told her, and everyone else at the table, how my real name was Ethan, and that Spoon was short for my last name, Spooner.

"Well, Ethan, you've worked harder than any of us could have imagined over these past six weeks. Not just physically, but mentally and emotionally. It feels as if you're growing into a man right before our eyes." Everyone nodded at the elder's statement, except for Roban who stared down his nose, and tattooed arms crossed over his chest. "And we'd like to give you something to show you our appreciation."

Jana set a wooden box on the table, pushing it towards me with a tear in her eye. "Open it."

Chapter 30

I OPENED THE LID of the box. A silver chain rested inside. It was made of small links, fit so close together that they looked like a rope. It was a necklace. The chain was connected by a thick clasp, and miniature, metal talon hung from its center.

"It's amazing," I said, lifting it out of the box.

"I had a Byroc in Gaelwallia make that while you trained," explained Melik. "It's so you won't have to carry Quaren's verve stone in your pocket anymore."

I reached into my pocket and set the red stone on the table. It glowed dimly. The talon seemed to be the right size, but it would need to open to fasten around the verve stone.

"How does it work?" I asked.

Melik put his elbows on the table. "Press the stone against the talon," he said.

I arched an eyebrow.

"Trust me," he said.

I picked up the red stone and did as I was told. Clinking together, the claws of the talon opened as if they were alive. I gasped, losing my grip on the necklace. The talon closed around the glowing stone as it fell.

"No way," I said, staring at the metal talon that was rigid and hard once more.

"My people are master craftsmen," said Melik. "And some of us have a flare for the dramatic."

I lifted the now complete necklace to my neck, leaned forward, and clasped it behind my head. Quaren's verve stone hung below my collarbones.

"I don't know what to say," I stammered.

"Thank you," grumbled Roban.

"Thanks," I said, nodding to the table of guild members.

Jarvis arrived with our plates. Everyone ate. Roban, Melik, and Fey discussed the latest Gramhammer news. Vadin talked to a somber Jana about horses. Not having anything to add to either topic, I glanced around the inn.

A new group of Lyosians huddled together in the corner. A woman, dressed in fancy clothes, passed me with so much perfume on that my eyes watered.

With a ring of a bell, the inn's door opened. A teenage girl with brown hair and a teenage boy with pointy sideburns entered the inn.

The girl wore a yellow dress, which she fussed with constantly, and walked with graceful strides. The boy wore a collared shirt and lightweight jacket. She weaved her way to the bar. He followed her, rigid as a post. It didn't take long for Jarvis to spot the two newcomers. Surprisingly, the innkeeper shook the boy's hand and reached over the bar to hug the girl.

Pulling my attention off the girl, I tried to focus on the conversations at my table. But every four seconds my eyes had to find her. She was beautiful, with high cheekbones and a cheerful smile. Her brown hair hung to her shoulders and had a bounce all its own.

"Spoon," Vadin said.

I spun around and folded my hands on the table. Vadin had a mischievous look in his eyes. He turned his head towards the brown-haired girl, and back to me. Vadin sucked in a breath to say something, or laugh, but at the last second Fey elbowed him in the ribs.

With my attention on our table, I kept my eyes down so Vadin couldn't make fun of me. I listened as the conversations changed from horses and Gramhammer to me.

"He'll need a real teacher soon," Fey said.

"Isn't Roban good enough?" asked Vadin.

"I won't have the time to babysit this kid when I'm fully healed," snapped Roban.

"Who would you send him to, Roban?" asked Fey. "Your old teacher, Master Yonn?"

Roban shook his head.

"Isn't her school in Sely?" asked Jana.

"Yes," answered Fey.

"But she'd be perfect," said Vadin.

Melik asked, "Fey, do we have anyone near Sely who could get in touch with Master Yonn for us?"

"It doesn't matter," interrupted Roban. "Master Yonn doesn't take anyone over 7 years old."

"She could make an exception for Spoon, right?" asked Vadin.

Roban answered, "She never has before."

I was shocked to find myself rooting for Roban. I didn't like all the talk about shipping me off to learn how to fight. I didn't want to leave Melik and the others. They were the only people I knew on this world.

"But we could ask her," Roban added.

Fey asked, "What do you mean?"

Roban drank from a large mug and wiped his mouth with his sleeve. "Every year Master Yonn takes her two top students to participate in the Archstone

Tournament. She uses Gaelwallia as a stopping point each way. We might be able to meet up with her before she leaves for the tournament."

"How?" Vadin asked.

"We have a spy network at our disposal," said Melik, stroking his beard. "I'm sure we can think of something."

A sinking feeling grew in my gut.

Vadin grabbed the jug of water on the table, filled empty glasses, and downed the rest. Droplets fell from his chin. Keeping an eye on someone moving over my shoulder, he shoved the empty jug into my chest. "Go and have Jarvis fill this up for us," he insisted.

"But," I whined, looking at the overflowing glasses.

"Don't argue with me or it's a hundred push-ups with me standing on your back," ordered Vadin.

I sighed, turning toward the bar.

"Good," Vadin said.

I zigzagged between tables, slouching my shoulders. I reached the bar and waited for Jarvis to appear. I didn't see him anywhere. I tapped my fingers on the wooden counter top. Why I had to be out of my seat was beyond me. Could Jarvis go any slower?

While I waited, I snuck a sideways peek at the brown-haired girl. Her seat was empty. "Where did she go?" I whispered to myself.

"Where did *who* go?"

Standing behind me, with a water jug of her own, was the girl in the yellow dress.

Chapter 31

MY MIND WENT BLANK. "Umm," I stammered. Panicking, I glanced to Vadin, who flashed me a toothy grin. Noticing an empty chair next to Fey, I said, "My friend Jana. I was just wondering where she ran off to."

The brown-haired girl scanned the noisy room. "Is that the woman you were sitting with?" she asked.

I nodded, cheering in my head that she knew where I was sitting.

"Is that her?" asked the girl, pointing to a dark corner of the inn.

I followed her finger and found Jana talking with a thick-browed man and his three friends. "Yes, that's her," I said.

"You twos need som'n?" asked Jarvis from the other side of the bar.

"Water," we said as one.

"Comin' right up," said the innkeeper.

Jarvis grabbed our jugs and walked into the kitchen. I tried to think of something to talk about, but the girl beat me to it. "Are you always this nervous?"

"Not usually," I said, trying to not let my voice crack.

Her cheeks reddened.

"What brings you to the Krusty Dragon?" I asked.

"My older brother and I are visiting our dad. It's his birthday tomorrow," she explained.

"You don't live with your dad?" I asked, worrying that she'd be offended by my question.

"No," she said, not showing signs of being upset. "We live with our grandmother in Sely, and our dad works on my uncle's farm here in Gaelwallia."

I saw Jarvis emerge from the kitchen, a water jug in each hand. Oh sure, now he was on time. "Here you two go," he said, giving me a wink that the girl didn't see.

The brown-haired girl and I reached for the same water jug, our hands banging together.

"You take that one," I said, grabbing the other jug.

"Alright," she said smiling.

"It was nice talking with you," I said, giving her a dorky wave.

"You too," she said, tucking a stray strand of hair behind her ear.

She headed to her table. I walked in the opposite direction, humming a quiet tune. I chose a chair and sat down, making it five at our table. The others were talking, but all I heard was my heartbeat in my ears.

"Did you get her name?" asked Vadin, interrupting my thoughts.

"What?" I asked, distracted. "Her name...oh man!" I slapped my forehead. "How could I've been so stupid?"

"But you talked to her forever," cried Vadin.

"At least I talked with her," I declared.

"Thanks to me," said Vadin, pointing his thumb at his chest.

"Leave the boy alone," said Fey.

I replayed my conversation with the brown-haired girl over and over in my mind – every word, nod, and smile. Even the times I acted like a loser.

Vadin ordered a whole pie to celebrate my foolishness. I bit into my slice as a farmer with a graying goatee joined the girl and her brother. He greeted the boy with a handshake that turned into an awkward hug. He gave the girl a bear hug, lifting her off her feet. I figured that the new guy was their dad.

"Spoon," said Vadin, bringing me back to reality. "We're about to take off. Do you want to join us? Or, do you want to stay and talk with your girlfriend more?"

"She's not my girlfriend," I said, feeling my cheeks burn. I looked at my piece of pie. I'd taken two bites.

Jana spoke up, returning to our table. "I have to finish my pie too," she said, sitting in front of her slice. "I can walk home with Spoon."

I liked that idea a million times better than Vadin making fun of me all the way to Fey's place.

"We won't be far behind," said Jana, as the others left, leaving her and I at the table.

"See you later," Melik said.

Vadin waved goodbye as the guild members exited the Krusty Dragon.

Jana and I were left sitting at the table. The guild woman poked at her pie with a fork. I ate my slice, while checking over my shoulder to see the brown-haired girl. Jana and I left when our plates were clean.

On the way out, I waved goodbye to the girl. She waved back! I wiped the silly grin off my face as Jana and I walked over cobblestones, neither one of us saying a word.

If I hadn't been so focused on myself, I might have noticed something strange about Jana. She seemed to be thinking hard. Her brow was furrowed, and her eyes darted around. Feeling guilty for ignoring her, I decided to make some small talk.

"Thanks for saving me from Vadin," I said.

She nodded, not looking at me. Could she be missing her family?

"Is everything alright?" I asked.

No answer.

Looking up, I realized that I didn't recognize the street we'd turned down. "Where are we?" I asked.

A wind crept up. Clouds rolled in, blocking out the first stars of the night. My throat went dry. Pricks of sweat popped up on the back of my neck. Why was I so afraid? I had no reason to be.

Jana covered her mouth with her hands. "I'm so sorry, Ethan," she cried.

"For what?" I asked, my voice shaking.

With puffy eyes, Jana finally looked at me. She choked out, "Because I couldn't go another moment without my children."

"We can search for them right now," I said. "I can train later."

The guild woman sucked in great gulps of air as she wept. "It's too late for that," she wheezed.

"Why?" I asked, putting a hand on her quivering shoulder.

"Because they're coming," she stammered.

"Who?"

Jana fell to her knees and pointed. "Them."

Four men emerged from the gloom of the street. Each carried a weapon. One had a short sword, two more had matching curved blades, and the fourth wore bronze-colored armor, a helmet, a shield, and a mace. He also had a thick brow. These were the guys Jana talked with at the Krusty Dragon!

"What do they want?" I asked, taking a step backwards.

"You!" she wailed.

"Why me?"

Jana pressed her hand over her face. "He said I could have my family back if I spied for him. But not anymore," she said. "Now he wants you."

"Who is *he*?"

"The Soul Stealer," she whispered.

The thugs ignored Jana altogether, passing her on either side, and stopping a few feet in front of me. I tried to retreat, but the street Jana led me down came to a dead end.

A man in black appeared from the darkness, holding a baton with a serrated blade in his right hand. The long lost Marzzoe had returned. He walked behind Jana, who never heard him coming.

"Jana, watch out!" I shouted.

It was too late. The Marzzoe stuck its serrated blade into Jana's back. She crumpled to the ground. I ran, spitting and screaming. He'd murdered her! The four thugs blocked my way. One of them grabbed me by the shoulder and shoved me backwards; I fell and smacked my head against the wall.

A man with a face that resembled a weasel approached me, whispering to the empty space to his right. "I want to see him bleed, too," he said to his invisible friend. Then his eyes focused on me. One creepy hyena laugh burst out before he said, "My name is General Zambraza. I'm here to escort you to my king."

Chapter 32

THE DARKNESS GREW, thunder rolled, and the air smelled like rain. The shadows of the buildings swallowed up most of the light in the alley. No better place for four guys to kidnap a kid.

Standing over Jana's unmoving body, the Marzzoe stared at me. I wiped my nose with my sleeve, but I didn't see any blood. Was that a good thing or a bad thing?

"Why Baracus is concerned with this runt is beyond me," Zambraza grumbled. "You two," he ordered, pointing to the men with the curved blades. I could see the beginning of weaving black tattoos peak out from beneath his sleeve. They appeared similar to Roban's, but unique as well. "Let's see what the boy can do."

The two men faced me, and from the sick smiles on their faces, I had the feeling they liked to play with their food. They wore identical patched brown shirts, had darker skin, and smelled liked Fey's stables.

"I get the first crack at him, brother," said the older guy.

The other man sighed, but didn't object.

My heart felt like it might beat its way out of my chest. I wiped my nose a second time. Nothing. Taking a deep breath, I tried to think. At least I didn't have to take on four guys at once.

The older brother pointed his sword at me. His three friends moved back, giving him room to work. A lesson from Melik about waiting for an opportunity to attack came to mind. I hope he's right.

"Draw your weapon," he said.

I didn't need to be told twice. Grabbing my sword with two hands, and setting my feet shoulder-width apart, I pointed it at my opponent. A bolt of lightning sizzled down from the sky, lighting up the alleyway. A rumble of thunder wasn't far behind. Raindrops began to fall.

"What are you smiling about?" asked the older brother.

I hadn't realized I was smiling. "I like the rain," I blurted. "It reminds me of home."

"I don't care if it reminds you of your teddy bear," he teased.

The older brother charged me, swinging his curved sword at my head. It was easy to block. He came at me two more times, probably testing me. I remembered Jana telling me to not let anyone test me. Like a reflex, I did what I was taught. Rushing the man, I feinted to my left, slid away from his backswing, and sidestepped an overhead chop.

"You're a good dancer, runt," he said, bringing his eyebrows together as if rethinking his current strategy.

I tilted my head and smiled at the compliment.

I sent three jabs to his side, doing some testing of my own. I know I'm new to fighting, but this guy felt sloppy. I used a move from Vadin's bag of tricks. I charged him like a maniac, hacking at him from every angle. The thug didn't know which way to block. He backpedaled into a wall. Vadin would've been proud.

He countered with several slashes at my torso. I avoided each without the need of my sword.

The thug wiped the rain from his face, cursing me. He stepped towards me, sword tip pointed at my chest. I brought my blade against his, and flicked my wrist. The move sent the curved sword spinning out of his hands. It clanged to the cobblestone. The thug was left without a weapon. He wasn't a happy camper.

"Brother?" asked the other man with the curved blade.

"I'm fine," he spat, gritting his teeth.

The younger brother joined the fight anyway. To evade his frenzied slices, I dropped to the ground and rolled to my right. He left a glaring hole in his defense, allowing me to strike with my sword. Crying out with pain, the younger brother didn't advance on me.

"You alive?" asked the older brother, his sword returned to his hand.

"Yes," whined the guy, holding his bleeding thigh.

I hadn't noticed before, but the brothers had intricate black tattoos covering their forearms. Just like Roban. I wanted to ask the guys about their tattoos, but I got distracted when they attacked me.

The oldest brother stabbed at my sword shoulder. His brother swung for my legs. I elbowed the older guy in the chest, spun around on my heel, and kicked the younger in the bicep. They both staggered into each other.

"Get out of my way," said the older brother as they untangled themselves.

They attacked as one, blades slashing. Taking a step to the right, I planted my feet and twisted the younger brother's sword out of his hand. I slid to my left, and brought my sword down on the handle of the second curved blade, forcing it out of the older brother's hand. The brothers were left standing in the center of the alley, staring at the tip of my sword. I let out a surprised burst of laughter at the sight.

"Pathetic," said Zambraza with venom. Baracus' general turned to his right, where nobody was standing, and whispered, "I didn't think the boy would be able to fight either. But I'd get in trouble if *I* hurt him," He nodded in agreement with some invisible friend. "I agree," he said, turning his attention to the large man in the bronze armor. "Gramble, you're up."

The two brothers managed to pick up their weapons and limped to the side of the weasel-faced man. "You're going to get it now!" shouted the younger of the brothers.

Gramble, the guy who looked like a pro wrestler wrapped in a bronze wartime tank, stepped forward. He had bulging muscles, a thick brow, and sausage-like fingers.

His bronze helmet was shaped like a bear's head, complete with snarling teeth. "Warm-up's over, kid," he said, unbuckling a circular bronze shield from his back and strapping it onto his forearm. What had me most freaked out was the spiked mace and chain he held in his gauntleted hand.

I should've been scared out of my mind, but what was more surprising was my nose still wasn't bleeding.

Jana constantly preached about finding your opponent's weakness. I wondered if Gramble's movements suffered from his armor. I would be faster than him, but causing him damage would be the obvious challenge.

Gramble didn't wait for me to come up with a plan. He swung the handle of his mace around his helmeted head. Its long chain whistled through the rain. He slammed the spiked mace down at my feet. I rolled away as the cobblestones below exploded like a shards of ice, spraying rainwater and rock in every direction.

This guy wasn't messing around. He repeated his attack, making contact with the stone wall behind me. I thought the building might crumble from the impact.

I dodged his wrecking ball a third time with a quick spin. With an overhead chop, I brought my blade down on his right shoulder. Guess what? I hit bronze. Fingers vibrating, I struggled to keep a grip on my sword. I tried to get another slash at the giant's upper arm. The blade clanged off the giant's armor again.

Gramble used his shield to shove me back. I was in his mace's range now. I got low and darted for the man's legs. Planting my right hand, I kicked the back of Gramble's knee. He stumbled, but did not fall.

He attempted to slam the edge of his shield into my skull. I deflected the blow with my sword, rolled, and got jabbed in the sternum with the handle of Gramble's mace. I skidded across the cobbles, gasping for breath. My lungs felt like they had been crushed. Wheezing, I heard the two brothers laughing. I rubbed my chest, wincing. That was going to leave a mark.

"Is that all you have?" I coughed.

The giant bent his head back, chuckling to himself. "I like your spirit."

"Gramble, we don't have all night," teased the oldest brother from the sidelines.

The big man nodded, never taking his eyes off me. "Shall we?" he asked.

"After you," I retorted, like I had a death wish.

"As you wish," he said, with a widening smile. He clearly enjoyed this more than me.

My entire body tensed up for his next attack, but it didn't come. The giant glared at me from behind his bear facemask, darkness hiding his eyes. Roban's advice about watching for your opponent's brasa came to mind. As if on cue, two burnt-orange lights cut through the night like a pair of high beams. The lights came from the eyeholes in Gramble's facemask. He had a verve stone, and I had no idea what superpower it gave him. The muscles in his legs and arms grew an inch in diameter. The pale white skin around his neck transformed to brown fur. Did his brasa make him hairier?

I had no choice, I had to use Quaren's verve stone. Though, I haven't been able to tap into it since I killed the nygar. It wasn't for a lack of trying. Roban has had me doing breathing exercises every morning, focusing techniques on the roof before lunch, and concentration workouts late into the night. The only thing these exercises gave me were headaches.

Gramble lifted his mace, started whirling it above his head, and then sent it at me with a flick of his wrist. I dodged his spiked ball, and his gauntlet. But not his bronze-toed boot. The contact flipped me backwards. I smacked my head against the hard ground.

The giant wasn't done. He swung three more times. Squinting through the rain, I jumped over, or ducked under, his next series of mace attacks. I never saw his bronze knee coming though. It rammed into my side, knocking the breath clean out of me. I heard a crack as I was sent off my feet. I slid to a stop. My ribs felt on fire, as if someone was sticking me with a hot poker. Something had to be broken.

"Get up, runt!" shouted one of the brothers from the sidelines.

The pain was so intense I didn't think I could get up. But a spiked mace sailing at my face proved to be very motivating.

I rolled to my right. I rolled to my left. The spiked ball-of-death left two craters in the cobblestones. Gramble's attacks were much faster now that he had his brasa on, and harder to see. I wobbled to my feet. I couldn't keep this up forever.

Changing tactics, I charged Gramble. I got inside of his mace, faking an uppercut. The giant brought up his shield. I somersaulted to the left. My sword twanged off a bronze chest plate. The juggernaut would not fall.

Running away crossed my mind. But I couldn't leave Jana's body. I could try and talk my way out of the situation? That would involve talking to Zambraza, and he didn't seem like the talking type, unless you were his invisible friend. I guess I have to try Roban's worthless techniques.

I breathed in and out, grimacing in pain because of my broken rib. I set my feet, stood up straighter, and focused on my racing heartbeat. I open my mind to what I needed to do to defeat my opponent.

"Finish him," cheered the younger brother.

His words sent a spark in the farthest reaches of my heart to flare up. Jana and her family, Melik's wife, Vadin's brother, and my dad all came to mind. Each one murdered in the name of Gramhammer. I focused my thoughts on these tragedies. I saw Jana's unmoving body on the rain-soaked ground. My pulse slowed as my breathing became steady. A warm tingling sensation rippled through my body.

"The rumors are true," said Gramble, sounding interested in me for the first time. "You do have a brasa."

Chapter 33

EVERY RAINDROP, PEBBLE, AND COBBLESTONE was painted red in the dim glow of the city. My muscles inflated, and the pain of my broken rib lost its edge. Maybe Roban knew what he was talking about after all.

"It's about time," said Gramble, looking like he was going to enjoy the fight.

The giant charged me like a bull, swinging his mace above his head. I made my move, heading for the belly of the juggernaut. Gramble's burnt-orange eyes shined as he hurled the spiked ball at my head.

I held up my sword with two hands, blocking the path of the metal ball. Without my brasa, the mace would've smashed me to pieces. But with my added strength, the collision caused my teeth to vibrate, my shoulders to ache, and the mace to rebound to the cobblestones.

Gramble's jaw hung open as he stared at the kid he outweighed four to one. He swung his mace again. This time he hurled it at me on the second go-round instead of the third to try and catch me by surprise. I adjusted, bent my torso to the left, watched the mace miss my nose by inches, and countered with a slash to the chest plate of the giant. Gramble stumbled a few steps, but he would not fall.

"Strong work," he said, feeling the new dent on his breastplate.

With my increased strength, my sword felt like a plastic bat in my grip. I could swing it with so much force.

Gramble lashed out at me with a kick and an elbow. I rolled and flipped out of the way. We exchanged blows as clangs of metal filled the alleyway. I was sure my sword would be bent out of shape, but I didn't have time to check.

We separated, catching our breaths. I decided to take a page out of Vadin's playbook. I sprinted for the wall to the right of Gramble. I jumped at the last second, planted both my feet against the stone, and kicked off its surface. I propelled myself through the air at the juggernaut.

Gramble was ready. He sidestepped my flying attack and tried to cut me in half with the sharp side of his shield. I was able to rotate in the air and turn aside the shield with my sword, but the collision bounced me into the ground like a basketball. I rolled to a painful stop.

The giant didn't give me time to rest. His mace rained down from above. I barely crab-crawled out of the way in time. A crater was created in the cobblestones beside me. Gramble pulled his mace free as I scampered back to my feet.

I sent a combination of swings at the giant. Sparks flew as I hit his shield and armor in various places. Gramble got some good shots in as well. I avoided or blocked most of them. But I couldn't find an opening. I jumped backwards, gasping for breaths. The rain continued to pour down.

"You're better than you look," said Gramble.

"Thanks, I guess," I said. "You're trying to beat up an eighth grader."

"An eighth what?" he asked.

"Never mind."

I figured the longer the fight continued, the harder it would be for me, but that wasn't the case. The more I used my brasa, the easier it was to use.

Gramble's armor warped with every hit I landed. Whirling his mace over his head, the giant rushed me. Dancing away, I cut him between two plates of armor on his arm. He roared. His eyes blazed burnt orange. He swung the sharp edge of his shield at my neck. I brought my sword up. Blade smashed into bronze, ripping the shield from Gramble's arm. The collision finally knocked the giant to the ground. The bronze shield skidded to a stop about ten feet away. His helmet clanged down beside him.

I was about to ask him if he needed those, but the sight of Gramble's face sucked the words right out of my mouth. His eyes were deep-set, his ears had moved to the top of his head, and he had a black snout. His verve stone had transformed him partway between a grizzly bear and a man.

Gramble's mace dangled at his side as he stood. I set my feet and held my sword with two hands. I attacked with a combination of slices. He avoided them with quick steps backwards. I had to get closer to overcome his added speed.

Gramble countered with a spin that hurled his mace at my chin. I evaded the blow, stepped inside the haymaker that followed, planted my feet, bent my knees, and launched myself into the air. He shoved me away with the handle of the mace, but not before I punched the bear-man in his furry chin. It was the only vital part of him not covered in bronze. And for the second time, he went down.

Sitting up, Gramble rubbed his jaw. He stood in the downpour. His transformation had increased the size of his muscles, stretched out his arms, and shorted his legs. "My turn," he roared through yellow fangs

Gramble whirled his mace at me rapid-fire. He missed my side, my shoulder, but grazed my hip. I recovered. He followed that with a mace to my foot. I leapt away just in time, but got caught in the hamstring. I went down to one knee.

In the split second it took me to stand, he got his mace circling above his head like a helicopter. I prepared for Gramble's previous type of attack, but he had something new in mind.

Instead of whirling his mace at the side of my head, he released his grip. The entire handle, chain, and metal ball spun through the air, straight for me. I blocked the spikes with my sword at the last possible moment. The chain wrapped around the blade and crashed against my forearms.

Gramble used his attack as a distraction. He'd charged me as soon as his mace left his hand. He caught me by surprise in his furry arms. I would have thought his *bear hug* funny if he hadn't slammed me into the cobblestones, back first.

Sparks of light went off over my eyes. The air in my lungs was gone. My red vision turned off. My muscles didn't work. My broken rib roared back to life.

"It's about time," complained one of the brothers with the curved sword.

The other three thugs splashed across the wet alley. "Tie up the kid," ordered Zambraza.

The brothers kicked me before holding my wrists. Someone got me in the eye. Zambraza just watched. I cried out. The metallic taste of blood filled my mouth. I couldn't focus. The pain made me want to vomit. I prayed I'd pass out before they hit me again.

"That's enough!" growled Gramble.

"Relax," jeered the oldest brother. "We're on the same side big guy."

Zambraza nodded to his invisible friend. "We can hit him later."

A snarl echoed off the walls of the alley.

Everyone froze. A feeling of cold crept into my chest. Searching the tops of the surrounding buildings, I thought I saw something, but it was impossible to tell in the darkness.

"What was that?" asked the youngest brother.

"Just a dog," assured his older brother.

A yellow bolt of lightning ripped to earth from the storm, lighting up the sky. The silhouette of a monster appeared on the building behind the Marzzoe. Thunder exploded a split-second later, shaking my chest. The steady rain turned into a monsoon. A roar rang out from above.

"That looks like something to me," whined the youngest brother.

Another flash of lightning exposed the creature jumping off the building. I felt the alley shake in the following darkness. The beast landed right in front of me. It faced the four thugs and the Marzzoe. It was Bigfoot.

The monster didn't wait around for an invitation. It picked up the younger brother by the back of the neck and tossed him against a bin of rotting garbage. The older brother was dunked inside the bin. Bigfoot kicked Zambraza against a wall. It snarled at the Marzzoe, but to the assassin's credit, he didn't flinch. The only thug willing to meet Bigfoot's challenge was Gramble.

In bear form, Gramble could be mistaken as a distant relative of Bigfoot. But at six and a half feet tall, he paled in comparison to the nine-foot monster. With burnt-orange eyes glowing, Gramble replaced his helmet and picked up his mace.

Swinging his spiked ball around his head, Gramble attacked from a distance. Bigfoot dodged with an unnatural quickness. The thug made craters in the alley and on the walls. Now I know what the surface of the moon must look like.

Bigfoot closed the gap. Gramble shortened his chain. The thug sent an arching bomb toward Bigfoot's head. Then another. The monster dodged each attack. Bigfoot roared, rolled, and jumped into the air. Then he landed a furry elbow right on top of the bear-man's helmet.

Gramble's legs wobbled. He shook his head. Bigfoot rushed the bear-man with its claws raised. The thug created a whizzing shield as he spun his mace in front of him. The monster skidded to a stop, right in front of Gramble. Backpedaling, it snorted.

Gramble swung his mace to the right and left. He charged the monster. Bigfoot didn't attempt to move this time. The thug jerked on the handle of his mace so hard the glow from his eyes flared. At the last second, Bigfoot sidestepped and grabbed the whistling chain out of the air.

The mace and chain were wrenched out of Gramble's grip. Weaponless, the thug sent a combination of powerful kicks and punches at the creature. Bigfoot blocked these with its forearms and shins. Gramble rotated to the opposite side of the alley.

He was the smaller, weaker, and a slower fighter, but he didn't seem to care. With enough space between himself and Bigfoot, he charged the monster with his head down. The monster was up for the challenge. The bear-man and beast met head to head in the center of the alley with a sickening thud. Imagine two trains colliding at full speed. It wasn't a pretty sight. At least, it wasn't for Gramble. His body rebounded off Bigfoot and flopped to the ground. He didn't get up.

Bigfoot capped off its victory by lifting the juggernaut over its head and tossing him at the feet of the Marzzoe. The monster pounded its chest and roared so loud that the rain stopped. The assassin glared at the creature with glowing yellow eyes. He bowed to the monster, as if he were showing him respect. The Marzzoe turned away, vanishing into the sleeping city.

The general placed a hand on the sword at his hip as he stood there giggling like a hyena. The guy oozed creepy. Bigfoot growled, causing the hairs on my neck to stand on end. Zambraza lifted his hand.

"He shouldn't have left," the general said under his breath.

Squinting through my one good eye, I got to my feet. My knees trembled, and my rib was on fire, but I kept my balance enough to retrieve my sword. I raised it to the general. I even managed to activate my brasa.

Zambraza stared at me with his empty eyes. "See you soon," said the general, shoving his hands into his pockets. He turned and walked out of the alley. The last thing he whispered as he hung a right was, "I want to stab him, too."

Too exhausted to hold myself up, I slumped to the ground. Grabbing my rib, I prayed for relief. None came. I couldn't even raise my head without pain blasting up my side. How can such a small bone cause me so much pain?

My body was trashed, bruised, and broken. My head was fuzzy. Roban had said that I would feel drained after using a verve stone. He couldn't have been more right.

The scent of tree sap and soil filled my nose as Bigfoot leaned over me. I should've been terrified, but the creature's amber eyes told me it wasn't going to hurt me.

"Thank you," I cringed.

Bigfoot snorted.

"You saved my life, again."

The creature reached out its arm towards me. The muscles in its forearm rotated beneath its thick fur as it placed its palm on my chest. Shocked by its light touch, I smiled with bruised lips.

The brown coat of Bigfoot appeared to shrink. Its fangs did, too. Its ears morphed to the top of its head, and its snout grew smaller by the second. Now everything from its head, shoulders, and legs were deflating. It wasn't long before Bigfoot was six feet; four feet; two feet tall. The last part of its body to change was its tail, which stretched out and grew smoother.

Despite the intense pain it caused me, I forced myself to watch the entire transformation. When it was all over, I breathed, "It's you!"

Chapter 34

WET AND SHIVERING, Moka jumped onto my chest. The moondoggy watched me with dark eyes. "You are good luck," I exhaled.

Moka barked, as if to agree.

I wanted to sleep, right there in the wet alley, but my ribs wouldn't let me. Sitting up, I gasped from the pain. Standing was worse. Walking to Fey's place seemed like an unbearable journey. Carrying Jana's body might be impossible, but leaving her was not an option.

With Moka tucked into the hood of my shirt, and Jana in my arms, I trudged out of the alley. This trip wouldn't have happened without Quaren's verve stone. It gave me the strength I needed to carry my load, and take the edge off the mind-numbing pain.

My heart hurt as much as my rib. I thought about Jana's kids not having a mother. It was so unfair. Baracus used her family to get to me, and she was repaid with a sword in the back. Jerk.

When I finally reached Fey's place, I knocked on the grey door. Thank goodness I was ambushed relatively close to Fey's, I thought. Fey opened the tiny hatch, her eyes growing wide. "Spoon! What happened?!"

I held up Jana so Fey saw her face. "They killed her."

The door burst open. I guess I didn't need a tattoo. She rushed out. Fey ushered me inside. Limping into the circular room, I placed Jana in one of the empty beds. She appeared to be at peace with her eyes closed and head on a pillow. I could've sworn she was sleeping. Fey placed a sheet over Jana.

"Everyone else is out looking for you two," said Fey.

I nodded.

Fey lead me to the washroom, the same one Vadin had caught me flexing my muscles. It felt like that happened years ago. Not hours. I saw a face more purple than flesh colored. My left eye was swollen shut. Fey fussed over my numerous cuts and bruises. She scrubbed the dried blood off my hands.

I sat on a stool, without the energy to stop the tears from falling for Jana. Fey cut off my shirt, and helped me into a pair of shorts. She also whipped up a foul-smelling cup of brown liquid for the pain in my rib. She said it would help with the pain, and help me sleep. It tasted like vomit, but I drank it.

I cleaned up the moondoggy next. Her eyes were bloodshot, and she rubbed them with the backs of her paws. I guess transforming from a nine-foot monster to a tiny dog was harder than it looked.

I picked Moka up, walked to my room, and set her at the foot of the bed. I slipped under the covers. I didn't want to fall asleep with Jana's body in the other room. But after my fight with Gramble, the beating I took from the thugs, and drinking Fey's medicine, I didn't have a choice.

I slept until the stuff Fey gave me wore off. The searing pain in my side made it so even the weight of my bedding hurt. With Moka purring at my feet, I inched my way out of bed. I had to have more of Fey's medicine.

I limped to the kitchen. Fey was cutting vegetables at the counter. She walked right up to me with another cup of her fowl-smelling brown liquid. I drank it and thanked her.

"Would you like some tea as well?" she asked.

"Okay," I answered, but it turned out to be the same tea Jana made that tasted like dirt. I couldn't bring myself to drink the stuff.

Fey said Melik and the others searched for Jana and me all night. They returned early this morning and that Roban wanted to yank me out of bed the moment he learned I was home. Fey refused.

Guild members began to trickle into the kitchen for breakfast. Fey tried to get me to eat. I chewed on a piece of bread, and drank some water. I didn't have the stomach for anything else.

Roban grumbled to himself as he pushed scrambled eggs across his plate. He wanted to know what happened last night. Everyone did. Except me. Reliving last night was the last thing I ever wanted to do, but I couldn't risk Roban waiting another minute.

I took a deep breath and began my story from the moment Jana and I left the Krusty Dragon. I told them how Jana had been a spy for Baracus, how she was murdered, the fight with Gramble, and how Moka was the nine-foot tall Bigfoot from Anco.

Roban punched a cutting board the moment I finished. "Why didn't she trust us?" he demanded, glaring at me as if it was my fault. "We could've helped her."

Melik removed his tinted glasses and rubbed the top of his nose with his index finger and thumb. "What

I want to know is how long she's been giving Gramhammer information."

"They could have blackmailed her since Tarboo," said Vadin.

Fey nodded.

"Now that we know Jana's been working for Gramhammer, does this mean our mission to free Roon is in danger?" asked Vadin.

"Of course," said Fey. "However, Baracus knew we wanted to free Roon the instant we stole his blueprints. We can't be certain of how much Jana told Gramhammer. We'll have to adjust the details of the mission. But we will still free Roon."

Melik nodded.

The four guild members stood around the kitchen, staring at nothing.

"Who is Zambraza?" I asked.

"He's one of the Twelve Generals of Gramhammer," answered Melik.

"He talked to some kind of invisible friend," I said.

Fey said, "Our spies describe him as a blood-thirsty psychopath."

"What will happen to Jana's family?" I asked.

"If they're not already dead, they will be," scolded Roban.

My heart raced at his rude comment.

"She should have known *not* to trust him," griped Roban.

"Don't blame her!" I yelled, happy to have someone to take out my aggression on. "That monster had her family! What else could she have done?"

"Told us," countered Roban, up for the challenge. "She should've trusted us! Not the devil himself! Wouldn't you want to know if someone traded another's life for your own?"

"Roban!" warned Fey. "That's enough."

Roban kicked over a chair and stomped out of the room.

"He's upset, just like the rest of us," said Fey.

"Where will Jana be buried?" I asked.

"The Guild has a plot on the hillside west of town," answered Fey.

"Do you have a shovel?" I asked.

The weather was gray and cloudy, much like my mood. Melik, Vadin, Fey, and I brought Jana's body out of the city by horse and cart. Roban, of course, refused to join us. He was grumpy at me for insisting to bury her. I had no real answer to give, but it felt like the right thing to do.

This marked the first time I'd ridden Knight since we made our way out of Anco. I wish it were for a better reason. Fey made me enough of her foul drink to take on the trip, minus the part that makes me sleepy, but I still winced with each step Knight took. Moka rode along in my hood. I don't think she wanted to leave my side anymore.

We arrived on a grassy hillside overlooking Gaelwallia and Lake Tilvera. I set to digging the grave straight away. I couldn't help thinking about how today was a normal day for everyone else. No one in the city knew that Jana had died. They didn't have to bury a friend today. It was a regular day for everyone but us, and that didn't seem fair to Jana's memory. More people should be sad she was gone.

With every pile of dirt I moved, my broken rib caused me to almost lose my breath. My hands blistered. I almost stabbed the top of my foot with the shovel because I was so tired. But each scoop felt therapeutic, bringing back memories of Jana. Vadin joined me with a shovel of his own when I reached the three-foot mark. He didn't say a word. He didn't have to. We dug until the job was done.

We placed Jana's body in the grave. Fey said a few kind words. These were followed by a moment of silence. I hadn't realized the connection I'd made with Jana, but looking at her still face, I felt as if I'd lost an aunt.

As the sun broke through the overcast sky, Vadin insisted on covering the rest of the grave on account of my injury. But he never gave me a hard time about it. I said one last goodbye before we left.

As we rode away, Melik and Fey discussed the effect Jana's betrayal would have on the Guild. Vadin told me that I wouldn't be able to train with my rib. I didn't like the idea of sitting around brooding over Jana's death, but there wasn't much I could do about it either.

We made it into Gaelwallia without a hitch, through the maze of streets, and found ourselves back in time for a late lunch. Fey got off her chestnut horse and knocked on her own front door.

Without a word, the tiny window in the door opened up, Fey stuck out her arm, and silver candlelight flickered onto her skin. The shimmering outline of two crescents fitted together around a circle appeared on her forearm. The gray door opened an instant later. I expected to see Roban on the other side. Instead, a man with a large hood hanging over his blank face greeted her.

"It's been a long time," said Fey.

Chapter 35

THE MAN NODDED as the swirls on his face shifted from yellows to oranges. He seemed to square his shoulder at me. "You made it," echoed his voice in my head.

I put my hand on my chest. "I didn't have much of a choice."

"I guess you're right," said Quaren.

Fey said, "Let's get the horses put away and cleaned up before we sit down with Quaren."

"Agreed," Melik said.

It didn't take long to complete the chores. Everyone gathered around the table in the circular room where the stained glass window let in the afternoon sun.

"Roban told me about Jana," said Quaren. "He also filled me in on what's happened since Ethan's arrival."

The memory of the day I appeared in that ancient castle felt like a lifetime ago.

Quaren continued, "Roban wanted to know why I sent Ethan to Altrea. I asked him if my answer could wait until everyone was present."

"I bet he liked that," said Vadin with a wolfish smile.

Roban glared at Vadin, but he didn't deny the statement.

Hues of pink mixed together across the place Quaren's face should have been. "As you in the Guild know, I came to you looking for assistance rescuing my brother, Roon. Together we determined him to be hidden in Narbodonna. As your people investigated for a way to get him out, I searched for Kalven.

"I began in Yont, the place where Kalven and Roon had become friends. I determined that Kalven had been researching how to travel through the same ley lines that the three explorers from the Annals were said to have used. I found his notes on how to travel using a verve stone. Though he never admitted this in any of his writing, it was apparent that Kalven wanted to use the ley lines to get off Altrea altogether.

"With the help of Kalven's notes, I used the ley line at the bottom of the Annals. I came out in a vast field of grass, surrounded by stone blocks taller than four men. They were rectangular in shape, and some were laid on their side atop two others."

"That sounds like Stonehenge," I guessed. "I'd know that place anywhere because it's where my dad told me he was from, before I discovered his Altrean roots."

"Don't interrupt," snapped Roban.

My cheeks burned.

"Please continue," said Fey.

Quaren nodded. "I had configured my verve stone to detect its connections to other verve stones before I left Altrea. This would not have worked as well on Altrea — too many stones — but on your world," he said, turning to me, "your father had the only one. I tried to locate Kalven, but I found no sign of his verve stone anywhere. Either my stone wasn't working, or

Kalven wasn't there. So I returned to Altrea.

"I spent three days testing my verve stone, which was never broken. Pouring over Kalven's notes, I revisited a theory that claimed each Altrean ley line connects to its own Earth ley line. If it were true, Kalven could have taken another ley line and emerged somewhere too far for my verve stone to detect. It was my last hope for finding Kalven.

"According to Kalven's notes, the closest ley line he knew about was in Tarboo. I took a ship from Yont to Gaelwallia, met with Fey, and headed for Tarboo with Melik and Roban. We traveled south, entered Anco, and were soon attacked by a swarm of white monkeys. I got separated from my escort. But a moondoggy found me and led me through a maze of game trails until I came upon a lake."

Moka rustled in the hood of my shirt at the mention of her name, but didn't emerge from her comfy cocoon.

"A Larrabee flies out of a tree and tells me about the millions of possible future outcomes that she sees, and that one of them has Baracus being defeated by Kalven's son, who was on Earth. Her futures gave me pause," he declared.

"Tell me about it," I said.

"I made a decision," continued Quaren. "The moondoggy led me to Melik and Roban, and the three of us made our way to Tarboo. I found the ley line, prepared an extra verve stone for Kalven's son, and arranged to meet the guild members on the same day for the next three years, should it take time to locate Kalven."

"Which worked perfectly," added Melik. "I went out to Tarboo on the first and second dates. For the third date, Fey decided to make the ancient ruins our rendezvous point for the mission to liberate the blueprints from Vald."

"Which was successful," added Vadin, saluting the faceless man.

Quaren put his boney hand over his chest. "To Narbodonna?" he asked.

"That's right," said Vadin.

"My brother and I will never be able to thank you enough," he said as reds mixed in with the colorful hues of his face.

"Your brother is far from saved," grumbled Roban.

"Still, I'm most grateful," said Quaren.

Vadin smacked me on the shoulder. "I guess we know who thought you were special now."

I nodded.

"Where did the Tarboo ley line spit you out?" asked Fey.

"I arrived in a stone room, standing behind a red jaguar with jade spots. I exited the room, emerging from underneath a staircase at least eighty feet tall. It turns out the ley line was underneath a pyramid with four sides and a flat top. At the structure's base was a field of grass, a road, and a village. But surrounding all of that was dense jungle. Once outside, my verve stone was able to sense a faint verve stone due north. It took me more than two and a half years, and thousands of miles, to reach Kalven's stone. The rest you already know."

Everyone around the table nodded.

"Ethan said that you made him stand in a circle of white powder with your verve stone," said Melik. "What I don't understand is, how were you able to connect to the ley line from another location?"

"Kalven discovered that each ley line had its own kind of signature, and the trip to Earth had already preset my verve stone to that signature. All it needed was the means to penetrate the ley line and follow it to Altrea," said Quaren.

"Your father was impressive," said Melik, arching an eyebrow at me.

I smiled.

"How come you didn't arrive in Altrea after Spoon?" asked Roban.

"Ethan's mom barged into his room the instant before he disappeared. She chased me out of her house. I had enough materials to make another circle, but the local law enforcement kept me on the run for some time. I returned to Gaelwallia as soon as it was possible."

I leaned forward, set my elbows on the table, and rubbed my face. My brain was spinning with everything Quaren had told us. It was as if I could feel the weight of Luna's future on my shoulders.

"What's the matter, Ethan?" asked Melik.

"It's been a long day," I said, sitting up and crossing my arms across my chest. "And it's a lot to take in."

"It has been for us all," said Fey.

Roban grumbled, but said nothing.

"Let's take a break," Melik said. "We can come together tonight if there is anything else to discuss."

With my eyes on the stained glass warrior, I heard the guild members get up and march out of the room. I stayed put, my brain and body too drained to move. Moka stirred and came out from my hood, yawning and stretching on my chest.

"Is this the moondoggy the Larrabee sent to protect you?" echoed a voice.

I sat up, but Moka bounced to the table without a misstep. Quaren still sat at the table, watching me as his face churned from green to orange.

"Yes," I said. "Her name is Moka, and I'm certain that she's the same moondoggy that led you to Luna."

"Roban didn't speak highly enough of her," said Quaren.

"I doubt he knows how to speak highly of anyone or anything, except for Knight," I said.

Quaren nodded, but his attention had shifted to Moka. "Is she truly lucky, as the legends say?"

"In more ways than one," I said.

Moka looked up at the swirls on Quaren's face.

"Did you see my mom again?" I asked.

He shook his head. "No, I'm sorry."

A tear streaked down my cheek. "Could you send me home?" I blurted out, "If you wanted, I mean?"

"Yes," he said, his face going gray. "Is that what you want?"

My insides bubbled at the thought of being home with my mom. "Yes. No. Maybe. I guess it's nice knowing that I have that option," I said.

"I understand," he said.

"I almost forgot," I said, reaching up to take off my necklace. "I have something that belongs to you." My heart sunk. I felt a special connection to the little red stone.

Quaren held up one of his boney hands. "You keep it," he said. "I have the verve stone that brought me back from Earth, as well as the other one I would've brought your dad home with."

My hand dropped from my neck. "Really?"

"Yes. Two is plenty, and you've more than earned it," he said.

"Thank you."

"Is there anything else I can do for you?" Quaren asked.

I tapped my chin with my index finger. I nodded. "Do you know what my dad and your brother did to make Baracus' verve stone so powerful?"

"Yes."

Chapter 36

My BEST GUESS, from my brother's letters, is that it had to do with souls," he answered.

"Like taking them out of people and putting them into the stone?"

"That's exactly right," said Quaren.

"But what happens to the person's body when their soul gets sucked into a verve stone?"

"I have no idea," admitted Quaren, his face flushing with blacks and dark pinks. "I'd thought it would be the same as sucking all the life-energy out of someone and leaving a shriveled husk behind. But, after traveling to Earth through the ley lines, I'm leaning towards the entire person's body and soul breaking down to be stored within the verve stone."

I shivered. "Thanks for the nightmares," I said, and with that the faceless man excused himself, leaving Moka and me alone at the table.

Two weeks had passed since Jana died. Quaren fit right in with our merry group, acting as Fey's go-between with some guild members in Yont and Lyosa.

He's also been active in planning the rescue of his brother. Other than that, he's kept to himself.

I haven't been able to train with my broken rib, or do much else for that matter. I'd expected the pain to get better, but it's seemed to do the opposite.

It's funny how a few weeks without predawn runs, sweat soaked workouts, and bruised-up sparing matches had me missing my training.

Dealing with my boredom was hard enough without having to watch Roban make a full recovery. I know I should be happy for the guy. After all, it was my fault he got injured. But I wasn't.

Roban earned his fighting strength sparing with Melik and Vadin. I hated to admit it, but Roban was good. Really good. The three guildsmen sparred every day in Fey's backyard. I got to watch them use the skills they'd been teaching me firsthand. Vadin's spins and flips, Melik's momentum changes, and Roban's energy sword. They made it look like child's play.

Today's workout had Roban fighting with his black-bladed sword. He snapped it so fast that Melik couldn't counter. Vadin bounced across the stone diamond. Roban must've had an eye in the back of his head because he always knew where and when Vadin would strike.

Melik was overpowered with a combination of hacks and kicks. His sword clattered to the stones below, and he was left rubbing his wrist. Vadin didn't manage any better. He rolled away to avoid a jab from the black blade, and was surprised to see Roban's boot collide with his chest. He slid into the side of the planter.

Vadin attacked again with a childlike hoot. His actions caught Roban off guard, but only for a second. I heard three clangs before the weapon in Vadin's hand spun away from his grip. It landed at my feet.

I picked up the weapon, feeling the hot spike of my rib jab me from within. Stretching my fingers around the wooden handle, I admired the tree etched into the blade. I missed this feeling more than I'd realized.

"Does this mean you're done whining?" asked Roban.

The insult broke my train of thought.

Roban glared at me from the center of Fey's stone diamond. Melik and Vadin were behind him, hunched over with their hands on their knees.

I didn't answer.

"What's the matter, you go deaf and weak when your rib was broken?" he asked.

I white-knuckled the sword. "Why do you always have to act like such a jerk?" I said, clenching my jaw.

"You want to say that loud enough for everyone to hear, or are you going to keep standing there, talking to yourself?" he asked.

I'd never met anyone who could make my blood boil faster than this loser. I gritted my teeth. "I said that you're a jerk!"

The sides of Roban's mouth turned up as if I'd given him a compliment.

"Leave him be, Roban," said Melik. "He's injured."

"Pain is part of life," said Roban.

"He's just a kid," Vadin huffed.

"This lesson is best learned at a young age," was his response.

I took three steps towards Roban.

Melik called out, "You don't have to do this."

"Yes, he does," insisted Roban. "We're asking him to defeat Baracus, the Soul Stealer, and it's time he takes his fate into his own hands. Let the boy decide."

"You don't have to do this, Spoon," Vadin said. "You're rib is a long way from healed."

I closed the gap between Roban and me. "I'm not backing down."

Roban huffed, not taking his sword off his shoulder.

I was prepared to go to any means to make him take me seriously. It was in that moment that I realized what kind of trouble I was in. I was about to fight my teacher, a fighter who just beat two grown men without his verve stone's ability. Oh yeah, and I had a broken rib.

Instead of panicking, I began a breathing technique. I focused on the verve stone around my neck, which was almost impossible with the pain I felt in my rib with every breath. All the times Roban yelled at me, or was rude to me, surged within me like fire. My muscles tingled. And then my brasa switched on.

"I hate to admit it, but you've improved," said Roban. He'd mastered the talent of making a compliment sound like an insult.

Through my red vision, I saw the bully crack a smile.

I circled Roban the way Vadin had taught me. Roban kept his sword stuck to his shoulder. No brasa. I sent a jab at his back. With a flash of Roban's sword, he swatted it away as if it were a fly. The vibrations from the impact traveled into my arm, up to my shoulder, and into my rib. The pain made me want to puke.

Roban's face told me that he was enjoying my discomfort. I charged him again, going for the backs of his knees. Roban brought his sword down like a falling tree, smashing my blade into the ground. Without the verve stone giving me added strength, I'd never have held onto the sword.

I went after Roban three more times, but each one ended the same way, with Roban deflecting my sword with his own black blade. I couldn't get past Roban's defenses, even with my added strength.

"We're not done yet," he growled.

Half of my brain worked to keep my verve stone working, while the other tried to overcome the burning pain of my rib. I switched to a stance that Melik had taught me.

"That's not going to work either," said Roban.

Stupidly, I ignored his comment and let him come at me. Swinging his sword from side to side, Roban tried to move me off the stone diamond. I did what I could to redirect his attacks with the smallest amount of energy on my part. It worked if the defender's able to strike their adversary's blade in the exact spot, at the precise time, with the perfect angle. But Roban avoided the technique with ease.

"You'd better try something else," shouted Vadin.

"He's right," said Roban.

I'd fought like Vadin, and Melik, but only at that instant did I realize that Roban could beat both of them. It wasn't like I could use the moves Jana taught me either. I needed something else that Roban's never seen before.

I dug deep into my verve stone, pulling as much as I could into myself. I found a place deep within myself and put all my hatred for Roban there. The hairs on the back of my neck stood up and my brasa sparked.

Roban must've noticed the change coming over because he smiled as if he'd planned for this all along. "Come on," he urged. "Let's see what you can do with all that anger."

In a blur of speed I blasted forward with an overhead chop. I mixed in a bounce to my right with a cartwheel. He blocked it, but his mocking smile had vanished. I flicked my wrist to turn aside Roban's sword before rolling to my left and slashing at his side. The grumpy guildsmen blocked it with the side of his blade. But he couldn't stop the new speed of my leg sweep.

I darted around, moving so fast my eyes watered. His sword whistled through the air, missing me by inches. I blended the styles of all three of my teachers with my own skills. Roban was overwhelmed, unable to counter my attacks. I'd never imagined beating him, but the faster I moved, the more I could smell an upset.

"What's the matter, old man?" I called out. "Not fast enough?"

A wolfish smile spread across his face. I hate that smile. "Come and try that again," he said, switching on his blue brasa, and changing the blade of his sword to pure energy.

Chapter 37

I'D GOTTEN SO CAUGHT UP in accessing the Essenzian ability in my verve stone that I'd forgotten about Roban's own verve stone. I didn't let myself focus on my screw up.

Bursting forward, sword over my head, I circled Roban with my new speed. Moving this fast was a strange sensation. It was as if Roban moved slower, and everything around him was distorted.

Roban got onto the balls of his feet. His blue eyes shot sparks as he chopped, swung, and stabbed at me with his energy sword. I dodged each one without needing my sword, but not by much.

The hardest part of fighting against Roban's verve stone was that I couldn't block his attacks. He'd cut the Marzzoe's serrated blade in half like a hot knife through wax. I had no doubt he'd do the same to my sword.

I twisted and dove, feinted and lunged, always one step ahead of Roban. I pressed in as close to Roban as possible, probing for an advantage. He countered with a pummel to my chest.

I put a hand over my sternum, wheezing, and searching for where Roban would strike next. He charged me. Using my speed, I jumped backwards as he sliced into the stones under my feet, leaving a glowing slash.

Roban didn't let up on his assault. He followed me over the diamond, around the planter gardens, and behind the gazebo. I ran out of room in the corner of the yard behind the outhouse. Roban kept me cornered with his sizzling sword. I needed to get around his defenses and hit him.

A metal shovel and rake leaned up against the outhouse. Fey probably used them in her planter gardens. Roban grabbed the rake with his left hand and pointed it at me. He looked funny holding his glowing sword in one hand and a gardening tool in the other. But when the rake's four rusted claws transformed into pure energy, I was no longer amused.

Roban attacked with his rake. It moved slower than his sword, which he held at his side. But what the rake lacked in speed, it made up for in devastation. Roban put four glowing slashes into the corner of the outhouse with his energy rake. He almost took off my shoulder, too.

Roban continued to fight me with a rake. I combined my strength and speed to keep out of his reach. He countered with a twist of the rake. I avoided this. Roban mixed in a number of sweeps and stabs from the wooden handle of the garden tool. Every one of those found their mark. My thighs, shoulders, and forearms would be purple the next day. But the blow that dropped me to my knees was the hit to my stomach.

Between my broken rib, and all the air that exploded out of my lungs, my red vision disappeared. I dropped my sword with a clang. Roban stood in front of me, energy rake pointed at my neck.

"You're done," he commanded.

I was seeing spots from the pain in my rib. "I want to start training again," I declared.

The rake returned to its rusted metal state and his sword had changed back to normal. "It's about time," he said.

Turning away, Roban walked to Fey's backdoor. "You underestimated him, didn't you?" whispered Vadin.

Roban just huffed.

The next day, Melik and Vadin complimented me on my fight with Roban. They also told me that Roban was more of a get-things-done kind of guy. Someone willing to do whatever it takes to complete a task. Deep down, I was thankful for Roban pushing me to my new speed, even if it makes me sick to admit. He moved me farther than I thought possible.

Having discovered my Essenzian speed, I had twice as much to learn. I kept quiet about my aching rib, and soaked in everything Roban taught me. The best part was he began to teach me a new technique.

That night, Fey got a message from a Guild spy in Archstone. It read that Master Yonn, Roban's teacher, agreed to a meeting at Fey's house on their way to the tournament in three weeks. Roban said there would be a test involved.

This wasn't the first secret report or spy to come into Fey's place. But it was the only one not to bring word about Baracus' march north. The last detail I heard about that battle was the Gramhammer army would reach Sardic within the next two months.

The fear of meeting Roban's teacher made it impossible for me to sleep that night. I didn't want to leave the only people I know on this entire world to get turned into the next Roban.

Today marked the third week since I stood up to Roban. In that time, Quaren had left on a trip to Lyosa, promising to reunite with the guild members on the trip to free his brother; Vadin had gone, and returned, from Cannon on guild business; and my rib was actually feeling better.

I'd spent that morning, and afternoon, training with Roban. He had me using my extra strength and speed together, which is a lot harder than it sounds. We also prepared for Master Yonn's test with plenty of cardio and stretches.

These skills were not the only thing I learned over the past three weeks. Each day after dinner, Vadin would teach me how to play Talakic. The game involved two cards, three dice, and lots of betting. It took me four days to understand the rules, and another five to play without Melik's help.

The biggest drawback to gambling with Vadin was an increased load of chores, unless Moka was nearby. When she was around, I never lost. My first win without the moondoggy came with me out-bluffing Vadin. I celebrated by jumping up and down, and tripping over a chair. Vadin laughed so hard his side hurt.

It had been five weeks since the guild members had been to the Krusty Dragon, no doubt on account of it being the last place they saw Jana alive. But when Fey asks you to do something, you do it.

The walk to the inn brought back every bad memory I had from the night Jana was murdered. I found myself thankful for the daylight.

I did have one happy moment from that night, the girl in the yellow dress. She popped into my head about a hundred times a day. I fought off the guilt of having a happy memory mixed in with all the bad ones. Part of me felt I was dishonoring Jana's death. But no matter how hard I tried, I couldn't get that girl out of my head.

The five of us arrived at the inn's red door. Half the tables were filled with farmers in from a long day's work. The rest were split between some shouting merchants in their pointy hats, a group of Gaelwallian guardsman in their leather armor, and a single table of Lyosians watching each other without making a sound.

I didn't want to come. It was bad enough ordering mincemeat pies without Jana, but the conversation was about Baracus. Today's topic, which had been the same for weeks, was what the king of Gramhammer would do if he defeated Del-gard. Fortunately, Moka came with me, napping in my hood.

"His army is nearest to Locke," said Vadin. "My people have an army, but no castle."

"Baracus would never chance a war within those trees," said Roban, rapping his knuckles on the table. "Too much to risk and not enough to gain. What Baracus needs are more men to drink his soldier's brew. That leaves Tigard and Slatmor. Both are mighty castles, and each will bolster his fighting force before he can crack the dual walls of Gaelwallia. Only then could Baracus hope to overcome Silverwood and do what Gardleng, the first traitor of Gramhammer, could not."

The name of my father's homeland pulled me into the conversation. "Is Silverwood the strongest?" I asked.

"Yes," answered Fey. "The Essenzians are superior to the rest of us, though their numbers are much less. Any fight in their realm is deemed suicidal. But I'm certain the king of Gramhammer has a plan that he believes will grant him victory."

As the guild members continued to talk, my attention wandered to the front door. The bell above the door had been ringing all night, and each time I'd swing my eyes over to see who was coming or going. Though, at the sight of the latest person to enter the Krusty Dragon, I did a double take.

A girl with brown hair closed the red door behind her. Instead of a yellow dress, she wore a purple shirt and a sword strapped to her belt. I hadn't expected to see her ever again, but I wasn't about to let Vadin make fun of me any longer. I excused myself from the table and walked towards the girl, my hands sweating.

Chapter 38

THE BROWN-HAIRED GIRL SQUINTED at the tables, turning her head from side to side. But before she found whomever she was searching for, I asked, "I thought you lived in Sely?"

She turned around, eyes widening. "I do," she said. "My brother and I are traveling with our grandmother this time."

I tried to say something interesting, but this girl had a way of blanking my mind.

"Would you like to sit down?" she asked, breaking the awkward silence. "I'm early meeting my family."

"Yes."

She chose an empty table near the back of the inn. We sat on opposite sides of the table. "You look awful."

I resisted the urge to touch the tinge of yellow and purple still around my eye. "I got this the night we got water at the same time," I said, pointing.

"What happened?" she asked.

"My friend was murdered," I said, glancing at the tabletop. "And I was beat up in the process."

"That's terrible," she said. "I'm so sorry."

Out of the corner of my eye, I spotted Vadin giving me the thumbs up. It was something I'd taught him during Talakic. "Umm, by the way, my name is Ethan," I said, rubbing my hands together and trying to not appear nervous.

"That wasn't so hard, was it?"

"What?"

She tucked a loose strand of hair behind her perfect ear. "Telling me your name."

My cheeks heated up. "Well, now that you know mine," I said.

"My name is Emma," she answered. "It's my turn to ask you a question."

"All right," I said.

"How old are you?"

"Fourteen," I said. "You?"

"Fifteen," she said. "Where are you from?" she asked.

Emma wouldn't have believed me if I told her. "I'm from about as far from here as you can get," I said.

Emma wrinkled her nose at me. "Mysterious, aren't you."

"How about you?" I asked. "You go to school and live in Sely with your grandmother and brother. But what about your mom, where's she?"

Brown hair fell over Emma's face as she leaned towards me. "She died of a fever when I was four."

I felt like such a loser. "I'm sorry," I said, feeling as if I'd kicked myself in the gut. "That was a dumb question."

"No," said Emma. "It's okay."

"I should know better than to ask that kind of question," I tried to explain. "My dad died when I was two."

"Well, aren't we two peas in the same sad little pod," Emma said.

I sucked in a breath, ready to keep talking, but the ringing of the doorbell distracted me. A man wearing brown pants and a blue shirt, and a teenager with pointy sideburns and a collared shirt, entered the inn.

"Your family is here," I said, pointing my thumb at the door.

"I was hoping they'd be running late," she said.

Emma waved her dad and brother over to the table. I made my exit. "Have a nice dinner, Emma."

"You too," she said. "And don't be so shy next time."

"I won't," I said as I backpedaled, knocking into someone's chair.

After returning from the Krusty Dragon, I fed Knight and the other horses. This took more time than normal. I filled Knight in on what happened with Emma. I told him how Vadin high-fived me at the table, another thing I taught him while playing Talakic. I also let him know of my meeting with Master Yonn in the morning.

I got ready for bed. Moka snuggled into her usual spot at my feet. I scooted under the covers as a knock came from my door. "Come in," I called out.

Melik poked his head into my room. "Do you have a second?"

I nodded.

Melik walked in and stood at the end of my bed. "How are you feeling?"

"Like I have eagles flying inside my stomach," I said.

"Eagles?"

"They're large birds of prey back home," I said, spreading out my arms and waving my hands up and down.

"Right," Melik said. "Around here people say tumpers in their bellies. A tumper is just a colorful moth."

"I might have those, too," I said, rubbing my stomach.

"Do you want to talk about it?" he asked.

I nodded. "There has been one thing I've been wondering," I admitted. "Will I have to leave you guys if Master Yonn accepts me?" I looked at my feet, ashamed that the fate of this world rested on the shoulders of a selfish kid.

"That choice is up to you," he said.

"Isn't Master Yonn my best bet at defeating Baracus?"

"Yes."

"Roban might kill me if I don't train with his old teacher," I said.

Melik nodded. "He would be angrier than normal, but only because he cares about Altrea so much. It happens to be what I admire most about Roban. Just promise me that you'll do your best, and don't hold anything back. We'll figure out the rest when the time comes."

"I have to pass her test first."

"True," Melik said with a gleam in his eye. "If I told someone how much you've grown in these past weeks, they'd laugh in my face. Your Essenzian characteristics have aided your growth very much, but the main reason you've learned so much is due to you alone. You never accept defeat, and you're not afraid to make mistakes. You're an exceptional student. I'm very proud to have taught you."

"Thank you," I said, grinning from ear to ear.

Once Melik left the room, I rubbed Moka behind her ears. I thought about what on earth Master Yonn would test me on in the morning.

After an early morning jog through deep mud puddles, and a light breakfast, there came a knock at Fey's front door. Roban and Fey walked down the musty hallway to answer it. Melik, Vadin, and I waited in the circular room.

"Good luck, Spoony," said Vadin, punching me in the arm.

"Thanks," I said, massaging my shoulder.

Moka had stayed in my room. Maybe she didn't want to give me an unfair advantage.

"If you impress Master Yonn as much as you've impressed us, you have nothing to worry about," Melik said.

Roban introduced Fey to Master Yonn, and apparently her guests. "Welcome to my humble home," said Fey. "It's so good of you to have come."

"Thank you very much," said someone who talked like a grandmother.

Fey and Roban emerged into the circular room. An old lady in a flowered hat followed right behind them. She walked with a slight limp, carried a twisted wooden cane, and wore a sword on her hip. Her most vivid feature was a bright smile that leapt off her wrinkled face. At her side was a rigid teenager wearing a collared shirt and pointy black sideburns, and a girl with bouncing brown hair and bright gray eyes. They both had swords on their hips as well.

"Isn't that your girlfriend, Spoony?" whispered Vadin.

I elbowed him in the rib, praying that no one heard the big-mouthed guildsman. Between Emma standing across from me, and Roban's teacher being an elderly woman, my jaw was hanging open.

"Everyone," said Roban, reaching the center of the circular room. "This is Master Yonn." Turning his attention to his old teacher, Roban said, "Master Yonn, this is Melik, Vadin, and Ethan."

I was the last one to shake hands with the old lady, who had a firm grip.

Master Yonn was the next to introduce her guests. "This young man is my grandson Deecan, and this young lady is my granddaughter Emma," she said. "They also happen to be my most-prized students, both of which will be competing in the Archstone Tournament in three weeks."

Deecan had a fighter's body. His muscles warped tight around him. He looked all business. Emma was lean and athletic, with the same smile as her grandmother. I spotted a hot-pink verve stone set in the crossguard of Emma's sword.

Fey interrupted my thoughts. "How about the three of you join us for a cup of tea?" she asked.

Master Yonn answered with a bow. "That's very hospitable of you, but I'm most interested in seeing this boy Roban has talked about for myself. Can we do both?"

"Of course," said Fey. "How long will you need?"

My pulse tripled at the old lady's insistences to see me fight. "We'll be back before you finish your first cup."

"Ethan," grunted Roban, who had taken his teacher by the arm. "Why don't we show Master Yonn the backyard?"

I nodded, my mouth dry.

Once in the backyard, Roban and Master Yonn sat together in the gazebo, whispering to each other. With my sword on my hip, I made my way over to the stone sparing area. I tried to stretch out some of my nervousness. It didn't work.

"Ethan, please come over her and take a seat," said Master Yonn.

"Did I do something wrong?" I asked.

Master Yonn didn't answer, and her expression was blank and unreadable. "I want to hear your story."

I scratched my head. "You don't want me to show you how I fight, or use a verve stone?"

Master Yonn shook her head.

I glanced towards Roban, who grumbled his approval.

I began my story with Quaren showing up in my room, getting attacked by the Marzzoe, the nygar, meeting Luna, Jana's betrayal, and everything in between. Master Yonn didn't interrupt once, though I felt I was speaking super fast.

"Do you miss your mother?" she asked after I finished.

"More than anything," I answered. "But I can't face her until I've cleaned up my dad's mess."

Pausing, Master Yonn looked at me with focused eyes. "He'll do just fine," she finally said.

With that Roban helped his teacher off the gazebo bench.

I followed them into Fey's house, shaking my head. "What just happened?" I whispered.

"She said yes," said Roban, as if I were an idiot not to have figured it out myself.

"You said there'd be a test?"

"That was her test," said Roban, the edges of his mouth actually turning upward.

"Wait, what?!" I asked, confused.

"Motivations are important to a teacher," said Roban.

Master Yonn turned to face her former pupil. "Are you smiling?" she asked. "Since when did you get a sense of humor?"

"As of right now," he said, with a brief head nod.

Fey had taken her last sip of tea as Master Yonn, Roban, and I reentered the circular room. "She's good," I heard Vadin whisper to Melik as we sat down.

The rest of tea time was spent talking about me. It was decided that I'd leave with Master Yonn on her return tip from the tournament. Emma and Deecan listened to the conversation, but remained quiet. I had the feeling that they only understood that their grandmother was taking on a new student.

Melik told me yesterday that I could always reject the offer. I sat there in my leather chair, waiting for him to pull me aside and ask me if I wanted to go or not. That never happened. The isolation tore me up inside. I got up with a huff and stormed out of the room.

I slammed the kitchen door behind me, punching a cutting board with my fist. I'd given my blood, sweat, and tears for these people. Now I was nothing more than a tool for them to use as they saw fit. I thought they cared for me? I guess I was wrong.

Moka must've heard me stomping around. She entered the kitchen and jumped onto the counter. She glanced at me with her big, amber eyes.

"They didn't even ask me."

The moondoggy tilted her head to one side before darting up my arm and into my hood. A second later, I heard shuffling feet enter the kitchen.

"Are you okay?" came a voice from behind me.

I turned around and saw Emma standing in the doorway. "Never better," I lied.

Emma asked, "Would you like to talk about it?"

"Not really," I admitted.

"Are you sure?"

I didn't want to tell Emma anything, but the way she tilted her head at me was like a truth serum. "No one asked me if I wanted to go with your grandmother," I explained, louder than I'd intended. "After all, I'd be the one leaving my friends. Not them."

Emma stepped into the room. "Are they usually like this?"

"No," I confessed, crossing my arms across my chest. "Which is why it ticks me off so much!"

"You must be pretty special to have my grandmother agree to start training you," said Emma.

"Because I'm older than seven?"

Emma nodded.

"Is it hard?" I asked.

"What?"

"Training under your grandmother?"

Emma said, "It's harder than anything I've ever done. My grandmother is the best. You can ask any of her former students. Hard, too. But it would be nice to have a new student on campus," she said, the corners of her mouth turning up into a smile.

Being in the same place as Emma made my stomach flip-flop.

She took two steps towards me. "How long have you been training?" she asked.

"About ten weeks," I said.

Her eyebrows furrowed. "You're lying," she quizzed.

I shook my head.

"But that's impossible," she stammered. "You look like you've been training for years."

Thank goodness my Essenzian blood did more than give me an extra superpower. "I've had good teachers."

Her gray eyes widened. "It must be amazing learning from him," she said as she pressed a hand to her chest.

"Who?"

"Roban, of course."

"Why?" I asked.

"He's famous at our school," explained Emma, as if he were a movie star. "His records have remained the longest."

"He is good at what he does," I said. If what he does well is being grumpy.

I don't know how she managed it, but I'd almost forgotten why I was in the kitchen in the first place. Almost.

"Would you like to get out of here for a minute?" I asked. "We don't have to go far, but I need to get some air."

"I'd love to," she said.

Chapter 39

I couldn't have picked a better person to walk around Gaelwallia with. Emma was easy to talk with. She made me laugh, and the energy she gave off was electric. We strolled beyond the Krusty Dragon and discussed our mutual love for Jarvis' meat pie. We made our way into the market, where it teamed with shoppers eager to make an early morning deal.

"Did you know yesterday that I'd be meeting your grandmother?" I asked.

"No," said Emma. "My brother and I were told that grandma had agreed to meet an uncommon student candidate."

One stand we passed had a woven basket filled with the pear-shaped ivory fruit – the same ones Moka had me eat in Anco. I ran my finger over its bumpy skin when, to my surprise, Moka's head poked out of my hood.

"Is that a moondoggy?" Emma whispered with excitement.

I nodded. I introduced Moka to Emma before we left the fruit stand. Emma beamed at the mythical creature. Moka turned her nose up as if she smelled something foul, returning to my shirt's hood.

The next stand had a table full of expensive-looking fabrics. I didn't dare mess up the perfect piles, but that didn't stop Emma from running her fingers across each one.

We continued to walk and talk until we came to the chicken lady. Emma and I made sure to pass her on the other side of the street. We didn't want to get covered in floating, white feathers.

"Did you grow up in Gaelwallia?" I asked.

"Yes," answered Emma. "On our family's farm. My mom was a teacher before, well, you know."

We'd been trading off question for question for most of the walk. "Do you like to read?" asked Emma, standing next to a stand of books and scrolls.

"Yes," I said. "My dad was a librarian. I suppose books are in my blood."

"You mean your dad worked in the Annals?"

"No, but he went to school there," I said, lucky to have stumbled into a correct answer.

"Your dad went to school at the Annals, and you know Roban. No fair."

I wanted to tell Emma that I'd been beamed here from a far-off world where people can fly and everyone has a magic box that we watch shows on. But I didn't want her to laugh at me. Emma stopped walking in the middle of a hundred people pushing around the market street.

"When are you going to tell me where you're from?" she asked.

My eyes widened at Emma's ability to mention what I'd just been thinking. "Well," I hesitated, trying to find something other than her squinting eyes to look at. "You wouldn't believe me if I told you."

"You might be surprised," she said, rising on her tiptoes to look me in the eye.

"Shelton, Washington," I said, letting those names sink in. "Have you ever heard of those places before?" I asked.

"North?" she said.

"No, not exactly. More like farther up," I said, pointing to the sky.

Emma tilted her head back. "Another world?" she asked.

I nodded.

"My mom used to tell my brother and me about the three scholars who explored another world. But we always thought they were just stories," she explained.

"You believe me?" I asked.

"Of course I do," said Emma. "Why wouldn't I?"

"If you told me the same thing, I'd think you're crazy."

"Oh, that's too bad." I could tell from the tone of her voice that I'd said something wrong.

"Why?" I asked

"Because you would be the only friend I had there," she said, frowning.

I hoped my cheeks weren't too bright red.

We wandered through the entire market without buying one item. I pictured myself getting her some bright purple flowers. But I couldn't bring myself to get within twenty feet of the stand. We continued to stroll into the center of Gaelwallia. We arrived at the edge of the Westland River, sitting together on a patch of green grass.

"Ethan," said Emma. "Why are you coming to train with my grandmother?"

The thought of her being a spy did cross my mind, but something in my brain assured me that everything would be okay. I told her my story. Emma listened as I spoke. She nodded a lot, and clapped her hands at the part where the nygar got chopped in half.

Moka drank at the river's edge. The sun was warm, and the noise of the city had a calming effect.

"I'm sorry," she apologized.

"For what?" I asked.

"I can understand why your friends want you to train with my grandmother so badly," she explained. "Baracus is pure evil. He must be stopped. I can see why my grandmother would break her rule to be your teacher. The lure of training the hero that could defeat the Soul Stealer is too much to pass up." Emma pulled a pinch of grass from the ground and held them up for the wind to take away. "Would you want to go home if you could?" she asked.

"No," I said.

Emma reached over and grabbed my hand in her own. My head buzzed as her fingers set over mine. I lay there, too afraid to move for fear of her pulling her hand away. I would've stayed that way forever if it hadn't been for a slight movement to my right. I followed it and found three figures in black staring at me. Each one held a serrated blade, and had glowing yellow eyes.

Chapter 40

"HELLO CHILD," hissed the assassin and his clones in sickening unison.

Emma was on her feet before I could gasp in surprise. She'd drawn her sword and stepped in between the Marzzoe and me. "Do you know these guys?" she asked.

"They're the Marzzoe that almost killed Roban," I said, removing the sword from its sheath.

"A mistake that we're prepared to correct," one wheezed.

Moka emerged from my hood. She sent out a string of high-pitched barks. My nine-foot bodyguard was about to make her appearance. But instead of transforming into Bigfoot, she turned and ran.

"Where are you going?" I yelled.

Moka never turned around.

"I guess Zambraza was right about moondoggies only being able to transform at night," said a Marzzoe in an acid-like voice.

If the assassin was telling the truth, Moka might be half way to Fey's by now. It gave me a sliver of hope.

With her eye's glowing hot-pink, Emma charged. She whirled around like a cyclone with her double-bladed sword. She smashed two Marzzoe backwards. The assassins countered with slashes to her chest. Emma dodged, planted her feet, and kicked one in his thigh. The other in the stomach.

Emma was brilliant. Her fundamentals were flawless. Her skills were frightening. The assassins were not prepared for her onslaught. They were driven into the river as Emma brought her sword down like a blacksmith's hammer against one. The other she kneed in the ribs. They splashed around as I turned on my own brasa.

I jabbed at the heart of my Marzzoe. He turned my attack aside with the edge of his serrated blade. I mixed in a little extra strength to blast him back three feet. We exchanged blows. I landed a kick to his chest. He elbowed me in the shoulder. I caught him on the forearm with my blade.

The assassin slid inside my reach, bringing the handle of his weapon onto my wrist. I couldn't hold on. My sword flew out of my grasp. To my surprise, the assassin spun, not to finish me off, but to kick the sword out of my reach.

Attaching his weapons to his belt, the Marzzoe picked up my sword. "The only reason you live is because Lord Baracus wishes it," says the assassin.

Swords crashed together in the background, but I didn't take my eyes off the Marzzoe. "What is that supposed to mean?" I asked, stalling until I could figure out how to get my sword back.

"Your red-headed friend told us about the futures where you and Lord Baracus conquer Altrea," explained the Marzzoe. "Your power would grow unmatched under Lord Baracus. All that is required of you is to swear your allegiance to our king."

"That isn't going to happen."

"Do not take this invitation lightly," he said with venom.

"Over my dead body," I spat.

"That can be arranged."

The assassin pointed his weapon at my heart. He would have had his way if it weren't for Emma. I chanced a glance towards the river. Emma had a Marzzoe on either side of her. She kept them at bay with precise footwork and form, but the assassins were inching closer.

She rushed at the guy on her left, jumping out of the water and placing a roundhouse kick to his chest. As he crashed into the water, Emma pivoted, raised her arm, and blasted a streak of hot-pink energy from her palm. It hit the second assassin in the shoulder, sending him spinning into shallow water. Then she leapt towards the smoking Marzzoe and jab him with her sword. His body burst into an inky mass. The dark cloud spiraled around her sword before disappearing with a pop.

My Marzzoe glanced at Emma long enough for me to charge up my strength and speed, bend my knees, and punch him in the chin. The figure wrapped in black landed on a stairwell in a heap.

"Emma!" I shouted. "Let's get out of here!"

We ran away from the river and into the streets of Gaelwallia.

"What do those things want?" Emma asked.

"Me," I said, turning towards Fey's place.

Our feet slapped against the cobblestones as Emma took the lead. "We can lose them in the crowd."

We made our way through a hundred shoppers in the market, all unaware of our dire situation. I looked back over my shoulder a number of times as we made our getaway. I never saw a single Marzzoe. But that didn't stop us from being careful. We kept our heads low to blend in.

"You were incredible!" I whispered, turning to search for the Marzzoe.

Emma's cheeks reddened as she turned to find the Marzzoe, too. "You're wel...". Her eyebrows furrowed and she reached a hand up to her neck, as she stumbled to the ground.

"Emma?" I cried, shaking her shoulder. She wasn't moving.

I ran my eyes over her, hunting for what could have caused this. I found my answer. A black dart was embedded into the base of her neck.

Chapter 41

PEOPLE CIRCLED US. I yanked the dart out of her neck and tossed it to the ground. The Marzzoe remained hidden. I didn't have a moment to waste.

Tapping into my verve stone, I used its extra speed to strap Emma's sword to my waist, and added some strength to fireman-carry Emma. The next thing the market goers saw was a tall boy with glowing, red eyes sprinting through the crowd.

My plan was to get Emma to Fey's place. I dug deep into my verve stone to move as fast possible. Everyone around me appeared as a blur.

At the next corner, underneath a balcony, a man wearing a triangle hat dug into his bag. I veered behind him as he found whatever he was searching for. He stepped onto the street, and in his place stood a Marzzoe. I skidded to a stop.

"What did you do to my friend?" I asked, breathing hard.

"Do not order me around, filth," said the Marzzoe. "If it were up to me, you'd already be dead."

The second assassin appeared from the shadow of the building to my left. He pointed my sword at me. "Our poisons are swift. Your girlfriend has a limited time to live, unless you agree to pledge your loyalty to our king."

"No way!" I said, spit flying from my mouth.

The assassin leaned closer to me. His breath smelled like rotten meat and made me want to gag. "You don't really have a choice, your girlfriend will be dead in five minutes without our antidote."

I wasn't about to let Emma take the fall for me, not like Roban and Jana had. I sucked in a breath to answer the Marzzoe, but Emma cut it short by resting her hand on my forearm. "You can't trust him," she whispered. "Fight."

She was right. Baracus had lied to Jana about her family, and the Marzzoe killed her after she'd given their king what he wanted. He couldn't be trusted.

I set Emma in the doorway behind me. Drawing her sword, I started towards the original assassin with his glowing, yellow eyes. I swung Emma's blade in a circle, cutting the two poles that held the balcony above me. The heavy beams crashed onto the street in an explosion of snapping timbers. Both Marzzoe were caught in the wreckage. I picked Emma up before the dust cleared. I ran away as fast as my legs would carry me.

"Excuse me," I said, weaving around carts and between horses. "Pardon me."

At the end of the next block, I saw the Krusty Dragon. The inn had never looked so good. I was about to pass its red door when Emma's body started shaking. I tried to keep running, but I couldn't without dropping her.

I barged into the Krusty Dragon, finding the inn empty. I lifted Emma on the nearest table. The dread of watching Emma die made my throat tighten up. I gasped for breath.

With her body still for the moment, I felt for her pulse. It was almost too faint to sense. I had to do something. The poison had been allowed to work for too long, and Emma didn't have a second to spare. I racked my brain for an idea to save Emma's life. If Fey or Melik were here, they could help. But I'd never reach them in time.

Emma's face cringed in my red vision. My brasa allowed me to see Emma's life-energy seeping out of her body, as if it were evaporating under a blistering sun. I was helpless.

An insane idea popped in my head. The instant I realized what it required, I tried to think of another idea, anything else would be better than what I had in mind. Nothing came. I prayed that I wasn't about to kill Emma before the poison had its chance.

I placed Emma's sword over her chest and turned off my verve stone. Experimenting more than anything, I focused my thoughts on her hot-pink verve stone. Its link to me was easy to detect. The verve stone had a different pulsing than mine. In thirty seconds the inn was bathed in a hot-pink light.

My plan was to force Emma's life-energy into her stone, the same way my body was sucked into Quaren's verve stone when I traveled through the ley line, or how Baracus put real people into his verve stone. I didn't know what the poison would do to her body in the verve stone, but I figured I could get her out of the stone when I actually had an antidote ready.

Forcing Emma's verve stone to only collect her life-energy took all my efforts. I set my jaw and gritted my teeth. More and more of her life-energy transferred into her stone. With sweat pouring out of me, and my head pounding, an intense dizziness washed over me. I grabbed the side of the table for balance, not prepared to let up.

Emma's body shook again. Had I quickened her death? I got my answer when the tips of her fingers began to glow hot-pink, followed by her nose and cheeks. A blast of warmth came over me. I manipulated her particles into her stone where, hopefully, they would be safe.

"Come on," I urged myself, "just a little bit more!"

My eyes burned with the hot-pink brasa as every blood vessel in my forehead popped out. I couldn't lose consciousness. I had a job to finish. I slapped my face to stay awake. I don't remember how long I forced Emma into her stone, or when I passed out.

"Who goes there?" called a man from the door.

I opened my eyes, staring at the dark beams of a ceiling.

"What happened to ye boy?" came the voice again.

I rolled over and saw Jarvis holding three parcels wrapped in brown paper. "Did it work?" I asked.

"Did what work?" Jarvis asked, stepping into his inn.

I pulled myself up and looked at the table where Emma had been moments before. "It worked," I breathed. Its surface was scorched in the center, and all that remained was her sword.

I couldn't imagine how I'd explain everything to the skinny innkeeper. "Do you know where Fey lives?" I asked.

Jarvis scratched his head. "Yes."

"Go and get Fey. Tell her that Emma's been poisoned by an assassin!" I urged.

"She's been poisoned?" he said, his words sounding shaky.

I nodded. "She might die at any second. Go!" I said. At least it was mostly true.

"Right," he said, dropping his parcels and turning to the door.

I picked her sword up off the table, staring at its crossbar. My hands trembled at the thought of Emma trapped in her own verve stone.

"I'm afraid you're not going anywhere," said the Marzzoe, walking through the inn's front door, and blocking Jarvis' exit.

Chapter 42

"I'LL TAKE CARE OF THE MARZZOE!" I shouted, tapping into my verve stone. "You bring Fey and the others back!"

I didn't hear Jarvis' answer as I lashed out at the assassin with Emma's sword. The Marzzoe blocked my attack with his serrated blade and kicked at my side. I rolled, slicing at the assassin's back. He ducked, flipped backwards, and cut at my heels. The Marzzoe backed me into a wall of the inn with a combination of strikes. Without my added speed, I'd be full of holes and gashes.

I swung at the Marzzoe with all the strength I could muster. My sword bit a chunk out of the doorframe. The Marzzoe stopped me with his serrated blade. But the force of my swing sent him sliding into the side of the bar.

I rushed the assassin. We came together in a storm of clanging swords. I deflected a barrage of jabs and kicks. I also saw Jarvis crouched behind the bar. I backpedaled between tables and chairs in an attempt to get the innkeeper some running room. Jarvis must have seen his chance to flee. He made a break for the front door, staying low as he walked along the walls.

"Where do you think you're going," said another voice.

Jarvis stopped at the door. The second assassin emerged from the back of the inn, darting for the innkeeper.

I dug deep into my verve for any remaining life-energy. I manage to gather enough to speed ahead of the Marzzoe and stop the assassin from taking the innkeeper's head. I heard Jarvis's footfalls behind me as the second Marzzoe joined in the fight.

The assassins worked together in perfect unison, bouncing over and under each other as blades flashed at me from every angle. Three barstools were turned to scraps, and my clothes were shredded. I got in a few shots, but most of them felt more like luck than skill.

The assassins paused to trash talk me. "Are you going to run and hide this time?" asked the Marzzoe with my sword.

"Or have another girl defend you?" asked the other.

"No," I said, "I'm done running."

With my sword tip hovering between the two men in black, I racked my brain for a way to separate them. I went on the offensive, trying to make something happen. I used my added strength to toss a table at the pair. They cut it in midair, rushing at me through its center. I avoided their blades, twisting and jumping in one move. I countered with powered-up slashes that sent both Marzzoe sliding against the bar. Again, they didn't stay down for long.

The Marzzoe seemed to keep their distance after my last set of pummeling blows. I jumped onto the bar. The assassins did the same. They came at me with one hacking at my legs and the other at my eyes. I blocked the lower assassin with my sword, and tilted to avoid the other. I sent an overhead slash back. It missed.

The Marzzoe got on either side of me. Using my Essenzian speed, I went back and forth, dodging and attacking the assassins. I landed a few slashes, and received some hits of my own. The fight moved down the bar, knocking over a barrel of ale and a row of mugs. I couldn't keep this up much longer.

I needed an advantage. Waiting for the last possible second, I caught the shoulder of one, digging my fingers deep into his black clothes. With most of my strength, I threw the assassin at his friend. They came together like a pair of cymbals. I used that moment to sprint for the stairs that led to the second floor.

"He moves like a demon," screeched one of the Marzzoe.

"No matter," hissed the other. "He still bleeds when we cut him."

I greeted the assassins on the top stair with the sharp end of my sword. One kicked off a wall, slashing my sword at my knees. The other leapt off the handrail, his serrated blade slicing for my neck. I planted my left hand on a stair, ducked my head, and pulled my legs toward my body. The assassins missed.

I kicked out with one leg, connecting with an assassin. He flew to the bottom of the stairs. The next Marzzoe dodged my blade by twisting his body. This bought me three seconds before the first Marzzoe could rejoin the fight. It would have to be enough time for me to use the new technique I'd been learning from Roban.

I focused most of my strength into my right hand. This always made my fist feel heavy. Roban had explained that I'd done the same thing when I cut the nygar in half. Ever since Jana died, Roban has been teaching me how to repeat the process without the need of a weapon.

The second Marzzoe landed to my left, bent his knees, and launched himself at me again. I blocked a serrated blade with my sword, rotated my hips, and smashed my fist into his chin.

"That's for Jana!"

A flash of red light flared as my hand imbedded into the assassin's face. The only sound I heard after that was my sword clattering down the stairs. I spun around to see the inky wisps spiraling together before they vanished with a pop.

Roban told me that I was able to slice through the lizard so easily because I'd focused most of my strength into one single attack. He taught me how to master the technique with my punches and kicks. It does have a drawback; it requires a lot of life-energy. I didn't make it two steps before my brasa switched off.

Having absorbed his final clone, the lone Marzzoe faced me. "All used up," he hissed.

He was right. I was unable to tap into my verve stone. A lump grew in my throat at the sight of the Marzzoe approaching me. If I didn't turn on my brasa right now, this fight would be over.

The blood vessels in my forehead popped out as my red vision flickered back to life. I brought my sword up just in time to divert a serrated blade from slicing into my calves. This kept the assassin from getting a step above me. He somersaulted to the inn's floor. I should've stayed and kept the high ground, but I didn't have the life-energy to wait around.

Launching myself at the assassin, I rotated, sword leading the way. The Marzzoe set his feet and raised his weapon. We collided in a choir of crashing swords. I landed a knee to his head as the assassin spun me over his shoulder.

Gathering myself, I sent three jabs at the Marzzoe, who blocked each one. Those were followed by an overhead chop, which missed altogether. The Marzzoe was faster, stronger, and had better reflexes. Having to share his life-energy with his clones no longer held him back.

My legs felt like they were filled with sand, and my arms were numb. I was out of life-energy. My body was shutting down. I no longer saw the assassin's black-clad face bathed in red. My brasa vanished once more. I was about to die. No guild members to come to my recue. No Bigfoot to save me.

"This ends now," said the Marzzoe.

I held my sword out in front of me. But there was little I could do without my verve stone. The assassin slashed his blade at my chest. The force of his blow sent me flying off my feet. I crashed through a window and landed in the street.

I was covered in glass, my cheek and elbow were bleeding. I heard a loud pop in my knee. Grimacing, I rolled over and got to my feet, unable to put much weight on my right leg.

The assassin stepped through the broken window. He tilted his head to the side, no doubt happy to see me in such bad shape. I tried one last time to turn on my brasa. Nothing. It was all I could do to remain standing.

"I'm sure Lord Baracus will understand," said the Marzzoe.

Within my next breathe, an image of my mom flashed before my eyes. Would I ever see her again? Would Emma ever be released from her verve stone?

Emma! I felt for the familiar rhythm of her verve stone. I latched onto its pulsing with my will, mixing its life-energy with my own. Every muscle in my body tingled to a new beat. It felt wonderful. The best part was the street, inn, and Marzzoe were all bathed in its hot-pink glow.

Chapter 43

"THAT'S IMPOSSIBLE!" shrieked the assassin.

I didn't wait around for my newly found hot-pink brasa to switch off. I charged the Marzzoe, ignoring my injured knee. Emma's sword flashed in front of me, but the assassin dodged it with ease. I swept at his legs with my own. He jumped over them without a problem.

It was hard to believe Emma took out a clone without extra strength and speed. Her swordsmanship must be off the charts. She was able to shoot energy blasts from her palm. How did she manage to do that?

The Marzzoe cut me on the thigh, bringing my attention back to the fight. He hacked at my face. I tripped, but caught myself, blocking his serrated blades with the broadside of my sword. The assassin laughed, no doubt enjoying his advantage. I had to figure out Emma's verve stone. Now.

Coughing up blood, I concentrated on the bubbling life-energy of Emma's verve stone. It had a different beat than my own. It felt more fluid. I focused on finding the stone's release valve, so to speak. But the Marzzoe was very distracting.

The assassin came at me with a bombardment of flips and kicks. I limped for my life. He feinted for my neck. I fell for it, and received a kick to my injured knee. I cried out from the pain. Another hit like that and I wouldn't be able to stand.

Roban had taught me how to focus most of the strength from my verve stone into a single attack. I attempted to copy the technique where I focus most of my strength into a single attack with Emma's verve stone. Life-energy churned inside me. I was able to collect the energy in my right hand, the same way Roban taught me. It was surprisingly easy. It must have something to do with me accessing Emma's verve stone already.

The Marzzoe circled me with flips and twists, launching himself off a post. He let gravity carry his serrated blades to me. This was my chance. As I staggered back, I pointed my arm, palm first, where the assassin would land. A blast of hot-pink energy, the size of a baseball, erupted from my right hand. It sizzled across the street. The ball of energy missed the Marzzoe by ten feet.

My brasa flickered as I struggled to maintain my hot-pink sight. Emma's verve stone would reach its limit at any time. I needed to do something drastic. I put every last drop of life-energy into my final move. I focused it into the palm of my right hand. My eyesight shimmered. The assassin must have caught on to what I was planning. He sprinted for me.

With pink light swirling around my hand, the Marzzoe chopped down on me, over and over, with all his strength. He'd let go of his acrobatic ways, choosing brute force to finish me off. Unable to avoid the volley of overhead blows, I fell to my knees. I used my sword like a shield, holding it above my head with two hands. It was all that was keeping me alive.

The Marzzoe kept up his barrage of overhead chops. I used the split-second between hits to pump the last of the hot-pink life-energy into my palm. I was ready to fire. But I had a problem; if I let go of my sword the Marzzoe would chop me up like a piece of firewood.

I pushed up on my sword, trying to get to my feet. The assassin changed tactics, choosing to push down with his serrated blade, instead of chopping. The Marzzoe forced me back down to my knees. With veins popping out of my neck, I held my present position for what felt like hours.

Sparks flew as my blade slid against his. My muscles burned from the struggle, but I now had my legs under me. The Marzzoe countered my climb by pulling his blade off my sword. I was not prepared for this change. I stumbled. The assassin positioned his serrated blade above his head. He whipped it at my hip, but his blade never reached me.

I let myself fall. But not before releasing my sword with my right hand, and pointing that hand, palm first, at the assassin's chest. I was too close to miss. A beam of hot-pink energy, the size of a basketball, caught the assassin in the center of his chest. An explosion of light lit up the street. The assassin was blown off his feet. He landed against the stone wall across the street.

The thrust of the blast shot me in the opposite direction, smashing my head against the cobblestone. Opening my eyes, I saw that my hot-pink eyesight was gone. I sat up, rubbing my head. I had a bruise the size of an egg at the base of my skull. The Marzzoe was slouched against the wall. His black clothes had melted between the waist and neck. He wasn't moving.

The Krusty Dragon was trashed. Jarvis would have a heart attack when he saw his beloved inn. Emma's sword dropped next to me. I didn't have the strength to hold it anymore.

The weight of the moment crashed down on me. I'd been running from the Marzzoe since I landed on Altrea. They'd almost killed Roban, poisoned Emma, and murdered Jana. But now it was over. I'd won. Now all I needed to do was find a cure for Emma, and get her out of her verve stone. We could get back to her grandmother's school to train, together. It wasn't the happiest of endings, but I'd take it over the alternative.

Rubbing my eyes, I felt exhausted. I wanted nothing more than to lie down and sleep for a week. My knee wouldn't let me put any weight on it. I shook my head, trying to shake the dizziness away. I gave in and rested my head on the hard ground. A pair of dark leather boots walked through my line of sight.

"Tired, are we?"

I recognized the voice immediately. It belonged to the man who Baracus sent with the Marzzoe to return his blueprints. The same man who'd blackmailed Jana. General Zambraza. He kicked me in the side, telling his invisible friend, "Baracus won't have to feed me to his dogs now."

A tiny purple light, like a firefly, landed on my chest. Two attached to my legs. Two more stuck to my arms. My body had gone limp. I tried to roll away, to call for help, but it was as if my body had been paralyzed.

"You're coming with me," said the general.

Chapter 44

WITH A GLOWING-PURPLE BRASA, General Zambraza attached Emma's sword to his belt. He lifted me over his shoulder and carried me like a sack of potatoes. As the Krusty Dragon disappeared from sight, I heard someone calling. It might have been any Altrean, but I wasn't about to miss an opportunity.

"Help! I'm being kidnapped!" I screamed.

The general jarred his shoulder into my stomach as he ran. "That's enough out of you," he said.

Another purple firefly fluttered in front of my face before disappearing beneath my chin. I assume it landed on my neck because everything went numb in that area. I couldn't talk. I couldn't turn my head.

"He will pay," he whispered, but not to me.

As he continued to make his escape, I got intermittent views of the city with my floppy neck: a mom holding a new baby, shop windows, and a cart of garlic. Twice I heard the rushing waters of the Westland River, but we never got close enough to cross it.

When all I could see was the back of the general, I prayed Melik and the others would know where to find me. All I knew is that it was too early in the day for Moka to charge around a corner in Bigfoot form.

We had traveled for twenty minutes. I kept trying to figure out how he was going to get me out of the city. I had the feeling General Zambraza thought we were being followed. He seemed to be making a point to not go in a straight line as he jogged. Surprisingly, no one asked him who he was carrying in such a hurry.

Ten minutes later, the general came to an abrupt stop. He even darted into an alley. It was impossible to see why. He did slow his breathing, waiting for some unknown reason. I received my answer when I heard someone call out, "Spoon? Spoon? Are you here?"

A horse clopped past.

The voice belonged to Melik. Moka must have warned them in time. But with General Zambraza paralyzing me with his glowing-purple fireflies, I couldn't break free, let alone scream for help. Not being able to move gave me a claustrophobic sensation. My heart raced.

My gut burned with acid that help was so close, and yet I couldn't do a thing about it. I strained my ears for Melik. Nothing. I listened for Bomber's hooves on the cobblestones. Nothing. Melik had passed me by. The general must have come to the same conclusion. He went on the move again.

We didn't run into anyone else from the Guild, though I prayed constantly for it to happen. I received my first idea of where we were with the help of my nose. The air gave hints of dampness, algae, and spoiled fish. It must be Lake Tilvera. I got a glimpse of women selling clams in a fish market, and an old man trading a wrapped parcel for some coins.

The general's feet sounded different as he carried me over some wooden boards. The docks. Vadin and I had passed them on our morning runs. They looked like a floating city all to themselves; a patchwork of planks, pilings, and boats. Beyond the docks, in its continuous circle around Gaelwallia, were two enormous walls blocking the way in or out of the harbor. The only ways through were two heavily guarded gates that allowed ships to access the city.

We entered some kind of building. General Zambraza removed me from his shoulder. He set me down, letting the back of my head thud against a wooden wall. Before my chin fell onto my chest, I saw a man seated behind a counter. He wore a wool shirt filled with holes over a crème-colored shirt, and his skin appeared made from leather. Piles of papers, strands of rope, and boxes were spread out in front of him. He was writing in some notebook-sized journal with one of those pens you dip in ink. His eyes bugged out when he saw the glowing-purple eyes of the general approaching.

"I don't want any trouble," pleaded the man.

"Then answer my questions," said General Zambraza. "When does the next ship leave for Sardic?"

"It doesn't," the man replied, sounding nervous. "Gramhammer is marching to Sardic as we speak. They may have already arrived. No one is going there for some time."

I imagined the general grinning at the news.

"How close can you get me?" demanded the general.

The man behind the desk lifted a bent pair of spectacles to his eyes. He looked through the lens without a crack. "A ship is heading to Sely in the morning."

General Zambraza whispered, "Yes, I will make them." Then he spoke to the man behind the counter. "That will do."

"I must warn you," said the man, his voice filled with unease. No doubt from the general talking to his invisible friend. "The captain is known to charge quite a bit for last-minute passengers."

"That won't be a problem," said the general.

The man explained, "Take a left out of here. The ship is the last slot on the right."

I heard the general step towards me. He lifted me over his shoulder once more.

"What's the matter with the boy?" asked the man.

To his invisible friend, the general whispered, "I will stab him if he asks again." But to the man he said, "He's not well."

With a shaky voice, the man said, "I'm sorry to hear that."

Not surprisingly, he didn't ask another question.

General Zambraza emerged into the sunlight. He veered left, stopping near some men talking about having enough coffee for the trip. With me on his shoulder, the general asked, "Where is your captain?"

The conversation about coffee stopped. One of the voices said, "Who's ask-," but he cut his question off before he finished.

I'm sure Zambraza didn't appear to be someone these guys wanted to deal with, with two swords, a body draped over his shoulder, and glowing-purple eyes.

The other man said, "He's in his quarters."

The general carried me onto the vessel, crossed the deck, and then leaned against the mast. Two men holding boxes of citrus froze midstride to stare at us. General Zambraza cut some strips of rope from a nearby coil. He wrapped my arms backwards around the mast, and tied my wrists together on the opposite side. His knots were tight, cutting into my skin, and my shoulder's ached from the force and awkward angle. I faced the rear of the ship. He also switched off his brasa, giving me control over my body once more.

"Don't touch him," he warned the spectators.

They nodded in unison.

The general approached a closed door at the stern of the ship. He held back a hyena laugh as he let himself in. I have no idea what he said to the captain, but when they exited the quarters the captain ordered his men to prepare for departure to Sardic immediately. The guys complained about leaving without a full crew. The captain insisted they had more than enough to accommodate the needs of their special guest, Zambraza.

I watched the dock for any sign of Melik or the others. My heart hurt. If they didn't hurry up, I'd be on my way to Baracus. The thought turned my gut sour.

The general whispered on the other side of the ship to his invisible friend. With the slight breeze, I couldn't hear what he was saying. The captain and his crew flew around the ship and dock. It wasn't long before the food on the dock was in the hold, and sails were flapping in the wind.

As the docking lines were untied from the cleats, a voice almost stopped my heart. "Spoon!" It belonged to a man.

General Zambraza heard it, too. He scanned the dock, listening.

"Here. OVER HERE!" I yelled as loud as I could.

Nothing.

The general walked over to the captain. "We leave, now," he said through gritted teeth.

The captain's eyes bugged out. Sweat dripped down his brow. He yelled at his crew to unhook the dock lines. They did as he commanded. The gangway was pulled aboard as the ship floated away from the dock.

I attempted to thrash and kick to get free. I was close enough to hear someone calling my name, but for the second time today, I was helpless. The knots at my wrists cut into me more, but I didn't care. I had to get off the ship!

Just as my last bit of hope was about to be crushed under Zambraza's boot, the man's voice returned. "Spoon!" he yelled, and much closer this time. So close this time that I recognized the voice. Roban.

"ON THE SHIP!" I cried out with desperation.

Heavy footfalls approached on the nearby planks. Roban charged into view with glowing-blue eyes and his energy sword sizzling. The ship moved away with the wind, slowly. Roban could make the jump onto the stern, but not for much longer. He sprinted across the dock towards the ship. At the same time, General Zambraza sent five of his paralyzing fireflies at him. Roban was forced to dodge the attack. He slashed his white-hot blade through the air, vaporizing every firefly within range.

The ship moved parallel to the dock. Roban might be able to make the jump, if he hurried. The general sent ten more of his pesky fireflies. Roban slashed through them as well. "Spoon, you have to get off the ship!" he shouted. "Now!"

I wanted to tell Roban, "Duh," but he was busy at the moment. Twenty more fireflies came at him. Then thirty. General Zambraza wasn't letting up. He sent a swarm of fireflies to block Roban.

Roban was engulfed in the darting purple lights. He destroyed half with his energy sword. One got past his defenses and stuck to his calf, causing him to lose his balance. Instead of falling to the ground, he lunged into the water. Somehow he transformed the blade of his sword to black the second before he went under. The purple lights danced inches from the surface of the water. One got too close and fizzled out. They couldn't go in the water!

The longer General Zambraza waited for Roban to reemerge, the more he laughed. The sound was like nails on a chalkboard. Roban might have stumbled onto a weakness of the general's ability, but it wouldn't do him any good the moment he came up for air.

The fireflies flew around the ship in a protective circle. The general wasn't going to let Roban sneak up from the other side of the boat. The ship was twenty feet from the end of the dock, sailing towards the closest gate.

Roban finally surfaced in the boat's wake, but he was too far away to climb aboard. Fireflies zoomed for him. Roban sucked in a breath and swam underwater again. At this rate he'd never reach the ship.

"Spoon, is that you?" called out another man's voice.

"YES!" I yelled.

I glanced at the dock. Melik was waving his hands at me from atop Bomber. I tried to shake my head and kick my legs out, but I'm not sure he could see them. General Zambraza noticed him, too. He sent ten fireflies. Melik unsheathed his sword, facing the purple lights.

Roban's head popped above water in an area free of fireflies. He swam hard, splashing water with each kick. He had bare arms and legs. He must have removed most of his clothes underwater. The general was aware of Roban as well. His swarm would intercept Roban well before he reached the ship.

Melik saw his swimming friend. "Roban, I'm going to close the gate!"

Roban didn't act like he heard Melik. He just kept swimming. When the fireflies reached him, he dove below. They dive-bombed him from above. Two even fizzled out when they hit the water.

Melik spun Bomber on the spot, hooves taking him away. He had a long ride before reaching any guards that could get the gates closed. I doubted he could make it in time.

As the ship approached the first gate, the general attached fireflies to my neck, legs, and arms. Then he covered me in an oily tarp. I guess he didn't want to explain me to the guards.

On one of our runs, Vadin told me about the harbor gates. Three guards stood on a dock attached to the left side of the gate. Other guards were stationed on top of the wall in the gatehouse. I couldn't see the gate up ahead with how I was tied up to the mast, but I could picture it in my mind.

"Why are we slowing?" snapped the general.

"There's a fishing boat in front of us," stammered the captain.

"Run it down," ordered General Zambraza.

"The guards would never let us through if we do that," responded the captain.

The general grumbled something to his invisible friend. Would the boat slow us down enough for Roban to catch up?

I listened for what felt like ten minutes beneath my tarp. Finally the captain said, "The fishing boat has been waved through. We're next."

I felt the ship move forward and come to a stop. I prayed in the dark for Roban to swim up to the ship.

I heard a guard ask questions about the ship's cargo and destination. The captain answered both honestly. I prayed one of the guards would notice Roban swimming behind us, or ask what was beneath the tarp at the base of the mast, but they never did.

"Have a safe trip," said the guard. "And watch yourself in Sardic. You don't want to get tangled up with any Gramhammer soldiers."

The captain cleared his throat. "Thank you."

The ship moved towards the last gate between Baracus and me. I wanted to see if the fishing vessel had made it through the outer gate, but that wouldn't be happening in my current state.

A splashing noise brought my attention to the port side of the ship. Something heavy and dripping climbed onto the deck. A tattooed arm pulled the tarp off me. Roban, soaked and in his underwear, unsheathed his sword. He was about to cut me free when a swarm of General Zambraza's fireflies landed on his chest. He never stood a chance.

Paralyzed, and with his brasa off, Roban fell to the deck. His eyes stared at me with sadness, making my throat tighten up. These were not the eyes of someone who hated me.

"The guards are waving us ahead. We're next," said the captain.

"I want to gut him, but the guards would notice the mess," the general whispered. "I will hurt him though."

General Zambraza leaned over and kicked Roban in the head three times, busting his lip, cutting him along an eyebrow, and causing him to lose consciousness. Then the general shoved him under a rail and off the ship, sword still clenched in his paralyzed grip.

He'd be free of the fireflies the moment he went underwater, but he wouldn't be able to swim while unconscious. My heart broke inside my chest. The general was about to cover me in the tarp again. I didn't care. I wished he'd just toss me in the harbor with Roban.

I would have sulked across Lake Tilvera if a shout from above hadn't brought me back to reality. "Don't let that ship through! We're closing the gates!"

Loud gears above began to lower the gate. Dropping the tarp, General Zambraza sent new fireflies behind me. I didn't have to see them to know they were heading for the guards at this gate. And Melik!

The general barked at the captain, "Don't stop if you want to live!"

The captain chocked out a, "Yes, sir."

Our ship pulled next to the dock, allowing me to see the guards on the dock unable to move. The captain and his men inched the boat under the closing gate. More guards emerged from the gatehouse above. Some carried bows and arrows, others swords, but each one got their own firefly to the back.

"The fishing boat is blocking us," reported the captain.

"Ram it out of the way before that gate crushes us!" snarled General Zambraza.

The gate continued to lower foot by foot, directly above the mast, and me. Two guard boats approached the area between the two gates, but they'd never reach us in time. The general paralyzed a few more guards attempting to climb aboard the ship.

"Brace for impact!" warned the captain.

The ship hit something big. A crack reverberated through the deck and into the mast, vibrating my spine. Did we hit the fishing boat? What else could it have been?

Staring straight up the mast, the gate was about to split the ship in two. The ship jerked forward, our speed increasing. We must have passed the boat. The crow's nest cleared the teeth of the gate with inches to spare. The ship wasn't out of the woods yet.

"Spoon! Spoon!" Melik called. He was on the dock with more guards. "I'm sorry!"

I wanted to respond, but the gate was fifteen, ten, five feet from taking a bite out of the rear of the ship. Then the gate crashed down, breaking off the stern rail. The ship was free.

I saw Melik jump into the water through a square hole in the gate, but there was nothing he could now.

As I sat there helpless watching the distance between Melik and me grow, I thought about how he was the first person I'd met when I landed in Altrea. Like a loving grandfather, he answered all my questions. He helped me learn to defend myself. Make a fire. He saved my life. He and the other guild members were my closest friends on this world, and now I would never see them again.

Tears streamed down my face. I thought back to Quaren's offer to send me home; I should have taken him up on that. Instead, I had a one-way ticket to meet the Soul Stealer.

Acknowledgements

First of all, this book would never have happened without my former college roommates and a group-story told over email that ignited my passion for writing. These men, their wives, and their children are a second family to me and my own.

I would like to thank my friends and family members who encouraged or offered feedback, shaping this story into what it is today. This includes (but is not limited to) Ben Morrell, Steve Gritton, Megan Melvard, Peter Plantenberg, Bob Gilam, Robin Puelma, Kate Shramek, Steve Gritton, Bill Johansen, and Carol Johansen.

I also want to call attention to two people whose contributions to this book have been invaluable: J Caleb Clark (jcalebdesign.com) for creating the amazing map and cover art, and Dustin Terpening for his tireless editing.

A special thanks to my daughter, Gwendolyn, for her bright smile and caring heart, and my beautiful wife, Ingrid, for being my biggest cheerleader, sounding board, summary writer, and my best friend.

Made in the USA
San Bernardino, CA
23 April 2015